Three Dirty Dads

EMMA FOXX

CHAPTER 1

Grayson

"MR. ROSS, there's someone here to see you."

I swivel my chair toward the conference room door where my executive assistant Andrea is poking her head in. I frown. Andrea knows better than to interrupt me during this meeting.

"I don't have any other meeting scheduled this morning," I tell her, giving her a look that says, *what the fuck are you doing?*

Andrea has worked for me for three years. She knows better than this.

She casts an apologetic look around the room, but nods. "I know. This was unexpected. But it seems important."

"It wasn't on my schedule," I repeat. I don't do things that aren't on my schedule.

"Mr. Ross," Andrea says, coming further into the room. "You really need to meet this person. It's kind of…an emergency?"

She says it with a clear question mark at the end. My scowl deepens. I just spoke to my mother this weekend and everything was fine in South Carolina, so any family emergency would have to be of the medical variety. I don't like that at all. My parents are only in their sixties, and in good health, but that doesn't mean crazy things like heart attacks and aneurysms can't happen. Or car accidents, which could involve my sister, her husband, or my niece or nephew.

I start to rise from my chair, then remember that Andrea said someone is here.

"Who is it?" I ask brusquely as I straighten.

"Um," Andrea says, and her brow furrows, as if trying to decide how to answer. "Her name is Evelyn."

I shake my head. "I don't know any Evelyn."

"I know. But Mr. Ross, it's very important that you come meet her."

For fuck's sake. This is all taking longer than it probably would be for me to tell Evelyn whoever-she-is 'no' to whatever she's here to ask me.

I swear to God if this is some woman walking in off the street thinking she's going to make a grand impression on me with her confidence and boldness—she is grossly mistaken. I do not like surprises. I do not like to be interrupted, and I do not like to be thrown off schedule.

I turn to the conference table full of employees. "I'll return as soon as I can. Peter, can you continue please," I say to my vice president of operations for my Chicago office.

Everyone came into the New York office for this meeting, but since I'm in the New York office, it, of course, runs like clockwork. The Chicago office and the Seattle office are the two we need to review.

Peter nods and picks up where I left off as I follow Andrea out to the reception area.

The only person standing by Andrea's desk is a woman I know well. Sara, Andrea's assistant, is holding a small child. I suppose the child could even be called a baby.

But there's no one else around. Certainly no woman barging into my office seeking one of our exclusive, highly sought after internships.

"Where did she go?" Andrea asks Sara.

"Bolted as soon as you left. Here," Sara thrusts a rumpled, folded piece of paper at Andrea. "She said to give him this."

I can't help but study the child on Sara's hip.

I don't think I have ever seen a more suspicious looking baby.

She's not fussing, not squirming or crying, but she's looking at Sara with a deep frown. As if she is not convinced that Sara knows at all what she is doing.

Did I know that Sara had a baby?

No, I did not.

I realize that I'm very work focused and sometimes am not the most... personable...boss, but I would have noticed if Sara was pregnant.

I'm eighty percent sure that's true.

Then again, this baby looks nothing like Sara.

And looks like she—or he, I'm not really sure, actually—thinks Sara is kind of a dumbass.

She's not. Sara is great. I'm just saying that's how the baby is looking at her.

Andrea takes the folded piece of paper, sighs, and hands it to me.

"What is this?" I don't reach for it.

Something tells me I do not want that piece of paper.

"Well, I'm hoping it's an explanation," Andrea says.

"Evelyn left?"

Andrea shakes her head. "No. I'm guessing—hoping—it's about Evelyn."

"Where is this Evelyn?" I ask. I'm feeling very suspicious myself.

Andrea looks from me to Sara. Or rather, to the baby Sara is holding. "Grayson," she says, addressing me by my first name since we're not in front of employees. "Meet Evelyn."

It takes me just a second to catch on. "The *baby* is Evelyn?" I ask.

"Yes."

Okay, so it's a girl. "This baby is who you thought I should meet?" I ask.

Andrea nods. Then she shakes the piece of paper at me.

"Why do you think I need to meet this baby?" I ask, a cold ball of tension forming in my gut as I still refuse to take the piece of paper.

"Because she's yours."

Fuck.

That's what I was afraid she was going to say.

I shake my head. "There's no way."

Andrea gives me a *really?* look. "Read the letter Grayson."

"No."

Her eyes widen, and she shakes the paper again. "Read the letter, Grayson," Andrea says firmly.

"No. It's probably going to say that Evelyn is my child. But that's not possible."

"Have you had sex in the past—" Andrea looks over at Evelyn. "I'd say she's about seven months, add in the forty weeks of pregnancy..." She looks back to me. "Have you had sex with anyone in the past seventeen to eighteen months?"

She, of course, knows the answer to that question.

"Not that it's any of your business, but I always use protection."

Andrea is about five years younger than me, but the look she gives me is a very motherly look. As in a *don't fucking treat me like an idiot, young man* type motherly look. My mother has given me that look a lot over the years.

"Everyone over the age of twelve knows that condoms can fail. Read the letter Grayson."

"She looks just like you," Sara adds.

I look at her with a frown. "What? She does not."

Sara laughs lightly and reaches up to trace the frown line between Evelyn's eyebrows. "She has your frown."

Andrea laughs as well. "And your eyes."

"Shut up," I mutter.

Evelyn looks over at me then. For the first time.

We make eye contact and all of a sudden, the little girl smiles brightly.

My eyes widen. The grumpy baby is smiling at me?

"Oh my God," Andrea says. "She literally hasn't done anything but frown since they walked in here."

"Who walked in here with her?" I ask, still watching Evelyn.

"She was twenty-something. Pretty. Blonde. She didn't give us her name." Andrea holds her hand up as if to stop me before I can say a word. "She said she was Evelyn's aunt. She said that you had a one-night stand with her sister and you probably won't remember her." Andrea looks at the piece of paper in my hand. "Now read the damn letter."

Fuck. A baby. There is a baby in my office that everyone thinks belongs to me.

I do the only thing I can. I open the damn letter.

Grayson,

Hi. It's Lacey. We spent a very fun night together in New York City last April. We met at a cocktail party at the art museum. I was wearing a short red skirt you really liked.

Yes, we used protection. No, I didn't mean to get pregnant. Yes, I remember us talking about not seeing each other again or getting in contact. No, I don't want your money.

Evelyn was a huge surprise to me, too. And she's kind of messed everything up, to be honest. I mean, I love her. A lot. She's actually great. And it's not her fault. I really tried to make it work. But I'm broke. I can't do the single mom thing. I wish I could.

The best thing I can do for her is give her to her dad. You're rich, successful, and have your shit together. You're going to be a lot better for her than I ever could be.

You're named on her birth certificate. You have a bunch of lawyers, so you should have no trouble with the legal stuff.

Please take care of our baby girl.

Maybe someday tell her that she was named after my grandmother, that I love the Beatles and peach pie, and I hope someday she gets to see Zion National Park. I took a trip there when I was eight and still think about it.

And tell her I love her.

Lacey

I take a deep breath and blow it out. I remember the red skirt. I even remember the girl. Lacey was beautiful and fun, and we laughed. And had great sex.

We did have a really good time that night.

We also both stuck by our promise not to contact each other afterward.

I guess until now.

I look up at the baby.

Evelyn.

This is hardly proof that she's mine, of course. The fact that her birth certificate lists me is also not proof.

"We're going to need a DNA test."

"Oh my God," Andrea mutters, almost like she's disappointed in me.

She grabs the letter from me and starts reading. I let her. I'm probably going to need as many people in on this as I can. I don't know what the fuck to do.

"Come on," I tell her, my tone a lot less boss-in-charge than before. I hate that. "I can't just take this woman's word for it. That's downright irresponsible."

Andrea gives me a look. "*That* would be irresponsible? Look, it's not like she's trying to get your money or get you to marry her or something. She just wants you to take care of the baby."

"Just?" I repeat. "*Just* take care of a baby?"

"*Your* baby," Andrea says.

"*Allegedly*," I return.

"Really, your only options at this moment are to take her home or call child protective services," Sara says.

Andrea looks at me. "I swear to God, Grayson, if you call CPS for this baby, I will quit."

I believe her. It wouldn't be the first time Andrea threatened to quit, but the last time she threatened, she actually did it, and it took me three weeks to convince her to come back. And a ten thousand dollar a year raise.

"So I'm just supposed to take her home?"

"Yes," Andrea says.

"I don't know what to do with a baby."

Andrea props a hand on her hip. "You are thirty-three years old, a multimillionaire, graduated *summa cum laude* from business school at Columbia, and despite how you act much of the time, you're not actually an asshole. You'll figure it out."

"I know the first thing I would do," Sara says.

"What's that?" I ask with a sigh.

I'm studying Evelyn. She's looking at Sara again, frowning.

"I'd call my mom," Sara says.

That's actually the first thing anyone's said that's made sense since I walked out of the conference room.

CHAPTER 2

Grayson

THREE WEEKS LATER...

"Yes, so push that meeting back to Thursday," I tell Andrea, absently pouring creamer into my lukewarm coffee. I have a headache from lack of sleep and notifications from the office are pinging repeatedly from my phone in my ear.

"Grayson," Rose says from behind me.

I wave her off to acknowledge I hear her but to give me a minute.

Ping, ping, ping.

"Grayson, you can't reschedule that call. You've rescheduled it twice already in the last two weeks. You know Brandon doesn't like to be put off like that."

"Grayson," Rose repeats.

Ping, ping.

"I don't have a choice. I'm so fucking far behind," I tell Andrea. "I haven't even had a chance to look at the proposal."

Ping, ping, ping, ping.

How many fucking emails are my co-workers sending? For fuck's sake.

"Grayson," she sighs.

"*Grayson,*" Rose says.

I can't even think. Female voices are coming at me from all directions and I'm distracted and frustrated. It reminds me of a threesome I had a decade ago where both girls wanted my attention and I was forced to make a sex game out of gagging both of them so I could focus on fucking and not their competing demands.

"Can we just—" I start to say. To who, I'm not even sure.

A baby shriek cuts through my words. It's loud. It's shrill. It's at decibels that could shatter glass. It's incredible that so much volume can come from such a tiny, tiny human, but Evelyn has proven to be the most demanding female I've ever encountered in my entire life, and frankly, that is saying a lot.

It's entirely possible my head is going to explode.

"I have to go. I'll call you back," I tell Andrea and end the call, her protests echoing in my ear.

I turn to Rose, who is holding the baby on her hip, jiggling her up and down.

"What?" I ask, trying not to sound impatient and failing miserably. I drop my phone on the kitchen counter and reach for my coffee.

"You put formula in your coffee, not creamer," Rose says, gesturing to the mug in my hand.

I hear her words, but I don't process them. "What?" I ask, running my hands through my hair.

I'm exhausted. The baby was up and down all night and only agreed to sleep if she was on my chest on the couch. My neck hurts. I haven't taken a shower, and my coffee is officially cold. I take a sip, absently.

"That's formula, not creamer."

And...I'm drinking baby formula in my coffee. "I know that." I didn't know that. "I just don't care." I do care.

"Okay, I just didn't think you knew." Rose, who is probably

around sixty-five, with a chic gray bob and crinkles around her warm brown eyes, thrusts the baby toward me.

I take Evelyn, awkwardly. I still haven't gotten the baby transfer part down. The baby frowns up at me, her eyes wet with unshed tears. I settle her against my chest and run a hand over the wispy baby hair on her round head. Her tininess both amazes and terrifies me a thousand times a day.

"Grayson, I love you, but I quit."

Those words I comprehend immediately. "*What*? Rose, no, no, no, please, you can't quit. Why would you quit?"

"Because I'm old and you're a terrible boss. Too demanding."

The kitchen floor of my apartment feels like a black hole that is going to open up and swallow me. But there is nothing, and I mean absolutely fucking nothing, that money can't solve. "I'll double your salary."

"No." Rose picks her purse off of the counter and slides the strap onto her shoulder.

"Triple?" I sound as desperate as I feel. Maybe money can't solve this. But it has to solve this. I can't do this on my own.

She can't leave. It's noon. I have twelve hours of work ahead of me today and a baby who makes sounds I don't understand and who refuses to sleep unless she's draped on me like a weighted blanket.

"Grayson, I agreed to help you out short-term, but I'm retired. You need a young nanny. In fact, you need two, really. A day nanny and a night nanny."

"They have night nannies?" That sounds…amazing. Like God's gift to corporate single men who suddenly discover they have a child they didn't know existed, foisted on them in the middle of a midtown high-rise.

"Yes, of course. For people who have demanding careers. A day nanny does eight to five and a night nanny does eleven to seven."

"Who is supposed to watch Evelyn from five to eleven, then?"

I'm joking. I know the answer. I'm just not thrilled with what it's going to be.

I have serious doubts about my ability to parent in any sort of hands-on practical way.

Rose gives me a look. "You. Her *father*. That's who."

"We don't know I'm her father," I protest weakly. "We don't have the DNA results back."

Since the minute Lacey's sister dropped Evelyn off at my office like a damn DoorDash lunch delivery, my focus has been on logistics. Securing baby gear, making a pediatrician's appointment, filing for emergency custody, ordering a DNA test, finding a rental in my hometown of Honeysuckle Harbor, South Carolina and moving here.

I've barely had time to breathe between all of that and watching endless YouTube videos on what the hell I'm actually supposed to do with a seven-month-old baby. I haven't processed how I actually *feel* about it.

It doesn't matter now either, because I have yet another pressing logistical problem. Rose is leaving me alone with this baby and it will be a miracle if somehow we survive.

Rose scoffs. "Have you looked at this child? She looks exactly like you. Same eyes, same nose, same chin."

"How can you tell? She just looks like any other baby to me." I'm not just saying that. I can't tell if she looks like me or not. I've ruthlessly scoured her features multiple times, and she just looks like a baby. A perfect, beautiful, adorable as fuck little baby. I lift Evelyn up so I can check her out again, waiting for some moment of genetic recognition. My heart does a weird flip in my chest like it does every time I just pause and take a breath and look at her.

As far as babies go, I haven't studied them much as a whole or individually. I was never interested in the whole create-your-own-mini-me trend. At thirty-three, I've yet to feel any sort of tug to start a family. I haven't even felt any real urge to get married. That doesn't mean I don't get the appeal of having kids—I just never saw it as part of my future.

I like my life. I work hard. I play hard. I'm busy, but I also have reached the point in my career where if I want to take a spontaneous trip to Vegas with friends I can. If I want to romance a hot supermodel and jet her off to Paris for a weekend of sex and good food, I do. I have a killer apartment in TriBeCa, a closet filled with designer suits, and arrangements with the finest restaurants in New York to always have a table available to me.

It's tidy, it's fulfilling, it's very controlled.

Or it was.

Nothing has been in my control since little Miss Hates Sleep showed up in my life.

Evelyn frowns at me. I frown back. She wrinkles her nose. I wrinkle mine back. "What?" I ask her, gruffly.

She lets out another shriek that sounds angry.

Maybe she doesn't like being dangled mid-air and scrutinized. I probably wouldn't either. I lower her against my chest again.

Rose eyes us in amusement. "That right there…same furrow between her brows and same skeptical little frown. She's a dead ringer for you, Grayson. I haven't seen a baby this naturally cynical since, oh, let me think, *you* were a baby."

I feel a grudging sense of kinship toward Evelyn. "Not cynical. Intelligent. Highly intelligent."

"Or just crabby, one of the two." But Rose pats my cheek to let me know she's teasing.

"That's why I was your favorite." Rose was a nanny for my sister and me for a decade. She was a second mother to both of us and is still a huge part of our family. After we were too old to need her care, she moved on to our neighbors, the Andersons, who had a son and triplet girls. She then went on to one other family with an only child before she retired ten years ago.

This isn't fair to her. I recognize that. "How do I get a nanny? I don't want just some random person. No one will be as good as you, anyway."

"Don't try to butter me up. I'm not staying. I'm exhausted from these last two weeks. A good agency can find you some wonderful candidates to interview in the next week or so. I'll send you the name of the best agency around. They service the upper echelon in Charleston."

"An upper echelon nanny sounds good to me. Let's Mary Poppins this shit. But what am I supposed to do in the meantime?"

"You'll figure it out." Rose gives me a smile.

Panic starts to set in. "Oh, come on. You can't just roll out of here. I don't know what I'm doing!"

"You know exactly what you're doing. Just feed her, change her, keep her from putting anything in her mouth."

"You say that like it's easy." To prove my point, I stride into my living room where there is a playmat on the floor for Evelyn. I set her down on it. She looks stunned, tries to reach for me, falls over, and starts crying. "She won't let me put her down. My kitchen is filled with dirty dishes and bottles. My trash is over-filled with shit-filled diapers that I can't even take to the trash chute in the hallway because she won't let me put her down and I'm afraid I'll accidentally drop her down the chute."

Rose laughs.

I don't. "I'm fucking serious. I had a nightmare last night that I did that. I woke up in a cold sweat."

"Don't swear in front of Evelyn."

"See? I swear too much. I can't do this." My chest feels tight. Evelyn is on her side like a potato, crying.

I'm still in my pajamas and I haven't showered. My arms are killing me from holding her half the night and I work out all the time. They shouldn't be this damn sore. Then again, I haven't made it to the gym in three weeks. I haven't had sex in four weeks. If I had known my life was about to take a serious left turn, I would have fucked my way across Manhattan in the weeks before Evelyn appeared.

But I didn't, because I thought I could have sex whenever I wanted because my life was my own, and now I'm wound tight, reduced to frantic jerk-offs in the shower while Rose is in my apartment tending Evelyn. It's hard to enjoy an orgasm with your old nanny and your baby (or not my baby) fifteen feet away, but if I don't jerk off, I'll crawl out of my skin.

While I'm having a damn existential crisis, the baby is still crying.

I bend down and wince at the ache in my lower back as I pick up Evelyn. She immediately stops crying.

"Grayson," Rose says, gently.

There's a stuffed bear on the floor and I step on it, my ankle rolling. I don't really lose my footing—it just pisses me off.

Now I'm just grumpy.

So I kick the stuffed bear. Seeing it go flying across the living room is stupidly satisfying. "Fine. Just go. It's fine. We'll be fine."

And the second Rose leaves, I'm calling my sister and my mom. One of them will help me. I think. Hell, I'm not above begging.

"Give her a bottle, put her down in her crib, and take a shower."

"You say that like it's easy." There is a spit bubble on Evelyn's tiny little rosebud lips and damp tears running down her cheeks. I use my shirt to wipe them up. It doesn't matter. I'm a disgusting mess right now anyway and I'm pretty sure I smell like formula and diapers. The entire apartment does. Why would I be any different?

Meanwhile, a glance down at my phone showed I have fourteen notifications and three missed calls from Andrea. I have a Zoom meeting in forty-five minutes with our West Coast team.

"It is easy. Just relax. Your stress is giving her stress."

"I actually think it's the other way around but whatever."

"Don't you whatever me. You may be a big shot in New York, but here you don't speak to me like that, young man."

Shit. "Yes, ma'am." I take a deep breath. "Thank you for helping me."

Rose laughs. "That killed you, didn't it?"

"Little bit," I admit. "But I do mean it. I couldn't have done this without you. I *can't* do this without you."

Rose gives Evelyn a kiss on the top of her head. Then she firms up her purse strap on her shoulder and stares up at me. "Man up, Grayson. You want to play, sometimes you have to pay."

I almost launch into a defensive explanation of how I wasn't irresponsible with any of my many one-night stands, but I stop myself in the nick of time. It's a losing argument.

"This could be life-changing for you in the best way possible."

Except that I liked my life exactly the way it was. When I could shower whenever I wanted and fuck whoever I wanted and sleep whenever I wanted.

"We still don't know if she's even my kid."

Rose rolls her eyes. "Keep telling yourself that."

I walk with her to the door and open it for her. I give her a hug and kiss the top of her head. Rose still smells like childhood to me, with her floral perfume and obsessive use of hand lotion. "Thank you. I mean it. I appreciate all the help."

She gives me a wave. "You'll be fine."

When the elevator opens for her at the end of the hall, I lift Evelyn's little hand and give her a wave. "Bye, Rose. We're probably going to die without you, but bye."

She snorts.

Then I momentarily forget about my problems when a woman steps off of the elevator and smiles at Rose, who eases past her.

She's gorgeous.

Late twenties, thick wavy reddish-brown hair. Sharp cheekbones and plump pink lips. I can't see her eye color from where I am, but they're warm and friendly.

She has long legs encased in leggings that show off her shape and outline her pussy in a way that makes my mouth water. She has on a crop top T-shirt with a knot at the hem so that I see a smooth expanse of skin above her waistband. She has big breasts. High, full, sensual breasts that I could bury my face in and...

Her eyes widen.

I realize I'm staring at her like a lust-crazed lunatic.

I clear my throat. "Hi."

"Hi." Her voice is low, very blues and jazz. Sexy. "Cute baby." She smiles at Evelyn.

"I know."

Why the fuck did I say that? I mean, Evelyn is a cute baby. She's a really fucking cute baby. But it sounds arrogant to admit that. I'm supposed to just say thank you, like a normal human being.

Not "I know" like a total prick.

The woman laughs lightly. She leans in and tickles Evelyn's arm. "You have a very proud papa. Lucky little girl."

She's too close to me.

I can smell her shampoo and see straight down her T-shirt, which has fallen forward with her lean. That's a lot of flesh spilling out of a bra that seems too small.

My sleep deprived brain can't figure out if she's somehow miraculously here to help me with Evelyn or to help with the raging erection I suddenly have.

But then she stands up and finger waves at Evelyn. "Bye, cutie."

And she sashays right on past me.

Oh my God, I really need a nap. She's not an angel of mercy, she's just there to visit another tenant.

She stops at the door next to my apartment. I call out after her, "Are you here to see James and Cas?"

I've barely had a chance to meet the two guys who live next door, but they seem cool. They have a baby as well—a little boy. Or is it a girl? I can't remember because the last few weeks are a fucking blur.

And of course she's there to see James and Cas. She's knocking on their damn door.

"Yes." That's all she says, but she does give me a friendly smile.

I retreat back into my own apartment and look down at

Evelyn. "That was not smooth," I tell her. "That was embarrassing."

Evelyn gives me a gummy grin and bounces up and down on my hip. She sticks her wet fingers into my mouth.

"We're calling Auntie Annabelle," I mumble from around her fingers. "We need help. So. Much. Help."

CHAPTER 3
Caroline

I HAVE KNOWN James through many of his eras. His fourth-grade Student Council President era, where he campaigned on the platform of puppies in the classroom, his middle school Paramore Super fan era, and his high school Gymnastics God era.

But seeing him holding his son makes it clear he's in his best era yet. "Oh my gosh, look at you!" I say, going in for a hug when James opens his apartment door holding his baby.

He's smiling ear to ear, and whereas the last time I saw him, he still sported a boyish vibe—now he has defined and sharper features, all vestiges of his youthful baby face gone. His green eyes are bright and his hair is a little long and shaggy, beard stubble across his chin. He's wearing joggers and a basic gray T-shirt, which shows off his fit chest and muscular upper arms.

All of that with him cradling a chubby little sleeping infant in his left arm?

It's the total package of hotness.

"Hot dad alert, wow!"

James laughs and gives me a one-armed hug. "Thank you." He pulls back and holds my left arm out to the side. "And look at you. All grown up and straight-up gorgeous."

I do a little curtsy. "Thank you. God, it's so good to see you. It's been forever."

"Since college. Come in. I'm so glad you reached out."

I follow James into his apartment, glancing around curiously. It's an adult apartment, with curated and expensive looking furniture. There's art on the walls and a gallery of photos that include wedding portraits and baby pictures. There is baby gear tucked everywhere.

"Can I get you water or a sweet tea?"

"Sweet tea would be great. Let me see this baby. Can I hold him?"

"Absolutely. Meet Noah. He was three months old yesterday." James gestures to the living room. "We are doing his three-month photo shoot today, so that's why there are beach balls. Summer theme."

My amazement grows as I take Noah from James and gently cradle him in my arms. Noah doesn't wake up. He just gives a soft sigh and his arms briefly lift and shake before he settles back into a deep slumber. He's light and smells like baby freshness. He is wearing little pastel blue and yellow plaid Bermuda shorts with a yellow onesie designed to look like a polo shirt. There is a tiny blue threaded dolphin insignia.

"He definitely looks ready to hit the golf course before a beach stroll with a sweater draped over his shoulders. It's adorable. He's adorable."

"Thank you."

That seems a more natural response to me complimenting someone's baby.

Unlike the neighbor, who managed to look both a complete and total mess and arrogant all at the same time. I'd have to ask James about his surly neighbor a little later.

"How has it been?" I ask James. "Becoming a parent, I mean. You don't even look tired. Your apartment is pristine. Your baby is an angel. I'm impressed."

"I love it," James says, reaching into a cupboard for two tall glasses. "Seriously. It's the best thing I've ever done. Sure, getting up three times a night is hard, and yes, I am plagued by self-doubt that I'm doing any of this right, but I literally just stare at my baby and the entire world is just…right there. Everything feels complete."

My heart softens. I always knew James was a good guy, but seeing him like this makes me so happy for him. "That's fantastic. Congratulations on getting married, too. I heard through the Honeysuckle Harbor gossip chain that it was quite the grand affair."

James laughs as he opens the refrigerator door. "You know my mother. She was born to throw a grand affair. It actually seemed to rejuvenate her so much she looks five years younger. Or maybe that's the Botox."

I snort, strolling with Noah over to the gallery wall to study the photos. "Tell me about Cas. Your *husband*," I add in a singsong voice. "Very handsome."

He is. He's taller than James, with very trendy glasses. The first two shots are them on the beach gazing at each other, but then there is one of them laughing and holding hands, clearly leaving their reception. Cas has removed his jacket and rolled up his shirt sleeves, revealing two fully tattooed forearms.

Arm porn at its finest. I'm a little jealous of James.

"Cas is great. He's Dutch. He's very tidy, orderly. He's thoughtful and protective and he loves to take care of us. I honestly couldn't ask for a better partner." He glances over his shoulder and grins. "Plus, he's really hot, in case you hadn't noticed."

"Oh, I noticed. Trust me. Please tell me he's good in bed too, so I can officially be jealous of you."

"Uh, yes. He is. I wouldn't have married him otherwise."

"Bullshit." I stand, rocking Noah back and forth. His little mouth is mimicking sucking in his sleep. "James, you are the kind of guy who would fall in love and make it work even if the man was, shall we say, *lacking*. You are probably the nicest human I know."

"I think you're giving me too much credit. Sex is important."

"I wouldn't know," I say, breezily. "It's been so long I'm not sure I remember how to do it."

"It's like riding a bike."

I would ride anything right now.

"If you say so."

James laughs. "How long are you back in town?" he asks, setting the glasses of sweet tea with lemon wedges on the coffee table. "Come sit down."

"Just a few months. Then I'm off to Colombia for my next teaching job." I walk slowly over to the sofa where James is sitting. I gingerly lower myself so I don't jostle Noah and wake him up.

"You always said you wanted to see the world. Good on you for doing it, Caro." James puts his feet up on the edge of the coffee table. "How was Germany?"

My last two year assignment had been in Munich and while I had loved the freedom and the ability to bounce around Europe on the weekends, the upscale international school hadn't been my favorite of my teaching gigs so far.

"Germany was great, but a little...stiff for me. You know I'm a free spirit. That's why I'm trying South America next."

"And where were you before Germany?"

I reach forward to grab my glass. "South Korea. The kids were adorable. I loved them. The food, too. It was an incredible experience. I'm glad to be home for a bit, though. I missed my family and friends. I just spent a week in Florida with my mom and my sister."

"Where are you staying while you're here?"

"With Fiona and Frannie. They have a house now." They are identical twins in a group of triplets, with their sister, Finley, being fraternal. We've been friends since grade school.

James nods. "I run into them sometimes. We love to go to Raw.

They're both pastry chefs there now, but obviously, you know that."

"They have three bedrooms and they're being very cool to let me crash while I'm here. But you know me—I travel light."

It's been years since I had more possessions than what can fit into a couple of large suitcases. The last time I owned furniture was in college. There are some random boxes stored at my mom's house, but other than some jewelry I travel with, I'm not huge on having stuff.

"So you'll be a beach bum for the next few months?"

That makes me laugh. Noah reacts by jerking in his sleep. "Oops," I whisper. "Can't wake the baby."

"He's actually a dream baby. He'll fall right back asleep, trust me."

"No wonder you look so chill and well rested. Unlike your next-door neighbor."

"You saw him?"

"Yes, looking surly and forlorn in his doorway, walking an older woman out. What's his story?"

"That's Grayson Ross. Remember him?"

"*Grayson Ross*? No way. Of course I remember him. Every girl in middle school had a massive crush on the high school star quarterback, me included." I sip my sweet tea and muse on how we all primped and dressed to impress at thirteen for the older guy who was never going to give us the time of day. We sat in those stands every Friday night and cheered him on with heart eyes.

"Middle school girls and me." James sips his tea. "He's been living in New York since college and just moved back."

"With a wife and a baby?"

"Just a baby." James reaches out. "Here, I'll take Noah so you can relax."

"No, I'm fine," I protest. "You get him all the time—don't be greedy." I'm enjoying the weight of him on my arm. "So where is the baby's mom?"

I was curious before, but now I'm *really* curious.

Grayson might have looked exhausted and cranky as hell, but he's still hot. Maybe even more so.

"From what I hear from my mother, who apparently heard from Grayson's mother at the hair salon, he had a one-night stand who had the baby dropped off at his office and then disappeared."

My jaw drops. "What? Holy shit, that's *awful*."

James shakes his head. "I know. I can't even imagine. I guess for whatever reason, she just couldn't handle being a single mom. Grayson hasn't said much to me or Cas about it, but he's clearly in over his head. He moved down here so his family could help out. His old nanny has been watching little Evelyn."

"That's why I recognized that woman. She was the triplets' nanny, too. She made the best chocolate chip cookies on earth. I loved going to their house after school."

"I give him credit for jumping in. That had to be one hell of a curveball. We had the whole process of finding a surrogate, then her pregnancy, to mentally prepare to be parents. Grayson just woke up one day and found himself with a seven-month-old baby girl."

No wonder he looked so exhausted. I feel bad for him.

I also am more excited that he's single than I have any right to be. A little sexy no-strings-attached fun would be very welcome right now.

"It says good things about him that he took the baby. That's intense, though. Poor guy."

James gives me an 'I-know-your-dirty-fucking-mind look'. "Why do I get the feeling you want to comfort him with your pussy?"

"James!" I cover Noah's tiny ears. "Not in front of the baby."

"I'm right though, aren't I?" he says dryly.

"You're not *wrong*," I admit. "Though he looked like he needed a shower."

"You can offer to scrub his back for him."

"If that man is naked, I'm not focusing on his back." I shrug. "It's been a minute. What can I say? How's your new gym venture going?"

"Good, actually. Hey, if you're looking for some extra money, I could really use a part-time teacher."

James has opened up a storefront downstairs that hosts Daddy and Me classes, Mommy and Me classes, and toddler tumbling. Given his background in gymnastics, it seems like a great fit.

"I'd love to. You know I love kids. I was planning to take on a serving job at the boardwalk, but we're toward the end of the season, so that is probably a long shot. This would help me out a lot."

"It would help me, too. Now that Noah is sleeping less, it's becoming more challenging to manage my schedule. Cas is a lawyer, so he works in Charleston and has long hours."

"Sleeps less?" I lift Noah a tad. He's just dead weight. "This baby?" I joke. "I don't believe you."

"He used to sleep eighteen hours a day. He's scaling back, I swear."

I'm about to respond when there is a hard knock on the apartment door. It's so demanding we both jump. Noah stirs in his sleep.

"Jesus, who is that?" James stands up and goes to the door right as another pounding knock booms through the room.

When he opens the door, Grayson Ross strides in with his daughter in his arms. He's still wearing pajama pants and a T-shirt that has unknown stains on it. His hair is sticking up, and he looks frantic. James didn't even invite him in and he's already standing in the middle of the living room.

"Can either of you watch Evelyn?" he asks without even so much as a greeting.

I sit up a little straighter, taken aback. He doesn't even know my name, and he wants me to watch his *child*?

"What?" James asks, closing the door behind him. "Why?"

"I have a work call in twenty minutes, and I need to take a shower before it starts. I called my mom and my sister and they can't get over here in time."

"Where did your nanny go?" I ask.

"She quit." Grayson waves his hand in the air. "I'm desperate. Please."

"Dude, you can't just leave your baby with random people," James says, looking visibly appalled.

"You're not random. You're my neighbor. You have a baby yourself. Your mother knows my mother. I trust you. I meant in my apartment, anyway. Evelyn doesn't like change. If I try to leave her here, she'll scream."

I have to admit she is a very suspicious-looking baby. She is eyeing us like we are about to kidnap her, her little hands digging tightly into Grayson's arm and chest. Every time he moves, she turns her head so she can track us.

My heart goes out to the little girl whose mother has left her with a total stranger, biological father or not.

I'm not sure what to say. I want to help Grayson, but he seems a little…ferocious. "I have lunch plans in an hour."

"It will only take thirty minutes, I promise. I'll give you a thousand dollars."

I stand up instantly with Noah in my arms. "Happy to help. James, are you coming with me?"

James looks like he wants to object, but doesn't have a good reason to say no.

"I guess we can help you for thirty minutes. What are neighbors for?"

"You're a lifesaver. I owe you, James. Seriously. Whatever you want. I'll buy you a car."

"Just pay your rent on time."

"Let's meet your friend," I tell Noah as I walk past Grayson.

I swear he glances at my chest.

"I'm Caroline," I tell him. "By the way."

He doesn't even have the decency to look shamefaced that he hasn't asked my name.

Nor does he offer his.

CHAPTER 4

James

I DON'T KNOW Grayson Ross well.

He's from Honeysuckle Harbor, so I've known *of* him, of course. The town's not big enough to have too many complete strangers. But we've never been more than passing acquaintances. Until now, I guess. He's our new tenant and neighbor.

All that said, I've definitely had an impression of Grayson Ross, of someone in control. An impression that completely shatters when I follow Caroline into his apartment. Grayson himself looked like a mess, and I wasn't letting her come over here by herself. But it's not just Grayson that's a mess. His apartment looks like a tornado hit it. A baby tornado. I don't mean a small, baby-sized tornado, I mean a tornado of baby *stuff*.

His couch is draped in baby blankets, a couple of onesies, and there's a package of diapers where throw pillows should be.

His coffee table is covered in more diapers, a canister of formula, some toys, some manila folders, and a couple of empty coffee cups. There is a baby swing, a jumper, a playpen, and a stroller sitting haphazardly around the room.

A highchair sits near the breakfast bar, covered in smears of various colored mush.

And the whole place smells like baby formula, and dirty diapers.

"Excuse the mess," Grayson says roughly. "It's been a hell of a few days."

"You sure you only need help during the next thirty minutes?" Caroline asks, looking around curiously.

Grayson watches her. "Oh no, I definitely need more help than that. But right now, I'm taking life thirty minutes at a time."

He looks at the clock on the wall, sighs heavily, and hands his baby girl to Caroline.

"This is Evelyn."

Evelyn scowls at Caroline.

Caroline takes her. "Hi Evelyn," she says sweetly. "I'm Caroline."

She balances the baby on her hip, smiling at her, bouncing slightly.

Evelyn is studying her carefully but looks perturbed.

I stroke my hand over Noah's head. He's sleeping peacefully right now, but I have never seen my son frown other than a few times before he filled his diaper.

"I..." Grayson looks around the room. "Hell, I don't know. Make yourselves at home, I guess. There's water and soda in the fridge. And Evelyn's stuff is—" He moves his arm, indicating the entire room. "Everywhere. I'd love to tell you where to find certain things, but I have no fucking idea."

Caroline laughs lightly, a pretty sound that makes me smile in return. God, everything about this woman is pretty.

More than pretty.

She was pretty as a teenager. She was also kind and carefree and so easy to be around. I'd definitely been looking forward to seeing her again and catching up.

But it turns out I wasn't prepared at all to see her again, given she's not a girl anymore. She's a woman. She's a confident, gorgeous, smart woman who has been traveling the world and becoming even more interesting and intriguing and, yes, beautiful.

"We'll find whatever we need. I'm not worried," she assures Grayson.

"Well, that would make one of us." He shakes his head. "I don't mean I'm worried about you being here. I'm just worried in general."

"Go do your meeting or whatever. We'll be right here."

He seems to want to say more but just shakes his head again, turns on his heel, and heads for the bedroom.

As soon as the door shuts behind him, Caroline turns to me. "Wow, I think he's really in over his head."

I cast a look around the room and chuckle. "What makes you say that?" I ask dryly.

Caroline looks down at the baby in her arms. "What do you think? Is your daddy having a hard time?"

Evelyn's brow furrows and her bottom lip pushes out.

"I'm gonna take that as a yes," Caroline says. She reaches up and rubs the little girl's bottom lip. "That is quite a pout you have going."

Evelyn's face scrunches, and the lip begins to tremble.

Caroline looks at me. "Uh oh."

"Don't worry, Evie," I say. "We're going to help. How about we work on making your apartment smell a little better first?"

Evelyn's pouty lip goes away as she looks at me. I step closer and turn so she can see Noah's face. "This is Noah. Do you want to be friends?"

Evelyn studies Noah but doesn't say anything.

"Maybe Noah can borrow your swing," I say, moving toward the swing next to the couch. I lower Noah into it and press the button to start it gently rocking.

Evelyn is watching us with clear suspicion. Fair enough. Three total strangers are here in her space, taking over her stuff, and her dad just disappeared.

We're lucky she's not screaming.

Caroline carries her over to the jumpy-seat toy. "Evelyn, you sit here and watch Noah."

She puts the little girl in the seat and twirls a couple of the toys on the tray. Evelyn isn't impressed.

I chuckle, and Evelyn looks up at me. Then she practically knocks me over with a sudden toothless grin. I can't do anything but grin right back at her.

"There you go," Caroline tells her, propping her hands on her slim hips. "We're not so bad, are we?"

Evelyn looks at her. And frowns.

Caroline's eyebrows arch. "Say something else," she tells me. "Talk to her."

"What do you have to be so grumpy about at only seven months of life?" I ask Evelyn. "Or was it your past life that's got you so down?"

Evelyn looks up at me, and sure enough, grins before putting her fist to her mouth.

Caroline laughs. "Maybe she just likes men. You little flirt," she tells Evelyn.

That gets her another frown.

Caroline puts both hands up. "Okay girl, I got it. I'm leaving you alone." Caroline looks at me. "I'm gonna go clean up in the kitchen. How about you do the living room? I think Evelyn would prefer you stay out here with her."

I grin down at the little girl. "I can do that."

We spent about fifteen minutes cleaning up Grayson's apartment. Not only are there a ton of dishes to gather and rinse and put in the dishwasher, making a full load that we then start, but there's just general straightening to do.

Not to mention the garbage.

In the end, we have an overflowing trash can in the kitchen and another half trash bag filled with sandwich wrappers, takeout bags from a taco place, and probably forty-seven to-go coffee cups.

"He doesn't even make his own coffee?" Caroline asks, dropping the final cardboard cup into the bag I'm holding. "Do you think he doesn't know how or he doesn't have time?"

"Did you know Grayson at all when he lived here in Honeysuckle Harbor?" I ask her.

She shakes her head. "No. He's what? Five years older than us? I know the Rosses have lived here forever. Really nice people, right?"

I nod. "Very nice. And I've never heard that Grayson's not. But he's some big-shot business prodigy who quickly moved up the ranks, became CEO, and then started his own company. I don't know what exactly he does, but he's very successful. It would not surprise me at all, despite how this apartment looks and the fact that he clearly has no idea what to do with a baby girl, that Grayson Ross doesn't do anything for himself when it's possible to order or pay someone else to do it."

"Was he ever married?" Caroline asks, bending to pick up three socks—one man's and two baby socks that do not match.

"No. If you're asking about the origin of Evelyn, it was a one-night stand that showed up at my office a few weeks ago with a baby girl who she handed to my assistant and then walked out the door."

We both spin at the sound of Grayson's voice.

Dammit. You never gossip about a person in their apartment when they're home. Of course, he was going to walk out and catch us.

"Grayson, I—" I start.

But Caroline doesn't act guilty to be caught. "She just showed up and handed you the baby?"

Grayson tucks his hands into the pockets of his slacks. He's studying Caroline with an unreadable expression. "No. It was her sister. And she handed her to my assistant. I didn't even see her."

"That's very unfortunate." Then Caroline tips her head, clearly curious. "Did you remember her?"

So I'm standing here, embarrassed that he caught us talking about him behind his back, and Caroline is not only clearly unapologetic but is also pressing on this sensitive private matter.

I also tuck my hands into my pockets and settle in to watch. This is fun.

"I remembered the short red skirt she was wearing when we met. Once she mentioned it," Grayson says.

I'm surprised he's answering. He could tell Caroline it's none of her business. Because it's really not. But I think that might actually be a tiny smile tugging at the corner of his lips.

Caroline nods. "Oh, a short red skirt. That'll get you every time. This entire thing is so not your fault."

"Do you have a short red skirt, Caroline?" Grayson asks.

My gaze goes quickly from Caroline to him.

Is he flirting with her? Seriously? In the midst of...all of this? In front of me?

You're married to the man who lives in the apartment next door to this one, remember?

Right. There is no reason Grayson would think flirting with Caroline in front of me was strange.

Actually, there is no reason Grayson flirting with Caroline in front of me is strange.

What the hell are you thinking?

But him flirting with Caroline right now, considering the current circumstances, is a little weird. I mean, yes, Caroline is gorgeous, but they just met. And his apartment smells like dirty diapers.

"Actually no," she says. "Mine's hot pink. Oh, and I have a black one. But they basically serve the same function."

I watch as Grayson's gaze moves over Caroline from head to toe. Then he nods. "I bet they do."

Yep. He's flirting with her. Blatantly. In a stinky apartment. Despite the fact that he clearly can't handle his life.

I am irrationally irritated by this.

I step forward and thrust a garbage bag toward him. "We cleaned up a little while you were busy."

That pulls his gaze from Caroline, and he looks down at the trash bag. Now he at least looks a little sheepish.

"I would've taken all of this out, of course. But Evelyn doesn't like when I'm not with her, and I can't take her to the trash chute with me."

"She seemed fine with James while you were in the other room," Caroline pipes up.

Grayson looks over at his daughter. She's sucking on the knuckles of her hand, watching us. Frowning. Until she sees her dad looking, then she gives him a big smile.

I grin. That is one cute little girl.

"Wait, why can't you take her to the trash chute with you?" I ask.

"Because she might fall in," he says in a tone that indicates this should be obvious.

I exchange a glance with Caroline.

She's watching Grayson with a half-amused, half-puzzled look.

"You think you might drop Evelyn in the trash chute accidentally?" I ask.

"It could happen," Grayson insists. "What if I have it open, and I'm trying to put the trash in with one hand, and I'm only holding her in one arm? Then she gets squirmy, and I lose my grip? She could tumble right in. She's top heavy."

"Surely you have a better grip on her than that," I say.

"Does she wiggle that hard? And try to get away from you?" Caroline asks.

It's clear she's fighting a smile.

Grayson frowns, and I'm struck by how much he looks like his daughter.

"Well, no," Grayson admits. "Evelyn prefers when I hold her and never tries to get down."

His tone makes it clear that her never wanting to be put down is somewhat of a pain in the ass, actually.

"Well, we are happy to help you take your trash out," Caroline says sweetly.

That might be a little flirty too, as a matter of fact.

Since when is talking about trash, or talking while surrounded by trash, flirtatious?

"Sure," I say. "Or you could just put Evelyn in the swing or the playpen for the two minutes it takes to take the trash down the hall."

Grayson shakes his head immediately. "She doesn't like when I leave."

"So you let the trash pile up rather than let little miss be upset for even two minutes?" Caroline asks, her smile breaking free this time.

Grayson is still frowning. "There's no reason to upset her."

Caroline shakes her head. "Wow, I wish all the men in my life were so accommodating as to keep me from being upset for even two minutes." She looks at Evelyn. "You're going to have to teach me your ways, baby doll."

I roll my eyes. I am certain this woman has men tripping over themselves, trying to make her happy.

"Or you could just put Evelyn in the stroller and take her down the hall with you to take the trash out," I suggest.

Grayson looks at me thoughtfully. "That's actually a good idea. She does like the stroller."

I snort. "Glad I could help."

I shouldn't tease the guy. Clearly, fatherhood is not something he's taking to naturally. And it can be overwhelming. I at least have a partner helping, and Noah is an absolute ray of sunshine. He loves to be held, of course, but we can put him down when we need to do other things.

"You really need to get some help," Caroline tells Grayson.

He runs a hand over his face and gives a heavy sigh. "I'm aware. I had help until this morning. Rose. You met her on her way out."

Caroline's eyes widen. "What did you do to make that sweet woman quit?"

"I needed her to work a lot. Too much. My expectations tend to be very high for lots of other people. Particularly ones who are picking up the slack in my life where I…"

"Kind of suck?" I offer.

I don't know why I feel the need to point out that this man is drowning. I definitely get the impression that not being good at something is very unusual for Grayson Ross.

He doesn't look pleased with my suggestion, but he doesn't deny it either. "I'm not above asking for help, and I'm not above paying very well for it. But I do expect that help to do an exceptional job."

"Especially for your daughter," Caroline says.

Grayson looks over at Evelyn. "We don't actually know that she's mine."

Caroline and I look at each other again, and I snort. Again.

"What?" Grayson asks. "We're waiting on the results of the DNA test."

"She looks just like you, man," I tell him. There's no way this kid isn't his.

"So I've been told," Grayson says. "But I need to be sure."

Caroline looks around the apartment. "But you still did all of this? Even before you knew for sure?"

He shrugs. "She needed things. It's not her fault that the woman in the red skirt dropped her off with me."

"What was her name?" Caroline asks. She's studying him closely. "I know you know."

He sighs. "Lacey."

"And you were in New York when you 'met' Evelyn?"

"Yes."

"And then you picked up your life and moved here."

"Yes. My family is here. I thought they'd help."

"But they're not?"

"Not as much as I need them to."

"Why not?" Caroline asks.

"Because I'm a full-grown man who has money and brains and no excuse not to be able to do something literally millions of people around the world do every single day," he says. It's clear he's quoting someone.

Caroline smiles. "Is that what your mom said?"

"My older sister. But my mom concurred."

Caroline's smile grows. "I—"

"Don't say it," Grayson tells her.

"What?" Caroline asks, blinking with fake innocence.

"That you also concur."

She laughs. "Why not?"

"Because I know you do." He looks over at me. "I know you both do."

I do. I mean, he is all of those things and there isn't really an excuse.

But I'm annoyed by his easy camaraderie with Caroline and how comfortable she seems with him.

Which is stupid as hell.

"Do you want me to ask around? See if anyone's available to help?" I ask.

Grayson shakes his head. "I've already filled out applications for a nanny agency. I'm actually looking for two. A daytime and a nighttime. I should be getting resumes soon."

Of course, he's going with some high-end service. The nannies probably all went to Harvard and are pediatric neurosurgeons in their free time.

His eyes are on Caroline again. "I could use help until I hire someone, though. Are you available?"

No, she's not available. She's…

Not anything to me but a friend, I remind myself. Sure, we were a couple in high school, but that was a decade ago.

I don't need to feel protective of Caroline. She's been traveling the world on her own. Teaching all over. She is quite capable of taking care of herself.

Still, there's something almost predatory about the way Grayson studies her. Something that makes me think that, in a different circumstance, he would want much more from her.

Or hell, maybe in this exact circumstance.

"Caroline is going to be teaching some classes at my gym," I say.

"But that's very flexible. And Grayson said this is temporary." She looks at Evelyn and smiles. The baby frowns back. "Sure, I can help you out. I won't say I'm any kind of baby whisperer, but if all you need is a couple extra pair of hands—" She lifts her hands and wiggles her fingers. "I can do that."

"That would be amazing." Grayson's sigh of relief is long and heavy. "I would really love to have the use of your hands, Caroline."

And the idea of Grayson enjoying Caroline's hands for anything at all—Should. Not. Bother. Me.

But despite the cleanup Caroline and I just did, things suddenly feel very messy in Grayson Ross's apartment.

CHAPTER 5

Cas

JAMES MOANS. "This is absolutely fucking amazing. God, I need five more. *Please.*"

Frannie Anderson laughs. "God, you're hot, an amazing dad, and you're always willing to try my crazy concoctions, and you actually like them. Why did you have to meet Cas before you came back to Honeysuckle Harbor?"

She casts me a look and I give her a wink.

I know Frannie is teasing James not only because he's married, but because she thinks he's only into men.

But he's actually bi and Frannie is gorgeous and if he had come back to Honeysuckle Harbor single, he probably would've taken her up on this not-really kidding offer.

I study my husband across the table as he and Frannie chat. They've known each other for years. They're the same age and went to school together all the way from kindergarten through senior year. I've gotten to know both Frannie and her twin sister Fiona and have even met the other triplet, Finley, once since we've moved back. Their older brother Ford owns our favorite restaurant, Raw, where we're having dinner tonight while James's mother gets her grandson fix.

James is really happy back here in Honeysuckle Harbor. He's a naturally happy, laid-back guy who makes friends easily wherever he goes, but there has been a change in him since we moved back. He's more relaxed, he doesn't worry about things like finances and the crime rate like he did when we first started talking about having kids.

I was very happy to give him this small town life when we finally decided to start a family.

I would do anything for him.

There is truly only one drawback to living here.

Small town life, especially small town life where he grew up and knows everyone, has put the kibosh on one part of our lifestyle.

James and I both like women.

We're in love with each other and very happily married, and we have an amazing sex life, but we've always enjoyed bringing women into our bedroom from time to time.

It was something we did when we first started dating and we easily made it work with adventurous women in the city who were happy to be a one-night or even weekend-long third. They were never relationships, but we definitely liked the women and even had a couple over the years who we hooked up with regularly.

It's been a fun, consensual part of our relationship from the beginning and has actually brought us closer as a couple.

And we're both missing it since we moved here.

We agreed coming to Honeysuckle Harbor would end all of that. Having a situation like that in this town would be far too complicated.

It's fine. We're very happy and our sex life is great. As great as two working new dads to a three-month-old can be.

We're a very typical couple in every way.

It's just a little like no longer being able to get salted caramel cold foam on my iced caramel lattes. They're still amazing without it, but that extra sweetness on top just makes it a little more fun sometimes.

"Caroline said she's living with you and Fiona right now," James says as I tune back into their conversation.

After reminding myself that Frannie is not an option for a third with us, no matter how gorgeous and funny and sexy she is.

"She is," Frannie says. "It's been really fun having her back. She said she stopped over and saw you today."

Yes, this is the fifth time James has mentioned Caroline tonight.

The Caroline.

He told me his old friend had stopped by to say hello and meet Noah. Apparently, she's been out of the country for several years and is back in town just for a few months between jobs.

James told me it was great to catch up with her. He told me they had a great afternoon and that Caroline will be nannying for our neighbor Grayson. He also told me that he hired her to work part-time at the gym.

I have heard a lot about Caroline.

Add that to my previous knowledge about Caroline and I find this very interesting. Caroline isn't just one of James's old friends from high school, like Frannie or Fiona.

No, Caroline is an ex. She and James dated, and she's probably the most serious girlfriend he's ever had. She was also his first.

And I can't help but notice the way my husband's eyes light up a little and the extra tilt to his mouth when he smiles, talking about her.

"It would be so fun for all of us to get together," Frannie says. "We'll have to set something up."

"That would be awesome," James agrees. "I definitely want her to meet Cas." He looks over at me with a smile.

I lift my tumbler of scotch. I really want to meet Caroline too.

Because she's important to James and they have history. But also because I have an idea forming.

Frannie moves off, returning to the kitchen. She's a pastry chef here at the restaurant so not free to stand and chat for too long.

James turns back to me, his smile warm and wide.

"I love seeing you happy like this," I tell him.

He picks up his water glass and takes a long drink. "I had a great day."

He's also mentioned that three times now.

I smile. "I'm glad. Sounds like it was eventful."

He chuckles. "It was. Wait until you see Grayson with Evelyn. He's a mess. But it's kind of adorable." He leans in. "I'm sorry. I know you've seen Grayson and Evelyn together. I just mean, now that Caroline is going to be right next door and around more, I'll be seeing more of her, and that probably means more of Grayson, too."

"Not to mention she's now an employee," I say, fighting my smile.

He really has no idea how much he's talked about all of them. We've met Grayson and his daughter before this, of course, but haven't spent time with them. It seems now that James is enamored with little Evelyn as well.

James gives me a sheepish look. "I'm sorry I didn't wait and run the idea of hiring Caroline past you before I said something to her."

I shake my head. "It's your gym. You don't have to run those decisions past me. She's your friend. If you want her around while she's here in town, that's cool with me."

"It's not just that, though it was great to see her and I'm looking forward to spending time with her," James says. He chews on his bottom lip and then says, "I have to confess that it's been a little tougher to juggle all the business stuff and Noah than I thought it would be. The idea of having someone else around to help feels really nice."

Fuck. He's been doing an amazing job with Noah and everything while I'm driving to Charleston every day. I don't want him to get burned out. I'm the primary breadwinner and we agreed that he'd be more of a stay-at-home dad here in the beginning, but I don't want him overwhelmed.

I reach over and take his hand, stroking my thumb over the

back of his knuckles. "You're doing an amazing job. You have my full support, no matter what you want or need. If you want to wait on the gym until Noah is older—"

"No. The gym is great. I love it. And everybody coming in is telling me how much they love it. Plus, it's something I can do with Noah as he grows."

I was lucky to be taken on by the practice in Charleston, and only have a thirty-minute commute, but my hours are often long, and James is definitely left with the heavy lifting on the baby end of things. "We could hire a nanny, like Grayson did."

James laughs. "Maybe I'll ask Caroline if she just wants to watch Noah and Evelyn together."

"That would leave her with very little free time," I say.

He turns his hand over so our palms rest against one another. "True. I assume while she's in town, she wants to have a life and have some fun, too."

Yes. I would assume so, too. In fact, I hope so.

Caroline is obviously James's type. They have a past. She's only in town temporarily.

She might be the perfect thing I can give my husband to show him how much I appreciate him and that not everything in our life has to feel different and turned upside down.

Or at least maybe we can have some fun and work off some stress in the midst of everything that's turned upside down.

We definitely look like two nice guys who fell in love, got married, had an adorable little boy, and are now starting a business, putting down roots, and becoming part of a small town community.

But just like I've got tattoos under my very nice suit sleeves and a motorcycle in my garage, behind our closed bedroom door, we really love to have a dirty good time.

"So when can I meet Caroline?" I ask.

"Probably whenever you're free. She's going to be over at Grayson's a lot," James says. "And even though she told him that she's going to make him do the night shift on his own, I think she's going to feel sorry for him—or maybe for Evelyn—and show up really early and end up staying late."

I nod. "That's great. I'll try to get home early tomorrow night so you can introduce us. I'm looking forward to meeting her."

James smiles. "I think you're really going to like her."

Yeah, I think I'm really going to too.

Caroline Bell might just be exactly what we need.

CHAPTER 6

Caroline

IT'S good to be home.

I love seeing the world and I'm definitely not done exploring all the universe has to offer, but it's nice to have grown up in a place like Honeysuckle Harbor. It changes slowly, people are kind and gracious, and the pace is easy. When I come back for a visit, it still feels like home. The town and its people just open their arms back up for me and I love that.

Case in point—the older men who hang out in front of the cafe every day.

It's my first day babysitting for Evelyn and Grayson was pacing back and forth on the phone. Evelyn couldn't seem to focus on anything other than the fact that her dad was not holding her. I tried rocking her, distracting her with toys, putting her in the bouncer—that *really* pissed her off—and letting her suck on my T-shirt sleeve. But in the end, it seemed smartest to pop her in the stroller and go for a walk.

Sunshine and hopefully seeing other people and dogs might dazzle her into forgetting she's not being held by Grayson. That's my hope, anyway. She may be a baby, but she is a city girl and probably used to lots of stimulating sights and sounds. And maybe a messy apartment that still has the lingering scent of diapers is just trying her patience.

The apartment looks better today, but it's still a long way from clean and organized.

I'm a little surprised Grayson is letting me just leave with his daughter, but I also suspect he thoroughly vetted me last night via the Honeysuckle Harbor gossip chain, and maybe through a lawyer. That seems like something a wealthy man would do.

So now I'm outside on the sidewalk chatting with the men playing chess, who are all complimenting Evelyn and making faces at her. She's not crying, but she's not smiling either.

One of the men playing chess is Fiona and Frannie's grandfather, so I've known him basically my entire life.

"Mr. Anderson, I saw Rose yesterday, but I didn't realize it was her until it was too late to say anything. She was hot footing it out of Grayson's apartment."

He laughs. "Poor Rose. She probably needs to sleep for three days straight after all that babysitting. The word going around is Grayson Ross is a demanding boss."

Yikes. I already suspected that, but it's still a little daunting to hear it. Good thing I'm an easygoing person.

"Don't tell her that. She's working for the man," Sam Reed says.

"Well, this is only temporary," I tell them, pulling the stroller back and forth to soothe Evelyn. "Until he finds a couple of agency nannies."

"Make sure you find time to have some fun, too, while you're here," Walt says.

I laugh. "Don't worry, I'm here to relax and catch up with family and friends, too. I'm on my way to check out James's new baby gym right now, actually."

They all nod.

"Right, right," Mr. Anderson says. "James and Cas have that cute little guy. We're having a bit of a baby boom here in Honeysuckle Harbor. Must be something in the water. Be careful, Caroline."

I know it's just a joke—something he would say to any single woman—but I still have a few years of exploring ahead of me before I'm ready to settle down and start a family.

But, like I told James, I'm not having sex right now, so I have exactly nothing to worry about.

"Good thing I don't go in the water," I say lightly.

I mean that literally and figuratively.

The men laugh and I give them a wave and say, "No cheating at chess, gentlemen."

Evelyn throws her teething ring out of the stroller as I push the stroller in front of the baby gym's storefront. When I bend over to pick it up, I have the feeling there are eyes on my backside watching my movement.

I'm wearing another pair of skintight leggings. I live in them when I'm not at work, and I have a decent ass—thank you very much. I just really hope it's not the chess guys checking me out. But when I stand back up and flip my hair over my shoulders, a glance into the store shows it's James watching me.

A little sizzle runs through me.

Which I instantly feel guilty about. James is happily married. I can't sizzle around him.

Swallowing hard, I catch his gaze. He doesn't look away, even though he was obviously staring at my ass.

Mentally brushing it off, I smile when he opens the door for me to push the stroller through. James and I have history. We were two teens in the flush of first love, fumbling over each other's naked bodies in his dark bedroom. It must just be a lingering kind of nostalgic vibe.

Only my suddenly tight nipples might indicate otherwise.

Resolutely ignoring my body's reaction to his look, I glance around the gym. It's bright and colorful and clean. There are mats lined up on the floor and a wall with crates and shelves filled with balls and other items like pool noodles, block mats, and low skills apparatus. Noah is lying on his back on one of the mats, playing with his toes.

"This is so cute, James. That little balance beam, oh my gosh. How old are the students?"

For a second, he doesn't respond. I turn and see he's looking at me, but he just has a friendly smile on his face. I feel like I imagined it was anything other than that a minute ago.

I feel like that's confirmed when he starts talking, and it's casual and easy.

"We start at four months and go to six years old. It's movement based and imaginative play designed to build confidence and motor and social skills. I use music and games that are age appropriate. Right now we're doing three classes a day, but I'd love to add at least one more."

"This is so impressive. You know I love kids. I'm probably more comfortable with the older kids since I don't have the mommy experience, and I've taught kindergarten in South Korea." I step up onto the balance beam and go the length of it easily. "Hey, yoga has paid off."

"It's triple the width of regulation," James points out. "And flat on the floor."

"Let me enjoy my victory." I wrinkle my nose at him. "Not all of us were star gymnasts at Penn State."

"Most of us weren't," he says with a grin. James bends over and greets Evelyn. "Hi, sweet girl. What do you think? Should we blow some bubbles for you and Noah?"

She rewards James with a huge smile and some soft enthusiastic coos. She even kicks her legs and smacks the bar of her stroller.

"You really have the touch with her."

"It must be the dad vibe." James unbuckles Evelyn and picks her up. "Oh, you're so big." He walks over to the mat. "Noah has already changed so much. I can't believe in just a few months he's going to be sitting up like Evelyn." He sets Evelyn down on the mat and clutches his chest dramatically. "My heart can't take it."

Seeing James as a grown man—a father, a business owner—is really special to me. "Hey, remember that night we stole a bottle from my mom's case of wine and snuck into the boathouse?"

I sit down on the mat and cross my legs as I tickle Noah's tummy and smile at him.

James gives me a look. "Caroline. Of course, I remember that night. How the hell could I forget that night? I had big plans to get you out of your little denim shorts and instead you threw up all over me."

"It's polite of you not to mention what I was doing when I threw up." I had been drunkenly giving him a blowjob and… disaster. "At least I turned and aimed away from you."

He laughs and shakes his head. "It's best left unsaid. Really. Let's never talk about it again."

"Take it as a compliment. It was a lot to fit in my mouth."

James snorts. "Thank you. I guess."

"I still don't like white wine," I lament. "What was that?"

"Moscato. No one should drink an entire bottle of Moscato by themself. That's a lot of sugar."

"We've come a long way. That was literally the one and only time I've thrown up from alcohol."

"Lucky me, I got to experience that with you. Though I appreciate how hard you worked to redeem yourself the following weekend." He gives me a wink.

The next weekend had been when we'd both lied to our parents and said we were staying at a friend's house when, in fact, we snuck into his bedroom while his parents were at a fundraiser event. As far as first times go, it had been pretty damn sweet and eye opening all at once.

I squeeze his knee. "We shared a lot of experiences together. I'm glad they were with you."

James reaches over and plants a kiss on my temple. "I'm glad mine were with you, too."

It's a friendly kiss, nothing more.

Yet my heart rate kicks up a notch.

I had no idea I was going to be so nostalgic seeing James again. The last time I saw him, I had been a cocky twenty-year-old. Sure I knew everything there was to know about everything. We'd gone out clubbing in New York City when our schedules had aligned and stayed up all night, ending it at a greasy diner in Brooklyn. We'd discussed our future plans and how we were never going back to Honeysuckle Harbor.

Yet, here we both are.

"What made you move back home?" I ask.

James reaches over to the shelf and retrieves two bottles of bubbles and hands me one. "This. My husband, my son. Family. We lived in Philadelphia for years and it was great. I loved the food, the people. Hated the winter. Missed the small town atmosphere."

"Cas likes it here?" I uncap the top of the bottle and pull out the wand. I blow a bubble at Evelyn and she just stares at me. Not the bubble, just me. "This kid is a tough nut to crack."

"She's had a lot of changes recently. I'm sure she'll settle in. Cas is fine here. I don't necessarily think it's his first choice. He's from Amsterdam, and he's a city boy. But he loves the water, and he loves me. We do plan to travel with Noah to the Netherlands for Christmas this year to see Cas's family."

"That sounds incredible. I became a Christmas village devotee after living in Germany." I blow another bubble at Evelyn.

Nothing.

Noah is on James's lap now, giving little chuckles. James blows a bubble at Evelyn and she lets out a happy shriek. She even attempts to reach out for it. She wobbles a little but recovers.

"Okay," I say, delighted to see her reaction. "We're getting somewhere. Though she does seem to prefer men. Or maybe just anyone but me. Good thing I'm not easily offended, because I feel like she's just tolerating me."

"How was Grayson this morning?"

"I barely saw him. He just handed off Evelyn while talking on the phone. Speaking of, I should take Evelyn back up and see if she's hungry. I have no idea the last time he fed her a bottle." I unfurl my legs and stand up. "I'll text you later about when I can run a class."

"Perfect." James stands up with Noah as I pick up Evelyn.

He gives me a one-armed hug. "Don't let Grayson push you around."

"I can handle him."

Ten minutes later, I'm back in the apartment. I leave Evelyn in the stroller because she seems content there chewing on her strawberry shaped teether as I go on a search for the formula. The can on the kitchen counter is empty. A search in the cupboard reveals nothing. Truly, nothing. Grayson has no food. The man must be living on takeout and protein drinks.

Grayson isn't in the living room. His bedroom door is open, so I call out, "Grayson? Where is the—

I draw up short, mouth dropping open.

Grayson is naked in the bathroom. One hundred percent mouthwateringly naked, as he leans over the sink. I have a full view of his backside, and his front in the mirror that's hanging on the wall in front of him.

He has broad shoulders, a lean waist, strong, muscular thighs, and a very tight ass.

He also has a huge cock that he is fisting, stroking up and down with hard, urgent jerks.

Our eyes meet in the mirror.

"Oh, God," I say, both mortified and suddenly very turned on.

He doesn't break eye contact. He also doesn't stop.

Is he going to…

My cheeks grow warm. My inner thighs get hot and wet.

I'm frozen in place, torn between wanting to see him come and knowing I have no business being there.

His eyes narrow.

I jerk, returning to my senses and get the hell out of his bedroom, closing the door behind me.

CHAPTER 7

Grayson

I'M FACED WITH A DILEMMA.

Abandon what I'm doing or finish what I've started.

I decide to finish. Hell, Caroline already saw me beating my cock like it owes me money, so I might as well reap the reward of my efforts. I've been wound really fucking tight the last three weeks.

I'm poised over the sink for easy clean up, straight out of the shower. I could have jerked off in the shower, but I think I fell asleep under the stream instead. When I finally came back to my senses, the water was cold because this is an old building. I'd gotten out and decided to take care of business quickly before Caroline and Evelyn returned.

Not quickly enough, apparently.

But now, as I stroke myself a little slower, but tighter, my fantasy of a couple of blondes making out is replaced by the image of a certain woman with reddish brown hair who lives in tight leggings. Her expression—was she horrified? Yes. But I also think she was a little intrigued. Or maybe that's just wishful thinking.

Bottom line, I'm sure she's going to quit.

But right now, I'm visualizing what would have happened if

she had strode into the bathroom, got down on her knees and pulled my cock into her moist, silken mouth, cupping my balls with lithe fingers and gazing up over my length with a wanton expression…

I give a grunt and explode into my hand, the hot strands of cum spilling over into the sink. Letting out a deep breath, I release the tension in my shoulders and consider how I'm supposed to apologize to Caroline.

Not that I need to apologize. I was in my bedroom. Though the door was open.

But still. She invaded my privacy.

But she's also caring for my maybe-daughter and I should be available to her.

Though what happened to knocking?

The door was open.

Damn it. As I quickly clean up and get dressed, tension is already creeping back into my neck and shoulders.

At least I'm clean and I did a load of laundry last night. I have clean shorts to put on, though they're wrinkled to hell and back, and a golf shirt so I can look presentable on this afternoon's video call. I really need to research if there is a laundry service in Honeysuckle Harbor. In New York, my clothes just magically appeared on my doorstep three times a week in a tidy little hanging bag of ironed shirts and pants, as well as my towels and sheets in a bundle, a sprig of lavender on top.

Why do I feel like that's not a Honeysuckle Harbor staple?

I need a housecleaning service as well. Caroline and James ran my dishwasher and cleaned up a multitude of takeout containers the night before, which was really nice, but I can't expect Caroline to clean on top of caring for Evelyn. She's a pretty demanding baby. Hell, maybe all babies are demanding. I have no idea. I just know that I'm white knuckling this whole situation.

And Caroline is probably going to quit because I made her uncomfortable.

Though I still feel like she was in the wrong here.

I never gave her permission to be in my bedroom.

Of course, that's where the crib is.

Knowing I might actually be wrong doesn't improve my mood. It makes it worse.

I stride out into the living room, prepared for battle. I will argue my ass off to prevent Caroline from quitting.

She's on the couch, giving Evelyn a bottle.

I steel myself and open my mouth.

But Caroline speaks first. "Feel better?" she says, giving me a casual smile.

Caught off guard, I nod. "Sorry," I say, gruffly. "I should have locked the door."

I can admit, apologizing doesn't come easily to me.

Especially when I wasn't wrong.

She puts her hand up. "It's fine. Let's not make a big deal out of it. You close the door, I'll knock, we'll be fine. You've been under a lot of pressure lately, so I can't say I blame you."

"I have been under a lot of pressure." Deflated now that she's not giving me a reason to fight, I wander over to them and run my hand over Evelyn's downy hair.

She gazes up at me, making adorable little sucking sounds as she drinks her formula.

"Any port in a storm, right?" Caroline grins.

I grunt in acknowledgment. "This is a damn hurricane, that's for sure. Hey, what was it you wanted?"

"The formula. The canister on the counter was empty. But I found it in the bags of groceries by the front door."

"Sorry about that," I say, the apology easier this time. It just rolls off of my tongue. Look at me. Mr. Mellow. "Thanks for not running out of here screaming."

Caroline shrugs. "It's natural. A great tension release."

I wonder if she's getting fucked regularly, and that's why she's so calm all the time.

I envision some beefy gym rat sweating all over her and wish I hadn't.

I have no idea what her type is. Nor is her sex life any of my business.

Talk about a conflict of interest.

If I fuck the nanny, I'll really be complicating things, and God knows I'm in no shape to be in a relationship.

I've never been a relationship type of guy, anyway, preferring the freedom of being single and doing whatever I want. Now? Forget about it. I'm a mess. I can't learn how to become a parent—if Evelyn is mine—and navigate dating on top of that.

If I want to have casual sex, it needs to be with someone other than the nanny.

Caroline stretches her right arm out, which pushes her glorious breasts forward in her little tank top.

Or I can work really hard on finding a couple of permanent nannies so I can do whatever I want with Caroline, which is to strip her naked and lick her from head to toe.

With that idea in mind, as well as the fact that I'm undeniably drowning in domestic chaos, I check my email on my phone and find the nanny agency has sent me several nanny candidates' dossiers. I scroll through the possibilities. They're all young and have great backgrounds.

I turn my phone to Caroline. "What do you think of her? She was a senator's nanny."

Caroline eyes my phone. She reads with her lips moving. Then surprises me by reaching out and scrolling my screen until she gets to the woman's photo that has been attached. "She looks uptight."

I just see a woman who is giving a hint of a smile in an attempt to remain professional. She has high cheekbones, is attractive, and has sleek brown hair. "Shouldn't a nanny be, I don't know, disciplined?"

"Who else did they send you?" She glances down and readjusts Evelyn's bottle.

"This one. Her name is Primrose. She's twenty-one." I study

her picture. "She's also gorgeous. Like, wow, gorgeous. I better not pick her. Too tempting."

Caroline snorts. "Is that even real? She sounds like a catfish."

Is she jealous? I certainly hope so. This feels a little more fun than it should.

"These are from the agency," I protest. "It doesn't matter though, because she's too pretty. I'm going to set up an interview with the first one."

"Are there any grandmotherly type options? That seems like your best bet." Caroline is straining to glance at my phone again.

If not jealous, because she hasn't known me long enough to be jealous, she is definitely competitive. This is a *lot* more fun.

"Why is that?"

"They're reliable. And not looking for a rich husband."

"You think nannies are just trying to steal husbands?" That is a very cynical point of view. It sounds like something I would say.

"I don't mean they would *steal* husbands. But you're single, right?"

"Very single," I agree. "And not looking for a marriage of convenience with a twenty-one-year-old nanny." I give her a grin. "Sorry if that ruins your plans."

Caroline laughs. "You're safe with me. I promise I'm not angling for a husband."

It makes me curious what she *does* want in life. She seems very confident and easygoing.

"That's a relief."

"And I'm not twenty-one," she adds lightly. "I'm twenty-eight, so I'm basically aging out of trophy wife potential."

The corner of her mouth is turned up. She is enjoying teasing me.

"Oh, yeah, you might as well resign yourself to marrying for love at this point."

She laughs. "That's always been the plan. Just waiting for Mr. Wonderful to pop out of a bush because I'm not actively looking."

"Is that how people find spouses these days? Good thing I

don't have a yard." I give her a wink. "So tell me about yourself, Caroline. I've been too overwhelmed to ask you much, so I apologize for that. You're between jobs?"

"Yes, by choice. I teach overseas and I've been doing two year assignments. I start another in a few weeks in Colombia."

"Wow, that sounds interesting. Does it give you time to travel?"

"Yes, I've been all over Europe and Asia."

Caroline, the temp nanny, is even more fascinating than I expected. It's also nice to be around a woman who has no obvious interest in a long-term relationship. Though I am definitely curious to see if she might be on board with a little naked fun once she's no longer my employee.

"What was your favorite place?"

"Croatia. The water was gorgeous, and the people were lovely."

"I've never been there. I'd love to go." Though it occurs to me, my days of spontaneous weekend trips all over the world might be over.

With that in mind, I look at my phone screen again and go through three more nanny profiles. "What about her?" I ask Caroline, turning my phone so she can see.

This woman is around my age and she looks very…wholesome. Like she bakes bread and goes to church twice a week. Like she doesn't wear tight leggings and little crop tops to work.

"She's not bad," Caroline says. "She looks reliable."

Maybe she's right. Maybe I need a wholesome nanny. "I'll set up an interview." I realize that I'm bumping up against my next meeting. "Gotta go jump on a call. Are you good here?"

"Yes, we're fine. I'm leaving at five, just to remind you."

"Got it. Thanks." I retreat into my bedroom, which has become Evelyn's bedroom as well, and a makeshift office.

If I wind up staying in Honeysuckle Harbor, I'm going to need a bigger space. A house with multiple bedrooms and an office that is soundproof. Or at least far away from the main living areas. I'll have to ask my mom to look into that possibility.

Life is suddenly really damn complicated. I need a whole fucking staff.

The minute I'm in my room, I suddenly feel bad that I left the room without saying anything to Evelyn. I instantly feel guilty because her life has been turned upside down.

I also feel like I...miss her. Is that possible, given it's been thirty seconds since I saw her?

Whatever it is, I immediately return to the living room and approach the sofa. Evelyn is done eating and is attempting to stand on Caroline's legs. I give the top of her head a kiss.

"Have a good nap."

Evelyn starts and then looks up at me and smiles. She reaches for me and now I feel stupid for coming out here. I just made it worse. "Not right now, pretty girl. I have to work."

Her bottom lip juts out, and she starts to tremble.

Oh, God.

"Sorry," I say to Caroline and fast walk back to my room, feeling like the biggest dick to ever live.

Is this what being a parent feels like? You want to do everything right and feel like you're fucking it all up every step of the way?

I hear Evelyn crying and I decide that yes, this is exactly what being a parent feels like.

Overwhelmed. Exhausted. Terrified. Undersexed.

I'm going to assume it gets easier. It has to get easier.

It's already better in that I'm starting to understand Evelyn's moods and expressions and sounds.

I'll get more sleep with a night nanny.

And the sex part?

I'm going to work on that too.

All those thoughts are shoved aside though as I get dragged into a flurry of work calls and have to put out a dozen fires. The afternoon flies by and before I know it, Caroline is knocking on my door.

"Grayson? It's five. I need to head out. I have plans with Cas and James."

I shove my chair back rapidly and drop my phone on the desk. If I take it with me, it will just be pinging nonstop in my hand.

"Sure, of course," I say, yanking the door open.

She has Evelyn with her, so I reach out.

She comes readily to me, like she's been waiting all day for some attention from me. "Hi. Did you have a good day?"

She rewards me with a grin.

"She just had a bottle and some avocado," Caroline says. "She won't be hungry for a while."

"*Avocado*?" I ask. "Babies eat avocados?"

Caroline nods. "Sure. That's one of the best first foods. Good texture."

Well, shit, now I have to research what the hell I'm actually supposed to be feeding her because in my mind she is supposed to suck on a bottle until she tells me otherwise.

I rub my temple. "Oh, my god."

Caroline pats my arm. "It's okay. You'll get there, big guy."

That feels insulting. "Absolutely I will."

She smiles and turns with a hair flip, practically bouncing her way to the front door. "Bye!"

"Bye." The door is already closing behind her.

She's eager for her plans.

I suddenly feel a little lonely.

It's not a comfortable or familiar feeling.

"What should we do?" I ask Evelyn.

She smacks my arm before pitching forward and biting my shirt.

"You might have eaten, but I need to find something. I haven't eaten all day." I head into the kitchen and scrounge up some left-over Chinese takeout to eat.

Eating with one hand and holding Evelyn is harder than I

anticipated. She knocks multiple forkfuls of rice onto the counter before it makes it to my mouth.

It's when I'm cleaning up the mess that I realize Caroline's cell phone is on the counter.

It lights up. I glance at the screen automatically, not because I'm trying to be nosy.

It's filled with notifications from a dating app.

She's matched with Mitch.

And Trevor.

And Rashid.

I shove it in my pocket.

Food can wait.

"We have to return Caroline's phone," I tell Evelyn, then wonder if it's normal to narrate my whole life to a baby.

It just seems like common courtesy to tell her what the fuck is going on.

As is returning Caroline's phone. There's nothing more to it than that. Just common courtesy.

CHAPTER 8

Cas

CAROLINE BELL IS PERFECT.

She's even better than I expected.

She came over for dinner after she finished at Grayson's for the day and it's been delightful. She and James chatted while James made a simple but delicious Mediterranean chicken sheet pan dinner, and I put Noah to bed.

Caroline told me stories about James in high school while we ate herbed chicken and vegetables sprinkled with feta cheese and olives and drizzled with a tangy sauce, along with crusty bread and wine.

We laughed and talked, and I loved watching James and Caroline—or Caro, as he calls her—together. They have a natural, comfortable chemistry that comes with knowing someone well for a long time.

He casually touches her lower back when moving past her, squeezes her hand when she tells a story, even reaches over and brushes an errant hair away from her cheek. She puts her hand on his arm and even his chest when she laughs at something he says. And whenever they look at each other, it's with warmth and affection.

But when Caroline isn't looking, I catch James studying her mouth, her ass, her breasts.

My husband is very attracted to his ex-girlfriend.

That's awesome.

And if her flushed cheeks, hard nipples, and the way she also steals glances at him when he's not looking are any indication, she feels the same way.

Game. On.

I also find her incredibly beautiful. I expected to. One of the things James and I have in common is, conveniently, our taste in women. But Caroline is seriously gorgeous.

Her long hair falls in waves to her middle back, her lips are full and my favorite color of pink, her breasts are fantastic—and she's got hips and an ass I can't wait to run my hands over.

She's also funny, easygoing, and charming.

This will be such a fantastic way to fill the next few weeks.

It's too bad she's not staying longer.

No. I can't let thoughts like that intrude. Her temporary status in Honeysuckle Harbor is exactly why she's perfect.

"James was the best dancer in our class. Probably the entire high school," Caroline is saying as I lead her to the couch.

I ordered mini-dessert parfaits from Frannie at Raw and have laid them out on our coffee table. I've also got another bottle of wine open.

James told me that Caroline doesn't drink white wine, but I've been plying her with a delicious full-bodied red all night, and she's on her third glass. She seems relaxed and happy. I refill her glass and hand it to her.

"But you were his date to Homecoming and Prom your senior year, right?" I ask her. "And for more than his dance moves?" I give her an easy smile to let her know I'm open to discussing their past. "We don't have either of those in the Netherlands. Such a quirky and intriguing American tradition."

She giggles. "Probably a dangerous one for virginity as well."

James is standing behind where Caroline has propped herself against the pillow and the arm of the couch.

'*What are you doing?*' he mouths.

Caroline reaches for one of the lemon cheesecake mini-parfaits and I mouth, '*Trust me*' back to him.

"James, there's a peanut butter chocolate mousse parfait," she says, holding it out to him. "Come sit with us."

He starts to move toward the middle cushion, but I quickly reach out, wrap an arm around Caroline's waist and slide her to the middle.

She lets out a startled sound but doesn't protest.

James drops onto the cushion on her other side, but he's still giving me a '*what the hell?*' look over the top of her head.

"There, you fit well between us," I tell her. I slide my arm from around her slowly, letting my hand slip over the strip of skin between her T-shirt and leggings where her shirt has pulled up.

"I'm not going to protest being tucked between two hot men," she says, pulling her feet up onto the cushion and wrapping her arms around her legs. She gives a sigh. "It's been a while since I was tucked against even one."

"That's too bad," I tell her. Our hips are pressed together and her warmth seeps into my side.

"It really is," she agrees. She balances her wine glass on one knee, holding it with just two fingers and the little parfait on her other knee. She digs the tiny spoon into the lemon cheesecake. "Thank God for sugar."

I chuckle. "So you and James at Prom…were you the envy of all the girls?"

She nods as she licks the spoon clean, and my dick stirs, watching her tongue. "And some of the guys." She smiles at James. "If only they'd known they had an even better shot with you than the girls did."

"I wouldn't say better shot," James protests.

She nods. "Well, I'm so glad that I was…that you were…" She glances at me. "Never mind."

I laugh. "I know all about you and James, Caroline."

"You do?" She looks at James. "You told him?"

James grins. "Of course, babe. He's my husband."

She shakes her head and takes another bite. "I guess it's not as awkward to have an ex over for dinner when it's ancient history."

"What do you mean?" I ask, amused. I know what she means, but there are some details Caroline needs to be clear on tonight. This is the perfect segue.

"He's *married* to you, obviously. We were just kids." She giggles, and it definitely sounds a little tipsy. "Though we did enjoy learning to be adults together." She shoots James a smirk. "If you know what I mean."

James gives her an affectionate smile and stretches his arm along the back of the couch behind her. "I certainly do."

I laugh. "Oh, come on, J. Tell her how much you're still attracted to her. This isn't all ancient history."

Caroline looks from me to James, her eyebrows arched. "You're still attracted to me?"

James tucks a strand of her hair behind her ear. "I definitely am still attracted to you, Caro."

"But you're married."

I lean a little closer. Fuck, she smells good. "That doesn't mean that we can't appreciate what a gorgeous woman you are. Or that we don't still want to...*be* with women." I echo her words back to her. "If you know what I mean."

She looks from him to me. "I think so? Are you saying that you still do?"

"Very much."

She looks at James. He nods. "Yep."

I lean closer to her ear. "So you are still very much of an interest."

"Oh." Her voice is soft. Almost a whisper.

She looks from him to me again, then back to him.

"So, is this awkward, then? Me being around?" she asks me.

"Definitely not the word I'd use," I tell her.

"Oh," she says again, as if it's all sinking in. She takes the final bite of her parfait.

James takes the little container from her and sets it on the table.

She tips back her glass of wine, taking a big gulp. She blows out a breath. "How did you two meet?" she asks.

I look at my husband. We share a smile.

"A dinner party," he says. "We had friends in common who were trying to introduce us for a few months. We kept missing each other, though. Then, one night, we were finally in the same place at the same time."

"Was it love at first sight?" Caroline asks.

"Of course," I say. "Look at him. He's fucking adorable. He's funny, sweet. He lets me boss him around in bed."

James's cheeks get a little pink, but he doesn't deny it. My sunshine husband tells me exactly what he wants and needs too, but he does like it when I take charge.

I'm also aware of the change in Caroline's breathing. Her chest is rising and falling faster, her nipples are pressing against the front of the simple cotton tee she's wearing, and her cheeks are also a little flushed.

So, of course, I keep going. "He's amazing with his tongue," I continue. "He's got all those muscles and is very flexible." Caroline is staring at James. I drop my voice and say right by her ear. "And he's got that huge cock. You remember, don't you, Caro?"

She swallows hard.

"Jesus, Cas," James mutters.

"None of that is a lie," I say. "And you do remember, don't you, Caroline?"

To my delight, she nods. "I do. Of course." Then slowly she smiles. "And with the years of practice you've had, I can only imagine how much better you are with it," she tells James.

James coughs in surprise as I grin.

"Oh, honey, you have no idea," I tell her.

And then she giggles. "I might have a bit of an idea. I have a pretty good imagination and I read really dirty books."

The tension—the 'I-hope-I'm-not-pushing-too-hard' tension—evaporates. All that's left is the sexual tension.

"Can I tell you about one of my favorite dates with James?" I ask her.

"I'd love to hear it."

James gives me another of those looks but this one isn't *'what the hell are you doing?'* This one is *'are you sure this is a good idea?'*

But it is. I'm sure of it.

"We'd been going out for about three months. It was getting serious. But there was one thing we both really liked that would have been missing if we became committed and monogamous. We'd talked about it a little but hadn't really come up with a solution," I tell her.

"What was it?" she asks.

I squeeze her knee. "Patience. I'm getting there."

She presses her lips together.

I grin. "One night, I had planned the whole date for us. All James had to do was be ready at six. I had taken care of everything else. We were going to go to see one of his favorite classic movies in the park. I had the blanket, this amazing picnic with all his favorites, everything all set.

But it started to rain. A huge, unexpected thunderstorm. Ruined the whole thing. I was so bummed. Then James decided he was going to salvage the night. He drove us to a bookstore, said we had ten minutes to find our perfect idea for how to spend the rainy evening in front of the fireplace, and then we'd meet at the front door. Whatever we showed up with was what we were going to do.

We're both bookworms and we both like board games, so I spent my ten minutes searching for a great book to read together —I was thinking a mystery or thriller. Rainy night, lights off, fireplace only. That'd be cool, right?"

Caroline is watching me raptly. She nods at my question. "Very cool."

"I thought maybe he'd come back with a game or maybe a puzzle or something. We can be nerds sometimes." I give her a self-deprecating smile.

James shifts on the couch. He's not stopping me from telling the story, but he's clearly a little nervous about Caroline's reaction.

Yeah, me too. Not nervous, but curious.

We need to see how she responds to this.

"So I pick out a book and I go up front to meet James with what he picked out."

I stop. Caroline looks from me to James, then back. "What did he pick out?"

"Come on now," James said. "She wasn't a 'what', Hannah was a who."

Caroline's eyes widen. "*What*?"

"Right," I chuckle. "She was a who. Hannah. This cute, sweet little brunette who worked at the bookstore and who James had met there a month prior. And who was finishing work ten minutes later."

Caroline sits up straighter on the couch and turns toward James. "You picked out a *woman*?"

He grins. "Yeah." He shrugs. "We were talking about what we'd like to do on that rainy night together…Hannah was the perfect answer to the question."

Caroline's eyes are still wide when she looks at me. "And what did *you* say?"

"I said, 'it's very nice to meet you, Hannah,' of course. I'm a gentleman." Then I give Caroline a wicked grin. "At least I *can be* a gentleman. Hannah was totally fine with me *not* being a gentleman from then on."

Caroline just stares at me.

"You okay, Caro?" James asks.

She nods, still staring at me. "Yeah. Fine."

"Be honest. Are you something other than fine, too?" I ask, leaning in. "Like…curious, maybe?"

She wets her lips. "Do you…did you…do that a lot?"

"That?" I ask.

Of course, I know what she's talking about, but she needs to say it. We need to have it out on the table.

"*That*. Like with Hannah."

"What did we do with Hannah?" I ask. "What do you think happened?"

She looks at James. He smiles, almost encouragingly.

"I'm guessing you didn't take turns reading chapters of a murder mystery," she says.

His smile grows. "No. No, we didn't."

She takes a breath, then she looks at me. Our gazes are locked when she says, "You fucked her. Together. Right?"

I smile. "Good girl," I say. "And yes. That's exactly what we did."

She blows out a breath. "Got it."

"And no, not a lot," I say, answering her previous question. "Sometimes. For fun. With full transparency and consent between all parties. We make sure the women know James and I are together and that we're not looking for anything from them but sex, and we share limits and make sure everyone knows whatever they want or need to know."

"But not now?" she asks. "Now that you're married?"

I smile, but it's James that answers.

"Sometimes now, too. Though not since we came back to Honeysuckle Harbor."

She seems to be thinking that over. She's just opened her mouth to reply when there's a sudden knock on our door.

Caroline startles, and I frown. Damn it.

I look at James. He shrugs.

Begrudgingly, I get up and go to the door.

Grayson Ross is on the other side, his baby daughter in one arm.

"Hey, Grayson, is everything all right?" I smile at Evelyn and get a frown in return.

"Yes." He sighs. "Well, they're mostly all right." He holds up a phone. "Caroline left this at my place. She mentioned she was having dinner with you, and I hoped to catch her."

I step back and gesture for him to come in. "Yes, she's still here. Come on in."

"Oh, I don't—"

But Evelyn has caught sight of James and is squealing and reaching out her arms, her hands opening and closing.

My eyes widen as I look from the little girl to my husband. He's already off the couch and coming forward with a wide smile. "Hi, Evie girl."

He takes her from her father without even asking, and Grayson and I are both left standing with our mouths open, staring after them.

Caroline joins us, laughing. "Uh, yeah. They have a thing going."

"You left your phone next door," Grayson says as he hands it to her.

"Oh. Thank you." Caroline sets it on the table inside the door where we toss our keys and daily mail.

"She's like that with him all the time?" Grayson asks, still watching James and Evelyn as James sways in the middle of the room with the little girl, showing her one of Noah's toys.

"She is," Caroline confirms. She looks up at me. "But I thought she just liked men more than women. She didn't smile and coo and bat her big blue eyes at you, though."

"No, she did not," I agree.

"Huh," Caroline says.

We all look at Evelyn and James again.

Then Caroline looks up at Grayson. "That's so interesting. She apparently doesn't just like men and she doesn't seem to have a type. You and James are so different."

Grayson finally pulls his gaze away from Evelyn to focus on

Caroline.

"Are we?" he asks.

There's a change in his voice, and I swear a change in the electric current in the air.

What the hell?

"You are," she says. "He's such a sunshine. So laid-back and… nice."

Grayson arches a brow. "And I'm…" He trails off, clearly inviting her to fill in the blank.

I'm guessing the look he's giving her is one he's perfected in the boardroom with other hard-ass CEOs. I've seen my share of I'm-the-alpha-and-you-will-kowtow-to-me posturing around conference tables and in courtrooms.

But Caroline just grins up at him. "Not those things," she says.

She doesn't even seem to mind that he is very in her personal space.

"I'm not nice?" he asks.

"Not the first word that comes to mind," she says. "Or the first…" She pretends to think something over. "…twelve words that come to mind."

Grayson studies her. Intently. Like she's a puzzle he needs to solve.

Or an acquisition he wants to make.

Yeah, that last one feels more accurate.

"Good," he finally says.

Caroline rolls her eyes. "Yes, big bad CEO man—no one thinks you're nice. That's such a good thing. Very scary." She reaches up and pats him on the chest.

Grayson's hand moves swiftly, covering her hand and flattening it against his chest.

Her eyes widen as he leans in. "Since you're *not* scared of me, maybe next time you're in my bedroom, you won't run from me."

My eyes widen along with Caroline's.

Wait, what's going on here?

His bedroom? She ran from him?

Oh.

Oh.

Well, fuck.

Something is going on with Caroline and Grayson.

That might fuck up all the plans I had for her, and me, and James.

Caroline pulls her hand from underneath Grayson's. "That is *not* what happened," she says.

"Yes, I suppose scared and intimidated can be two different things," Grayson says.

"I wasn't *intimidated,*" Caroline says, sounding insulted. "I was being courteous."

Then I'm shocked to see the big, bad, broody CEO *smirk* at her. "It's a normal reaction to a brand-new situation where you feel unsure. Nothing to be ashamed of."

Caroline squares up with him. "Are you insinuating I've never seen a naked man before?" Caroline demands.

Oh. Shit. Something is definitely going on.

"I'm simply responding based on the information I've been given," Grayson says. "You acted like it was a new situation. Or at least, like seeing one like me, was new."

Caroline scoffs. "Like you? What's that mean? One with such a gigantic ego and huge head?"

Clearly, too late, she realizes how that sounds.

We all freeze. The apartment is completely silent for five beats.

Then James and I both snort at the same time.

Caroline rolls her eyes.

Grayson's smirk actually turns into a full-fledged grin.

"Shut up," she mutters. She turns to me and James. "I walked in on him…naked. Big deal. I'm taking care of his kid in his apartment. It just…happened. We're all adults. It's fine."

"Sure." I nod. "It seems just fine. You don't seem rattled by it at all."

Grayson smirks some more.

I might actually like this guy if he's not as wound tight as I thought he was.

And clearly, we have the same taste in women.

The three men in this apartment obviously all want Caroline.

Her phone buzzes on the table, and she looks over at it.

"It's been doing that a lot," Grayson says. "It's how I noticed it on the counter under the spit up cloth and the extra diaper."

Caroline grabs the phone and swipes over the screen. Her eyes go wide.

"Everything okay?" I ask, peering at the screen.

"Uh, yeah. Just…"

"Are all of those notifications from a *dating app*?" James asks, coming up behind her.

She presses the phone to her breasts. "No! It's not…well… fine." She pulls the phone away. "Kind of. It's a networking app. The company operates in every state and most other countries. People like me, singles who are traveling alone a lot for work, use it to meet friends and people with shared interests and ways to be social in new places. It's actually kind of hard to make new friends at our age."

"So you're meeting *friends*," James asks. "It's not to find dates or hook-ups?"

"Well…"

James frowns. I look up and see Grayson is also scowling.

I wonder if these two men realize that they've already got it bad for Caroline Bell.

"I have dated people I've met through the app," she says.

"And hookups?" Grayson asks.

She rolls her eyes. "A few. Nothing for a long time. But yes… sometimes the friendship turns into that. I travel a lot, and I never stay anyplace long-term, but I don't want to just never go out or have…fun."

"That doesn't sound safe," James says, frowning.

Grayson's scowl deepens. "It sounds like a really bad idea, actually."

Caroline looks from one to the other. "Well, thank you for the unsolicited advice, guys. I'll be sure to tell my mother that she doesn't have to worry or lecture me now that I have the two of you around." She looks at me. "Anything you'd like to add?"

I'm a little smarter than my husband and neighbor. You don't tell women what you think of their choices and decisions unless asked. And then, really, only if you're a very close friend, physician, or therapist. And even then, very carefully.

"Just that if you need any non-self-induced orgasms while you're in *this* location, just let us know. No need for an app."

Her eyes widen again. Then she looks at James. He just shrugs and nods. Then she looks at Grayson. His scowl is even deeper now.

"Oh my God," she mutters.

Then she steps past Grayson, pulls the front door open, and leaves.

Without a goodbye or even a look back.

At least she didn't slam the door and wake up the baby.

CHAPTER 9

Caroline

WHAT THE HELL JUST HAPPENED?

I hit the sidewalk outside of the apartment building and take a deep breath of warm air. I don't have a car in town and I'm a little drunk, anyway, so I order a car service. Cas was really plying me with red wine.

And I was downing it because my thoughts are all jumbled.

Pacing back and forth, I try to relax my shoulders as I wave a bug out of my face. I can smell the ocean, which normally is soothing, but tonight just reminds me of that summer all those years ago when I was drunk in the boathouse with James and we were frantically pawing at each other's clothes.

Cas said James was still attracted to me. James agreed. Cas also said he was attracted to me and that they on occasion open their marriage to a woman.

The very thought of that woman being me has my nipples tight and my pussy uncomfortably damp. Was that what they were suggesting? It certainly sounded that way.

I text Frannie.

Are you home or at work?

Home. What's up?

Good. I need emergency girl time.

I'll run out for wine.

I don't need any more wine. This calls for a clear head.

Well. As clear as it's going to get when I've had three glasses of wine and two hot men hitting on me. Because I think that's what they were doing. It certainly seemed that way.

Then there's Grayson Ross.

That man.

Fuck.

I wave my hand in front of my face, which is blazing hot.

I don't understand him. Was he flirting with me? Or does he genuinely believe that I've never seen a grown man masturbating?

It's been a minute, but I am no stranger to the naked male form—thank you very much.

My car pulls up and I jump in, glancing up at the apartment windows. I don't know what I'm expecting to see. It's not like any of the three men will be staring down, watching me leave with an expression of longing or anything.

The driver is chatty and I'm struggling to hold a conversation with him. Fortunately, it's a short five-minute drive to Fiona and Frannie's quintessential Carolina beach cottage.

I love this house. I thank the driver and hop out, instantly feeling less jittery and strange. The house is pink with white trim and a yellow door and has a deep front porch with four rockers on it. It looks worthy of two female pastry chefs.

Fiona has a habit of leaving the front door unlocked, so I'm able to go right in without digging for my keys. It drives Frannie crazy because she is definitely the more cautious of the two. She can fret about anything, whereas Fiona is willing to walk a little more on the wild side. Their triplet, Finley, is in law school and she loves live bands and drinks straight whiskey.

Most people who meet Fiona and Frannie have a hard time telling them apart, but I've known them for so long it seems weird to me that anyone gets confused. They have different expressions and subtle variations in their hand gestures.

Fiona is in the living room, feet up on the coffee table. Frannie is in the kitchen, making popcorn. She has an open lager can on the counter.

"Hey," I say, flopping down onto the chair opposite Fiona.

"Hi!" Frannie calls out. "What is going on? Tell us everything."

"Did you fuck Grayson Ross yet?" Fiona asks, her eyebrows rising up and down. She shoots me a gleeful grin.

"What? No." Though that doesn't mean I haven't considered it. "I walked in on him naked. Jacking off."

A bowl rattles in the kitchen. *"What?"* they both say simultaneously.

"How did that happen?" Frannie demands, juggling the popcorn bowl and her beer and coming over to the couch.

They're both in shorts and easy tank tops.

The cottage is small, but light and airy, with big comfy furniture that allows you to sink deep down into. The kitchen cabinets are soft pink and all the accent decor is shades of pink as well. They like to refer to the house as the pink palace. It suits them and it's very homey and comforting.

"I couldn't find the formula, so I went into his bedroom—the door was open, by the way—to ask him and he was just standing naked in front of the mirror stroking himself." I add an unnecessary hand gesture, but what can I say? I'm flustered.

Fiona snorts. "Damn. Did he stop?"

"No. We made eye contact in the mirror. It was…kind of hot. He looks really good naked."

"Did he say anything about it?" Frannie asks, setting the bowl down and curling up on the couch next to Fiona, tucking her feet under her butt.

"I asked him if he felt better, because I had to say something, and he said yes. He kind of apologized, but not really, and I kind of apologized for not knocking. It wasn't super awkward, it just made me very aware that I am severely in need of a good wall bang."

"Aren't we all," Fiona says ruefully.

"Yes," Frannie says emphatically.

"But then he started showing me a whole bunch of nanny candidates and they were all young and hot and I don't know. Getting involved with Grayson seems so dangerous. Like he could drag me into his hot rich guy orbit and I'll have to fight to get back out."

"I can see that. He's definitely alpha." Frannie nods. She tosses a handful of popcorn into her mouth.

I hesitate. I want to tell them about James and Cas and what maybe felt like a hint at a threesome, but I'm not sure it's my place to divulge what they shared about their marriage. That was told to me in what I have to assume was confidence, so I have to tiptoe around it.

"Then I had dinner with James and Cas, and well…it all felt so nostalgic and flirty and fun. I felt like I was sixteen all over again, hanging out with James, and yet we're both full-fledged adults now. He's married, he's a dad. I've traveled all over. I always knew he was my first love, but spending more time with him now just confirmed it."

I feel miserable and aroused and excited and confused, all at once.

Fiona pauses with a piece of popcorn at her lips. "Are you still in love with him?"

"No! Of course not." I'm not. "It was teen love, which is differ-ent. I still care about him, though. I just mean…it's nice to see him again," I finish, frustrated. I'm not even sure what I'm trying to say.

I don't know if I'm reading too much into what happened.

Was it really sexual tension or am I just really damn horny?

Or is it both?

I grab a huge handful of popcorn and shove it in my mouth.

"We should go dancing in Charleston this weekend," Fiona says, dropping her feet to the floor and stealing her sister's beer. She takes a huge sip. "Let's get our slut on. Dress up, grind on some guys."

"No, thank you," Frannie says.

It doesn't sound appealing to me either.

I don't think I want a random guy to hook up with.

But dancing would be a nice distraction. "I'll spontaneously combust if I grind on a guy, but I'm up for going out."

"Don't be a bore," Fiona says to Frannie. "You're going."

Frannie sighs. "I'm not wearing heels."

"It's Charleston, not Atlanta. We'll wear sandals and short dresses. It will be fun."

What would be fun would be to be naked between James and Cas.

Or Grayson Ross.

Or all three…

Oh, my God.

I reach out and grab the beer from Fiona and drain it.

My mouth is suddenly very dry.

CHAPTER 10

James

"SO, that wasn't how I expected the evening to go," I say casually to my husband after closing the door behind Grayson.

"I know, me too," Cas says, with a grin. "I was expecting Mexican. But the chicken was delicious."

"Cas, come on."

"What?"

"Why didn't you tell me you were going to bring women and sex up with

Caroline?"

"Because I wasn't sure I was," he says. "I was just going to see how things played out."

There's a little squawk from the baby monitor and Cas perks up. He doesn't go as far as waking Noah up to spend extra time with him, but he loves when Noah needs a little extra attention in the evenings. He's jealous of all the time I get with our baby boy, so he happily heads in at the slightest sound.

I used to worry that he'd spoil Noah, but our son is simply fully secure in how loved he is and knows that we're there for him no matter what, or when.

I follow Cas into Noah's room and prop my shoulder against

the door jamb, watching as Cas lifts Noah and nuzzles his face in Noah's neck.

"Hey, sweet baby," he croons.

God, watching my husband's thick muscular arms, covered in tattoos, bunch as he cuddles our baby is so hot. I move further into the room.

"You want to fuck Caroline?" I ask him bluntly.

I'll admit that it took me a second to catch on to what Cas was doing, but once I did, the lust had hit me hot and hard.

I love sharing women with Cas. It's always amazing. We love women. We love fucking women. We love making women come over and over. And it makes the sex between the two of us so damned hot.

But Caroline? She's different.

My attraction to her is stronger than any other woman Cas and I have ever hit on and taken home. I don't know if that's a good thing. I need to be fully transparent with him about it.

"I would love to fuck, Caroline," he says honestly. He's got Noah up on his shoulder, his big hand covering Noah's back. He's swaying gently and Noah is already falling back to sleep.

He'd probably fall back to sleep on his own if we just left him alone, but Cas figures Noah won't need him to cuddle him when he's off to college, so he won't listen about letting Noah comfort himself. I just shake my head and smile.

"But even more," Cas continues. "I'd love to watch you fuck Caroline."

I feel like I just took a big gulp of whiskey. Heat courses through me and my cock hardens. "Cas."

"You want to, right?" he asks.

"With you. I would never..."

"I know." He takes a step toward me and puts a hand on my shoulder, squeezing. "I know, babe. I'm not worried about that."

I cover his hand and put my other hand on Noah's back next to his. "Are you sure that's a good idea? She's not just some girl. We have a history. There were real emotions there, even if we were young. We're not starting at square one with her like we usually do."

"There *are* real emotions there, right?" Cas asks. "Not just were? In the past?"

"Cas." I blow out a breath. "I love you."

He smiles. "I know that. I am not worried about that. I love you, too. And I love our life. Everything we're building here. I also love our sex life. I could and would happily fuck just you for the rest of my life."

I snort. "So romantic."

He grins. "I thought that's how this was going to be when we moved here. I was cool with that. Now that we have Noah, we can't just be picking up women who are practically strangers, no matter how sure we are that they understand the situation. Before Noah, we could take some risks. We could have handled a little stalker, or getting robbed, and if there had been an accidental pregnancy, we would have dealt with it. But now, things are different. I won't put Noah in any kind of danger, and I won't put our amazing situation in jeopardy. I really didn't think we could do the woman-some-times-too thing again. Now though…" He trails off meaningfully.

Cas is so protective. He's also pragmatic. He doesn't make suggestions off the cuff and he doesn't do things spontaneously, even if it seems that way.

"Caroline isn't a risk?" Of course she isn't. But how is Cas so sure? They just met.

"Caroline was your first love. There is still a spark there and still real feelings. She's awesome. I really like her and we can trust her. And she's not staying long term. It would be great if she wants to come back between jobs and we could have a couple of months of fun once in a while, but we don't have to worry about adjusting our life in any way, we don't have to worry about hiding anything, or making any permanent changes."

See? He always thinks it all through.

And he's always right.

I nod slowly. "That all sounds really good."

His smile is wide. He tips Noah back from his shoulder. Our baby is fast asleep again, his face sweet and content. Cas kisses one chubby cheek. I lean in and kiss the other.

Cas carefully lays Noah back in the crib, then turns and slips an arm around my waist, steering me out of the room.

He pulls the door shut, then turns me, pressing me into the wall. His big hand cups the back of my neck, his breath ghosts over my mouth. "Fuck, you and Caroline would be so hot together."

I can't help the small groan that slips out. Yes, it has a little to do with the image of Caroline, naked, in our bed with us. But it's also my husband's lean, muscular body pressing close, one big hand holding me in place, the other running down the outside of my thigh, then up to cup my cock.

"That idea makes you hard, babe. You can't deny that you want this."

"I do," I admit. "You would fuck her so well."

Cas is an amazing lover. Honestly, sharing him with Caroline would be the nicest thing I could ever do for her.

"Yes." He squeezes my cock. "I would." He leans in, kissing me, stroking me through my jeans. Then he drags his mouth along my jaw to my neck. "Can you imagine her between us? You deep in her pussy, me fucking her ass?"

I shudder as lust snakes through me. "Why do you get her ass?" I manage, my hands sliding down his back to his ass, squeezing hard, pressing his cock against mine.

He chuckles, soft and rough. "Thought maybe you'd want to revisit that sweet pussy that you had so long ago. But if you want her ass, I'll happily fuck that tight little cunt."

"Jesus." I fist his hair and kiss him hard, our tongues stroking hungrily. Then I pull back. "Why do you make it sound like it's one and done? We can each have both. More than once."

"That a boy," he praises. Then he steps back, reaching over his head and grasping his shirt, yanking it over his head. "Let's go to bed."

"This has you all riled up, huh?" I ask with a smirk. I like that. A lot.

I want Caroline, for sure, but I want Cas to want her too. I *need* him to want her. And vice versa.

For all the reasons he laid out, she's a great choice. But also because the sex could be better than anything we've had with anyone else. I know her. I care about her. Sure, that sounds like it could complicate things, but not with Caroline. She's not staying in Honeysuckle Harbor. She's too independent, has her life all mapped out exactly as she wants it. She's not going to let two guys come along and make things messy.

This can be very hot, very fun sex, that's next level because there's true respect and affection and history between us. Friendship.

That will make it so fucking good.

"Very," he confirms. "We'll have to discuss how to approach it with her."

"I could—"

"Later." He cuts me off, nudging me toward our bedroom. "Take your clothes off and get on your knees."

Fucking *yes, sir*.

I strip on my way to the bedroom. Cas kicks his shoes off and shucks off his pants the second he crosses the threshold. We crash into each other, our mouths fusing, our bodies pressed together, rounding the bed as one.

Once we're next to the bed on the side with the drawer in the bedside table with the lube, Cas pulls back, staring into my eyes.

"I said, on your knees."

I slide down his body, kissing his chest, licking over his abs, and then nipping one hip.

His breath hisses out. "Suck on me, James."

I take his cock in hand, licking up the hard length with a firm, slow pressure.

His hand goes to my hair, gripping, but not guiding. He lets me have full reign over his pleasure here. I know exactly what he likes, and he only gives me words of praise and encouragement.

"You're so good at that. God, yes," he groans.

I lick up and down, swirl my tongue over his head, suck gently, then harder, but deny him fully taking him, instead only teasing.

"Yes, babe, just like that."

I lick down to his balls, cupping them, squeezing, licking over them, sucking.

"Fuck, James, more," Cas begs raggedly. He moves his hips, pressing harder against my mouth.

I give his balls a harder squeeze, nipping the inside of his thigh, then drag my tongue up the length of his huge, hard cock. "You put me on my knees. I decide what I do down here," I tell him.

He lets out a low growl. "Not how that works."

"No?" I swirl my tongue over the leaking head of his cock. "Who's really in charge here, Cas? You're aching and needy and begging *me*."

"I am. I want that perfect fucking mouth," he says. "Almost as much as you want to give it to me. You're on your knees because you'll do anything for me."

He's right. But admitting that isn't part of this game.

I suck just lightly on his head, then pull off with an audible 'pop'. "You've been hitting on, fantasizing about my *ex-girlfriend* all night," I say. "Do you deserve my perfect fucking mouth?"

I feel his hand tighten in my hair at the back of my head. His eyes are hot, his pupils dilated when he takes his cock in hand and leans over. "I *always* deserve your perfect fucking mouth. And especially after I get your pretty Caroline, who you still want so much you were aching to kiss her all night, worked up and wet over the idea of us taking her together, fucking her gorgeous brains out." He slides the head of his cock over my lips. "You're welcome."

I shudder as lust hits me hot and low.

It feels so amazing to be able to be open with him about my feelings about everything, even Caroline. Maybe especially Caroline. Sharing your sexual fantasies with your partner is important and immensely freeing. Finding out all of that is possible because they want to make them all come true and are fully confident in your relationship is incredible.

And God, I want to hear Cas talking dirty and being bossy with Caroline.

So. Much.

She'll love it. He's so damned good at it.

He's also always *determined* to make sex mind-blowing for me. And for the women we share. Cas is an amazingly generous lover. He's all about everyone's pleasure every time.

"I do thank you for that," I admit, running my hands up the backs of his muscular thighs to his tight ass. I squeeze. "But I don't need pussy right now. I need you."

"Then open your fucking mouth and take my cock. If you suck me well, I'll fuck your perfect ass instead of coming down your throat."

I open my mouth and Cas takes over.

CHAPTER 11

Cas

I SLIDE into James's mouth with a relieved groan. He's been teasing me and I've let him, but now I need release.

I don't have to take it easy on him. James and I have fucked each other every which way and know each other's turn-ons and limits, as well as our own.

I thrust, hitting the back of his throat and only feel his fingers dig into my ass, urging me on.

"That's right. Take me," I grit out, thrusting again. I'm not going to come like this. I need to fuck him. But I do love his mouth. He looks so beautiful on his knees for me, sucking and licking and wanting me this way.

James could have anyone. Male or female. He's not only gorgeous, with his always slightly mussed hair, his sweet warm green eyes, his easy smile, and all of those chiseled gymnast muscles, but he's charming as hell and such a genuinely nice guy, no one can resist him.

I'm a good guy too. I know that. I'm not bad to look at either, or so I've been told. But I remember being amazed that our first date actually ended in the bedroom, and that he called me first the day after.

I also remember thinking, *don't let him get away.*

I didn't.

I don't intend to.

I'd do anything for this man.

I thrust three more times, then drop to my knees in front of him and kiss him deeply. My tongue fucks his as I grip his head in both of my hands.

I lean back, resting my forehead on his. "I love you so damned much."

"Easy to say when you're about ten seconds from coming," he says breathlessly.

I laugh. "Always easy to say. But yes, I'm feeling *very* fond of you at the moment. Get up."

We stand and I turn him, bending him over so he has to brace his hands on the bed. I run my hands up and down his back, then around his sides and over his abs.

"What do you want?" I ask. "I'm going to take your ass. Do you want to come first, during, or after?"

He takes my hand and pulls it around to his cock. I grip him, stroking up and down. He groans. "Yes. That. Fuck me and jerk me off."

"Jesus. Gladly." I reach into our bedside table and grab the lube, flipping the top open with my thumb and squeezing a generous portion out.

I knead his ass—getting him ready—he presses back against me.

"Cas, stop playing."

"Greedy," I chide lightly. "I love when you get impatient for my cock."

"I'm always impatient for your cock."

I give his a squeeze and a long, firm stroke. "That's the right thing to say." I take my cock in hand, stroking with the same pace I'm giving him.

His head drops forward, hanging as he takes a deep breath. "Fuck, yes."

I stroke him faster and press against his backside, gripping his hip.

I love the way his shoulder muscles bunch as he braces himself, pushing back against me. His back muscles are like carved marble. I love just looking at him, running my hands over him, watching them flex as we fuck, but even as he works out, or fixes something around the house, or plays with our son.

I press forward, easing into him, relishing his ragged, *"Fuck."*

The feel of him gripping my cock is, as always, heaven. "James," I grit out.

"Fuck me, Cas."

"Gladly." I pull back and press back in, continuing to stroke his cock. "Just don't wake the baby when I make you come so good."

"Yes, sir." His voice is tight, and I know he's getting close.

I thrust into him harder this time and he grunts. I squeeze him, pumping firmly.

I continue fucking him, stroking him, talking to him.

"You feel so fucking good. God, you look good bent over our bed, giving me your ass."

I love his groans, his *'fucks'*, and finally, "Cas, God, *yes!*" as he comes, spilling all over my hand and our sheets.

I fuck into him harder, faster, then grip his hips tightly as my climax slams into me and I pump deep.

I slump forward, curving over his back, breathing hard, kissing his shoulder.

He continues to brace himself, keeping us both supported as we drag in oxygen and float back to earth.

After several long moments, I straighten, running my hands down his back, before I pull out.

He straightens and turns and we kiss, this time lazily, spent and happy.

James runs his hands through my hair and I run mine up and down his back.

When we pull apart, we share a smile.

"Shower?" he asks.

I nod. "Definitely."

I kick our discarded clothes toward the hamper. We'll get them later. In the bathroom, James turns the walk-in shower on and I grab the towels. We step in together and take turns dragging soapy hands over each other. We kiss and stroke, but it doesn't turn sexual.

We've had plenty of sex in the shower, of course, but tonight we just clean up, step out and dry off, then get in bed together.

We lie on our sides, looking at each other. He cups my face. I cover his hand.

"What?" I ask.

"I love you."

"I love you too."

"I intend to love you for the rest of my life. In other houses, with more kids, no matter what's ahead and what happens."

I nod. "Ditto."

"And if Caroline says no, maybe…we don't…" He trails off.

"No other women?" I ask.

"Maybe."

"We don't even have to ask Caroline," I say. She feels different. And I think that's a good thing. But if we don't go there, then we can't miss what we never have. "It's up to you."

He blows out a breath. "The thing is, I really want to ask Caroline."

That makes my heart do a weird thump. A good, weird thump. That's what I wanted him to say, but I didn't want to admit it until he did.

"Me too," I say. "So, let's ask. The worst that happens, she says no."

"Right. And it's awkward as fuck around her in the gym and just hanging out."

I laugh. "It won't be awkward. She's very cool. I think she'll just roll with it, honestly. She'll say no and we'll shrug and go 'okay, worth a shot' and we'll all move on."

I'm right. Caroline seems open-minded. And James will regret it if we *don't* ask her.

"And," I say, my grin getting a little sly. "She might say yes."

I can see hope in James's eyes. I also notice how his dick stirs.

"She might," he agrees.

"In fact, I think we should prepare for the chance that she does," I say.

He lifts a brow. "How do we do that?"

"Have Noah stay overnight with your mom. Get some condoms. Maybe some flavored lube."

"You think we're going to need it to be flavored?" he asks with a laugh.

"I just want *all* the incentives for everyone going down on everyone else."

He moves in, putting his mouth against mine. "Trust me, Caroline is going to want you between her legs. And to have your cock in her mouth. She won't need anything flavored." He kisses me deeply as I groan. God, I want that woman. More than I've wanted any of the others. Some of my relationships before James were with women. And we've shared some sweet, very sexy ones. But I've never felt the way I do about Caroline and I'm not even sure why.

She just has an 'it' factor that has my blood—and cock—stirring.

"Fuck," I say into his mouth. "I can't wait to see her gagging on your cock while I eat her pussy."

My graphic talk about Caroline makes his cock harden almost instantly.

We've never known the woman we've taken to bed ahead of time, so we've never planned like this. Sure, we've stocked up on supplies and made a general game plan, but we haven't been able to picture the specific woman lying between us, writhing in pleasure on our sheets, her legs spread, her mouth filled…

"Fuck," James curses, as I grip his now hard again cock.

"I love how much you want her," I tell him. "It's going to be so fucking good."

"*Cas*," he groans as I stroke him.

"Tell me what you're imagining," I demand, my voice and strokes firm. I intend to make every one of his fantasies come true.

He decides to be totally honest. "Me in her pussy, you in my ass."

"Goddamn," I groan. "Yes. Fuck." I pick up my pace on his cock.

"But you need to take her pussy too," he says, pumping his hips in rhythm. "I want to see you fucking her."

"Oh, I intend to," I say enthusiastically. "I'm going to spread those pretty thighs and make her scream, I promise."

And *that* is what makes my husband erupt into my hand for the second time.

And I love it.

James kisses me hard, then gets up to clean up.

When he gets back in bed and pulls the duvet over us, he says, "Now shut up and go to sleep or we're going to be up all night discussing our dirty Caroline fantasies."

"I can think of worse ways to spend our time," I tease as he curls into my side.

"I think we should discuss them *with* Caroline," he says. Then he yawns. "If she says yes."

I feel his body relaxing, but I say, "Or we could discuss them with her to help get her to say yes."

He tenses briefly. Yeah, the idea of telling Caroline all of our dirty thoughts is pretty tempting to me, too. I'm really hoping she's going to say yes anyway, but I also think we could give her a very good sales pitch. I smile and kiss the top of his head.

"Sweet dreams," I tell him.

"I'm going to wake up with a hard-on," he mutters.

Yeah, I assume I'll be having hot sex dreams all night, too.

"Well, maybe we should set the alarm a little early," I say. "We can definitely take care of early morning hard-ons."

He doesn't say anything, but he does roll toward the alarm clock on his side of the bed and bump the wake time back by thirty minutes.

•

CHAPTER 12
Caroline

I'M HUNGOVER. Not as bad as the morning after the infamous boathouse debacle in high school, but I have a pounding headache and a roiling stomach. I don't indulge very often and after the three glasses of wine I had three of Frannie's beers from the fridge. I regret it wholeheartedly as Evelyn lets out a shriek that makes my brain hurt.

It's a happy shriek of delight, which normally I find adorable, but now it makes me wince. I manage a smile though, because Evie is honestly a total sweetheart and it's impossible not to smile back at her grin, even when my head is splitting apart.

"I know," I tell her. "It's a good day, isn't it? It's not your fault silly Caroline threw back a few too many with the girls last night. And guys."

She gives another shriek of delight.

"Exactly," I tell her, wryly. I roll over and flop down onto my side on the soft area rug in Grayson's living room.

Evelyn is sitting up next to me, chewing on her hand and kicking a random block with her left foot. This position is much better. I have my giant water tumbler next to me and I tilt it so I can take a slurping sip of water.

"Hey, do you mind staying an extra few minutes?" Grayson says, suddenly appearing in the doorway of his bedroom.

It's been a very long day.

My fault. But still, a very long day.

Grayson, unlike me, looks delightfully refreshed.

He's wearing a soft blue button-down shirt and tan jeans that look expensive as hell with navy sneakers. He seems to have found his hygiene footing and looks showered, shaven, nary a clothing wrinkle in sight.

He looks gorgeous, and it's annoying.

He's responsible for my current situation.

Him and James and Cas.

All three of them.

They're all really damn attractive and sexy and sending out pheromones or something, because I can't stop thinking about each of them. Hell, maybe I'm ovulating and my body is taking over my mind in a quest to mate with men who are virile and masculine and sexy dads.

"Caroline?"

Grayson is staring at me expectantly, and I'm trying to justify my attraction with science.

"How long do you need me to stay?"

"Not long. I have a potential nanny dropping by for an interview."

My first reaction is *fuck that*. I'd rather go home and take a much needed nap.

"Why do I have to be here for that? Shouldn't you see how she interacts with Evelyn?"

"Oh, yes, of course. But I don't want to overwhelm Evie. I think she'd react better if you were here. It's the one who was formerly a senator's nanny."

On second thought. I remember that woman's picture. Elegant brunette.

"Sure. Okay. I can stay for a bit."

"Are you...unwell?" Grayson asks, eyes raking over me.

"I have the wine flu," I admit. "Mostly I'm just tired. Glad to see I'm fooling you, though."

He laughs. "You don't look terrible. Just not quite yourself. Too much wine with James and Cas?"

It doesn't sound like he cares one way or the other if I got drunk with his next-door neighbors. Nor is he offering to let me off the hook now that I've told him I don't feel great.

"Yes." I take another sip of water.

I can't blame Cas or James or even Frannie for my head pounding. This is my fault. I know better. It's why I don't really drink. I also have always gone with a safety first mentality since I travel so much. It's never wise for a woman traveling by herself to get drunk in an unfamiliar place where she doesn't speak the language.

"I'm not going to say I'm never drinking again, but I'm going to stick to my one glass of wine policy for the foreseeable future."

"That's smart. I don't see myself drinking too much either. I can't imagine taking care of a baby with a pounding head."

I blink. I stare. I wait for him to realize what the hell he has just said.

Nope.

He doesn't even register the irony of that statement.

Instead, he's clearing off the dining table of the mess from several meals. Grayson still seems to be running behind on general housekeeping, though he is taking the trash out every day.

It *is* hard to take care of a baby with a pounding head, like I've been doing all day.

But, temporary or not, I'm a hired employee, so I can't leave him in a lurch because I don't know my limit. Though I actually know my limit, I just ignored it and blew right past it, partly because of the man making a face at his own dirty dishes.

He's stacking plates in the dishwasher and loading it with bottles when his phone dings. "She's here."

He sounds excited, which annoys me.

I touch Evelyn's chubby leg, running my finger down over her soft skin. I'm going to miss this little girl. I feel a surge of protectiveness. This nanny better bring it.

Forcing myself to sit up, I straighten my sloppy bun and rest my back against the sofa as Grayson opens the door and enthusiastically greets the woman. All I can see is slim legs in a pencil skirt.

"Thank you for coming," he says. "So you're interested in the nighttime position? The hours are eleven to seven."

"Yes, I am. Thank you for meeting with me."

She has a nice voice. The right tone. Not too upbeat but not too flat either.

I pull Evelyn onto my lap and kiss the top of her head.

"Oh, is this little Evelyn?" she says, as Grayson leads her into the living room.

She's hotter than she was in her picture. She's dressed like she works in a law office. White button up shirt, navy skirt, sensible pumps. She has shiny, straight, non-frizzy hair, which reminds me just how rough my own hair is today. It's sloppy and frizzy and my skin is dull, my face puffy from the wine.

"Hi," she murmurs directly to Evelyn, dropping down into a squat like she's not wearing a slender skirt and heels. "I'm Kyle."

She glances up at me and gives a shrug. "My parents wanted a boy," she says, rolling her eyes a little and smiling at me. "Are you the day nanny?"

"Yes," I say, omitting that this is a temporary position for me. I'm feeling a little territorial. "I'm Caroline. It's nice to meet you."

Kyle gives Evelyn another smile, who is staring at her unblinkingly. Then she stands up and allows Grayson to pull a chair out for her to sit down.

"Thank you," she tells him with a warm smile.

"What makes you interested in the nighttime position?" he asks.

"I'm in law school."

Because of course she is. Pretty and smart.

"When are you planning to sleep?" I blurt out before I can stop myself.

Grayson gives me a *what-the-fuck* look.

Kyle just laughs lightly. "My classes are for working adults, so they're compressed from six to nine every night. I'll sleep in the morning and early afternoons. I like to stay busy."

"I don't mind if you study," Grayson says. "Evelyn is a challenge to put down, but once she's asleep, she usually only wakes up twice, around two and six. All I expect you to do when she's sleeping is some light housekeeping. Washing bottles, doing Evelyn's laundry."

"That sounds perfect to me."

I'm listening intently, so it takes me a second to realize my arm feels wet. I glance down and realize Evelyn has filled her diaper and then some. There is loose baby poop on my forearm and all up her back.

"Shoot," I mumble, forcing myself to my feet. "We have a blowout."

Neither of them acknowledges me. She is showing Grayson an app on her phone. "I'll log all of Evelyn's changes and sleep times here so you can view them at any time."

He's leaning very close to her. Their arms are touching.

I feel a surge of jealousy that makes me very uncomfortable.

I try to listen to their conversation from the bedroom where I'm undressing Evelyn, who is waving her arms and cooing.

God, she's cute.

Even covered in poop.

I can't hear Grayson and Kyle at all and Evelyn needs a bath, so I resign myself to not being able to eavesdrop as I carry Evelyn, still in her loaded diaper, to the bathroom. I fill the sink with warm water and finally remove the diaper.

Washing her off with her baby soap and a hand mitt sponge, I bend over to rest a little against the countertop. Evelyn is happily kicking and splashing.

By the time I have her squeaky clean and dressed in fresh

clothes, Grayson and Kyle are best friends. They're chuckling and smiling, heads bent together.

"We're going to take Evelyn for a walk," Grayson tells me. "I want to show Kyle the building and the neighborhood."

"Why? Everything is closed at night."

Normally I would have kept that thought to myself, but I'm tired, annoyed, and damn it, I'm jealous. I don't want either Grayson or Evelyn to like Kyle more than me, which is ridiculous. Me and Grayson are acquaintances and nothing more and I'm Evelyn's temporary nanny. I should be happy Grayson might have found someone who will stay long term and bond with Evelyn.

Grayson doesn't even bother to answer me. He just ignores me and retrieves the stroller.

"We're just getting the lay of the land," Kyle tells me, lightly.

Grayson comes over and reaches out for his daughter. "Hangovers make you cranky," he murmurs in my ear.

I bristle. "Maybe you make me cranky."

The corner of his mouth turns up. He's close to me. Too close. I can see the gold flecks surrounding his brown irises and smell his light aftershave. My gaze is drawn to his lips and I feel my cheeks grow warm.

Evelyn shoves a finger in his mouth, breaking my reverie.

"I think you need a nap," he says to me. "Lay down on the couch."

"Why can't I go home?"

"I want you here," he says simply. "I want to talk when I get back."

I swallow hard.

I should demand an explanation. Or just refuse to stay.

Instead, I say, "Okay."

"Good girl." Grayson gives me a panty-dropping smile.

I'm left standing there watching him leave with the amazing Kyle, law student by day, supernanny by night.

"Ahh!" I say out loud in frustration, stomping over to the couch and flopping on it.

Pulling a soft fleece blanket over me to combat the chill of the air conditioning, I punch a throw pillow a few times and lay my head on it.

"Get it together, Caro," I mumble. "James and Cas are married. Grayson is preoccupied. And you're moving to Colombia."

Keep it simple.

CHAPTER 13

Grayson

"IT'S BEEN a pleasure to meet you, Kyle," I say, sticking my hand out. "I appreciate you meeting me and I'll be in touch."

She takes my hand and smiles. "Thank you."

It's a calculated move on my part. I want to touch her hand just to confirm that I feel zero attraction to this potential nanny.

And I'm right.

Nothing.

No spark.

I don't get any vibe that she wants anything other than a job from me either, but even if she did, it wouldn't matter. I'm confident I can treat her in a completely professional manner, even under the unusual circumstances of having her in my apartment when I'm sleeping.

The agency provided a background check on Kyle, but I'll have my assistant Andrea run another one with a firm we use for hiring, just to be cautious. Evelyn seemed comfortable with Kyle, so I'm feeling a sense of relief.

We're at the cafe that is on the same block as my apartment building and Evelyn is content in her stroller, getting lots of waves and smiles from patrons as they enter, mostly tourists seeking ice cream. She is, of course, frowning at them in return.

I've asked another nanny to meet me here in fifteen minutes. This is the one I'm considering for Caroline's day shift.

The sooner I can find someone, the better.

I decide to text Caroline and tell her she can head home. It was selfish to ask her to stay, but I really want to talk to her about the fact that I want to fuck her six ways to Sunday. I can't get her out of my head. I don't know if I'm just wound too tight or if it's the obvious fact that she's gorgeous and sexy as hell, but I'm losing the battle with my self-control.

That's half the reason I'm so eager to hire a new nanny. I can't touch Caroline until I've hired her replacement because I can't blur lines like that. Not with the person caring for my child. But I want to let her know where my head—and my dick—are at and see if she's interested in me the same way I'm interested in her.

But she was clearly exhausted today, so I text her to let her know she should go home, feeling like an asshole that I didn't do that in the first place.

My head hasn't been on straight these last few weeks, but that's still no excuse.

As I watch two teens act like scooping ice cream behind the counter is the hardest thing they've ever done in their entire lives —with lots of sighs and snail-like movements—I decide I want a cone for myself. I've been eating poorly since I've been in Honeysuckle Harbor. I need to cool it with the takeout and find some kind of fresh meal delivery service.

But that's next week's task.

Right now, I'm getting myself a waffle cone filled with strawberry ice cream. I can't remember the last time I had an ice cream cone. Probably the last time I was back home in Honeysuckle Harbor last summer.

I'm standing in line when I hear, "Grayson? Hey, man, what's up?"

I turn and find myself face to face with Ford Anderson, one of my high school classmates. "Hey, Ford, good to see you."

We were friends and have bumped into each other over the

years, but I haven't been great at keeping up with people from my past. I've poured all my time and energy into my business.

"I heard you were back in town." Ford glances at the stroller I'm resting my hands on. "With your daughter."

"We don't know for sure she's mine," I say, automatically. I've been saying that since the second I clapped eyes on her.

At first, because I was terrified she was, but now, I think it's because I'm starting to get nervous that she's not. I don't know how I will react if the DNA proves she's not.

"Uh, she looks just like you," Ford says, giving Evelyn a grin. "Hi. What's her name?"

"Evelyn. I'm actually interviewing a nanny in a few minutes," I say. "Life is strange, right? How have you been?"

"Excellent. Harrison and I have a restaurant, Raw. I met the love of my life. Her name is Ivy. We live together with Harrison and his husband, Liam, because we're all together."

I remember Ford's best friend Harrison. He was a great guy, easy-going and charming. "Together, together?" I ask, a little surprised, though I'm not sure why. How the hell would I know anything about Ford's personal life or sexual preferences?

"Yep. Well, not me and Harrison." Ford grins as he rocks back on his heels. "I'm here grabbing some pints of ice cream for after dinner tonight. Gotta keep the polycule happy. Harrison can be a real asshole when he doesn't have his mint chocolate chip."

"That's great," I say, sincerely. "I'm happy for you. For all of you." I want to ask if the good people of Honeysuckle Harbor have been rocked to the core by a foursome openly living in town, but it seems like a rude question to ask. I don't want to put him on the spot.

"Let's get together sometime soon and catch up," Ford says. "My sisters—do you remember Frannie and Fiona?—they're hosting a bonfire next weekend. Got to get them in before fall arrives."

In my hometown, "let's get together" is real, not a fake suggestion like it is in my usual adult life back in New York. "I'd love to, but I'll have to see." I gesture to Evelyn. "Bedtime is seven-thirty."

Ford nods. "Got it. I'll text you though." He gestures. "You're up."

"Oh, right." I order my cone and turn when I hear the doorbell jingle. I think the woman walking in is who I'm meeting.

I now realize I've put myself in the awkward position of having ordered myself an ice cream cone and not offered to do the same for this girl. Plus, now I have to try to interview her while licking ice cream. Jesus. I'm really off my game. I blame it on sleep deprivation and lack of sex.

Grabbing an ice cream cup from the counter and a spoon, I tip the scoopers and dump my cone upside down in the bowl. Then I chuck the waffle cone in the trash. I feel pretty fucking sad I'm not going to be able to eat it, but hopefully I can refreeze the ice cream and salvage it.

I can't drink alcohol these days, so I'm holding onto anything I can with both hands.

The daytime nanny candidate is glancing around, searching for me. I walk up and introduce myself. Her name is Jane, and she's quiet, but she seems competent. I ask her if she wants anything, but she shakes her head rapidly. We sit down and I ask her some basic questions. It seems difficult for her to speak comfortably to me, which is concerning, but whenever she interacts with Evelyn, her face lights up.

She asks if she can hold her and when she takes Evelyn out of the stroller, my daughter goes with her readily. Evelyn touches the strands of long hair framing Jane's face.

"She's so sweet," Jane says.

We're sitting at a table and I ask, "Are you available long term? I don't want different care providers in and out of Evelyn's life more than is strictly necessary. She's already had enough change and trauma."

"Where's her mother?" Jane asks. "If you don't mind sharing?"

"She isn't interested in being a part of her life," I say, and for the first time, the enormity of what that means for Evelyn really smacks me in the face.

This innocent, adorable baby won't have a mother in her life, through absolutely no fault of her own. That fucking sucks. I feel a surge of protectiveness and love.

It's a good thing I'm sitting down because the force of it threatens to knock me over.

"Oh, no," Jane says softly. "I'm so sorry."

Jane has kind eyes and natural nurturing instincts, that's obvious.

This is the kind of woman you want your child to have for a mother.

Not that I mean Jane specifically, I just mean I feel bad that I can't give Evelyn that.

She's stuck with just me.

I pick up my plastic spoon and shove a spoonful of ice cream into my mouth.

What am I thinking, considering casual sex with Caroline? I can't risk another unplanned pregnancy. Evelyn isn't even a year old and I'm a hapless single dad. I can't let something like this happen *again*.

Caroline hasn't answered my text, which is bothering me. I shove my chair back without warning and stand straight up. "I need to head home. I'll be in touch."

I take Evelyn from Jane.

"I'm sorry, I shouldn't have asked," she says, looking mortified.

"It's okay. It's not your fault. I just remembered I have to...do something."

Run away from my emotions.

That's what I have to do.

I throw a one-hundred-dollar bill down on the table. "Here, get yourself some ice cream."

Which weirdly sounds way ruder than I intend it to. I meant it as an apology for cutting the interview short, but there are suddenly tears in Jane's eyes.

"This is a hundred dollars!" Jane sounds horrified.

"Oh, God," I mumble under my breath.

I'm used to New York girls. They would take the money and run.

It's a reminder that you can't always buy your way out of every situation.

I sit back down with Evie in my lap. I take a deep breath and let it out slowly. "I'm over my head," I tell Jane in a low voice. "I do not have my shit together right now. I'm trying but suddenly having full custody of a baby is a lot. So if you want this position, this is what you're getting—a demanding, short-tempered, busy as fuck businessman who until three weeks ago had never changed a diaper. Think about it over the weekend and if you're still interested, text me on Sunday." I stand back up. "Keep the money, please. I'm trying to apologize."

She stares at me for a second, her cheeks stained pink, before shaking her head. "There's nothing to apologize for. Have a good night, Mr. Ross."

"Thanks, Jane, you too."

I put Evelyn in the stroller, lock her strap, and exit the cafe. I'm halfway up the elevator when I realize I forgot my ice cream.

Fuck. Me.

When I enter my apartment, I stop short.

Caroline is asleep on the couch, curled up under a blanket.

She has her arm flung over her eyes in an attempt to block out the sun, which is cascading down on her face from the large front windows. Dust dances over her in the beams, reminding me I need a housekeeper.

So much to do.

And yet, I just stand here, gut clenched, watching Caroline sleep.

She's beautiful.

Her lips are slightly parted and her hair is tumbling down

over the pillow she's lying on. Her hair was in a bun before, but I see her hair band is on her wrist now.

As if I wasn't already feeling like a dick, I feel terrible all over again that I didn't let Caroline go home. No wonder she didn't answer my text. She fell asleep.

I need to feed Evelyn, give her a bath, and put her down for the night, but first I go over to the couch.

I don't even know where Caroline lives, and taking her anywhere with Evelyn in tow would be a pain in the butt, anyway. Caroline doesn't have a car. To be honest, I'm not even sure how she gets here every day, which again confirms my general dickishness.

She's going to sleep here, in my bed, and I'll sleep on the couch.

Evelyn seems content in her stroller still, which is a relief.

I squat down so I don't scare Caroline and murmur, "Hi, I'm back."

Caroline stirs, lowering her arm just slightly so that I can see her eyes. "Hey." Her voice is raspy.

"Come on. Let's go."

"Go where?"

"My bed."

Her eyes widen, and she scrambles to sit up. "Grayson! Where is Evelyn?"

"In her stroller."

"You can't just…take me to bed."

That makes me crack a grin. "I have to ask first? Is that it?"

"Yes!"

"Can I carry you to my bed?" I ask, even as I slip my arms under her back and her soft ass.

She feels incredible in my arms. It's a wonderful, terrible temptation. I need to stay strong, but damn, it's so fucking hard.

"No," she says.

"Too bad. I'm taking you to bed so you can sleep. I'll sleep on the couch tonight."

"I can just go home," she protests, even as she wraps her arms around my neck and leans against my chest.

"No, just stay. You're exhausted, and you have to be back in the morning, anyway. I'm a terrible boss, Caroline." I carry her across the living room to my bedroom.

"Is that an apology?"

"Yes."

"Well, it kind of sucks."

That makes me grin. "Yes. It does. I suck. Generally speaking."

"You don't look like you believe that."

I set her softly down on the bed and pull back my comforter for her to slip beneath.

She does so readily, with a heartfelt sigh. "How was the nanny?"

"Good. As soon as I get clearance on Kyle's background check, she can start working nights."

Unable to resist, I reach out and brush Caroline's hair back off of her face. I want to kiss this woman. I want to taste and touch every inch of her.

But I can't.

"Hey," she says, turning on her side to face me. "What did you want to talk to me about?"

I can't tell her now. "What kind of flowers do you like?"

It's an impulse question. I should get her flowers for helping me out this week. Sure, I paid her, but she has been a lifesaver.

"What?" Her brow furrows. "Why?"

"No reason."

Caroline smiles softly, her eyes drifting shut. "Wildflowers."

That fits her perfectly.

I retreat to the living room and pick up Evelyn and hug her close, kissing the top of her head. "You know what?" I tell her. "I love you, baby girl."

Evelyn sighs and nestles into me.

This is what matters—my daughter.

Not my neglected dick.

CHAPTER 14

James

CAROLINE RUSHES into the gym only five minutes before class is supposed to start.

She looks a little rumpled. Still gorgeous, but definitely a bit frazzled.

I give her and Evelyn a big grin, and the baby reaches for me immediately.

"Hey, Evie girl," I greet as I take her in my arms.

She smiles up at me, putting one hand against my cheek.

I don't quite understand why she's enamored with me either, but I like it. I love her grumpy side because it makes her sweet side even sweeter. She's been through a lot, and doesn't owe anyone smiles and giggles, dammit. And if I can be a comfort to her, something that makes her smile, then I'm all in.

I prop her on my hip and focus on her nanny.

I haven't stopped thinking about Caroline since the other night in our apartment, and my more extended conversation about her with Cas.

I haven't stopped fantasizing about her, either.

We haven't had a chance to bring our idea up to her, but the more I think about it, the more I want it. Her, me, and Cas. Together. Naked.

Honestly, I've built it up so big in my mind that, at this point, if she says no, I'll be crushed.

"You okay?" I ask Caroline.

She takes a deep breath and gives me a smile. "Yeah. Just kind of a crazy morning."

"Is Evie okay?" I look down at the baby. She looks perfectly fine as she grins up at me and blows a spit bubble.

"She's great."

When I glance back at Caroline, she's watching Evelyn with an affectionate smile.

"Grayson's been interviewing nannies."

I watch her face. Caroline doesn't seem happy about that.

"Right. I thought that was the plan," I say. "You were just filling in."

She nods. "I know. Of course, that was the plan. It's a good thing."

She doesn't seem to really think it's a good thing. "Have you met any of them?" I ask.

"One. The one applying for the night shift. Kyle."

She says the name with a touch of derision that doesn't make sense. "A male nanny?" That would maybe be great for Grayson to see a guy interacting with Evelyn.

"Nope. A very pretty, young, single woman who Evelyn seemed fine with."

I lift a brow. Caroline sounds irritated by all of that.

"And what did you think?"

Caroline shrugs, her eyes on the top of Evelyn's sock. She's running her finger over the embroidered duck on the side of the baby's sock.

"She seemed...okay."

Just okay. I don't know if I believe her. Caroline's getting attached. Of course, it's impossible not to fall for Evelyn, in my opinion, but I love seeing Caroline sweet for her.

Caroline is a teacher, so obviously she has a soft spot for kids, but I don't know that she's been around a lot of babies. I love how natural she's been with both Evelyn and Noah.

"You don't think she's qualified?" I ask.

I doubt that very much. Grayson Ross is not the kind of man to even bother to interview someone who doesn't check every single box on his likely ridiculous list of qualifications for any position. Nanny for his daughter? Yeah, I'm sure to even get a meeting, these women are more than qualified.

"She's qualified. She's just…stiff. She was wearing a skirt. And heels. Like she was dressing for an office instead of for taking care of a baby." Caroline runs a hand over her own rumpled clothes. "How's she going to get on the floor and play with Evie in a pencil skirt?"

"Maybe that was just because she wanted to look professional for the interview."

"Hmm." She sounds less than convinced.

"I thought it was the night shift, anyway," I say. "Won't Evie be sleeping?"

Caroline frowns. "Whatever. I'm just saying she doesn't *seem* like a nanny. Which she *isn't*. She's going to law school."

Smart too. "Wow, that's impressive."

Caroline glares at me as if I'm the one who talked Kyle into being a lawyer. "Is it? Or does it mean she'll be distracted from taking care of Evelyn? And does Grayson really need more suits in his life? Seriously? Did he even look past her uptight clothes or did he just see the button-down and think 'well, of course, she knows what she's doing'?"

I laugh. "I think Grayson Ross bases hiring decisions on more than wardrobe." I look her up and down. "Look at you. You've got possession of his daughter right now and you look like you just rolled out of bed."

Her cheeks suddenly flush pink. "Oh. Well…I did. And, I, um…I'm not… I mean, Grayson was…" She stammers to a stop and shrugs. "He was desperate when he hired me."

"True," I agree. There's no arguing that. "But still, he trusts you completely with Evelyn, and you don't wear pencil skirts and heels and aren't going to law school. I think he's basing this decision on more than all of that. Don't worry. Evelyn will be okay."

She runs her hand over Evelyn's head. "Yeah. Okay. You're right."

But I sense there's something more. She's a little jealous of someone else spending time with and being important to Evelyn. But she's also jealous of this person getting close to Grayson. This person she thinks is more his type than she is.

Dammit.

Caroline takes another breath and meets my gaze. "I don't suppose you could keep Evelyn and start class without me?"

I frown. "Sure. But that doesn't sound like everything's okay."

She waves her hand as if brushing that away. "No, I'm fine. I just really need a shower."

"Yeah, okay. Did you oversleep this morning?"

She puts a hand up to finger her messy bun and then looks down at her clothes. "I actually slept at Grayson's last night. I haven't had a chance to shower and get ready, and I am definitely feeling thrown off by that. If I can just shower, do something with my hair and get into a new set of clothes, I will feel much more ready for this day."

I know I'm staring at her like a dumbass, but I feel like she just slapped me across the face.

She's jealous of the new girl *and* she slept at Grayson's last night?

Well, fuck.

Have Cas and I missed our chance? If she's fucking Grayson, she's not going to go for our idea.

I clear my throat. "You, uh, slept on his couch? What happened?"

"Yes. Well, no. I mean, I did fall asleep on the couch. But then he carried me to bed."

Yeah.

Fuck.

"So you're okay keeping her for a bit?" she asks again.

"Of course," I say, my mind spinning. I'm definitely disappointed. My heart is pounding like I'm panicking, in fact. I need to call Cas.

"Okay, I'll be *right* back," she says, turning for the door. She hesitates, spins back, leans in and kisses Evelyn on the cheek. "Be back soon, baby girl." Then she heads out the door.

I immediately go for my phone.

Cas answers on the third ring. "What's up?"

I don't call him at work often. Usually I text if something comes up, and he calls back when he has a minute. If I call, it means I need to speak to him right away.

"Caroline slept at Grayson's last night. And she's jealous of one of the new nannies. I think she has feelings for him."

Cas is quiet for a few seconds, then he says, "We need to ask her out on a date."

I blink. "What?"

"We need to ask her out. We need to take her out on a date. A fun date where we can pitch her our idea. If she says no, we still have a good time and we can show her that we can still all spend time together while she's in Honeysuckle Harbor. If she says yes, we head straight home."

My cock stirs at even the *mention* of that idea. "She might be with Grayson," I say.

"Then she can tell us that," Cas says. "But we have to at least give her the chance to say no to us. If we don't, we'll always wonder."

I take a deep breath, my heart rate slowing a bit.

He's right. We have to at least tell her what we're thinking. If she and Grayson are together, she can tell us that.

But if they're not…

"When?" I ask. "When do we ask her, and when are we taking her out?"

"Ask her out when you see her," Cas says. "Just say the three of us should go out. Tomorrow night."

Yes. Tomorrow night. The sooner the better.

Before Grayson Ross can get even closer to her.

CHAPTER 15

Caroline

I'M NOT sure which one of these men is hotter—James or Cas.

They're completely different. Cas is tall, covered in tattoos, with an intense stare that makes me shiver. James is muscular, charming, with an adorable grin and hair that is perpetually in his eyes. Being around him is easy, comfortable, whereas Cas has a bossy edge that is slightly unnerving, mostly exciting.

I'm wildly attracted to both of them for very different reasons.

The good thing is, I don't have to choose. I get to be with *both* tonight.

A shiver runs up my spine as James opens the door to their building and Cas hits the button for the elevator, shooting me a sinful smile.

When they invited me to dinner, I thought it was just old and new friends spending time together over a delicious meal. Which it was. They drank two glasses of wine each, but I stuck with club soda, not wanting a repeat of the other night with my six drinks.

So I was stone cold sober when James asked me outright if I had been fucked by Grayson Ross. Then after I said no, Cas gave an emphatic, "*Good,*" and then suggested the three of us have sex together. Tonight.

I'm not easy to surprise, but even though I've felt a hint of sexual tension between me and James, I chalked it up to our past and that he's grown from a very cute teen boy to a sexy as hell man. And then with Cas that night on the couch, I assumed it was the wine and my low simmering need for an orgasm that isn't self-created.

But nope. That sexual tension was not imagined at all.

Cas just laid it all out there. They want to fuck me together. Tonight. And James backed him up on it, saying he couldn't imagine anything sexier than watching me and Cas. So I asked all of two questions before I said yes, because *I'm not sure which of these men is hotter and I don't have to choose.*

The second the elevator door closes behind us, Cas takes my hand and gently tugs me toward him. Then he pivots me toward James. "Kiss my husband, Caroline. He's been fantasizing about your lush mouth for days."

Cas's hands are on my waist now, stroking through the fabric of the floral dress I borrowed from Frannie to wear to dinner. He has big hands and they're sinking lower and lower on me, resting heavily above the curve of my ass as I stare into James's warm brown eyes.

"Is that right?" I ask him. "Have you been thinking about kissing me?"

"Nonstop since the second I laid eyes on you again. God, you're fucking gorgeous, Caro." He reaches out and brushes my hair back off of my forehead, stroking his knuckles down over my cheek and across my lips.

A shiver rolls through me.

Cas has invaded my space, running his hands down over my ass before coming to rest on my hips as he shifts in behind me, easing my wavy hair to the side and leaning in to land a brief, airy kiss on my neck.

A split second later, James is lowering his lips to mine and kissing me, his hand buried in my hair.

I moan softly, rocking into the kiss.

They're barely touching me, but the sensation of being

cocooned between the hard plane of James's muscular chest and the tall dominance of Cas is new and thrilling. James breaks off the kiss and I fall forward a little, unaware he'd been supporting my weight. I feel magnetically drawn to him, seeking another kiss, at the same time as I instinctively arch my back to allow Cas to run his hands over my ass and squeeze.

"I've never been with two guys before," I murmur, meeting James's gaze first and then glancing over my shoulder at Cas. "I've only had one threesome and it was a guy and another girl."

"Then you're in for a treat," Cas says, bunching the fabric of my dress up and rocking my ass back against his hard length. "Two cocks are better than one, I can fucking assure you."

"I'm starting to see the benefit of that," I agree enthusiastically, reaching for James.

He gives me another hot, panty melting kiss before we all realize the elevator has stopped moving and the door has been open long enough that it's closing again.

Cas sticks his foot in front of it to force it open again. "No, you don't," he tells the door. "We need to get in the apartment before we fuck Caroline in the hallway."

A sudden image of James lifting my dress up and taking me against the wall has me blurting out, "Oh, God, yes," before I can stop myself.

"Caroline, *fuck*," James grits out, pushing me backward gently. "Is your pussy wet, thinking about all the things Cas and I are going to do to you?"

"You'll have to find out for yourself," I tell him, letting Cas take my hand and pull me hard against his chest.

They're reversed now, Cas in front of me, James behind and Cas takes full advantage. He tips my chin up and takes my mouth in a hot, dominating kiss. He breaks away, his light gray eyes filled with lust behind his glasses. He's staring down at me as he says, "Check her pussy, James. The lady wants you to find out for yourself."

Heat floods my cheeks and slick desire coats my panties at his taunting, sexy words.

Note to self: Cas is dangerous. In a really good way.

"I'll do whatever you want, Caroline. If you want me to touch your pussy, I will." He tugs the hem of the dress up so he can slip a hand under it, tickling along my inner thigh. He murmurs in my ear, "If you want me to eat your sweet, hot pussy, I will. If you want me to fuck your tight, needy pussy, I will." He cups my mound over my simple cotton panties. "If you want me to spank this little pussy, I can do that too. You get whatever you want tonight. Times two."

Cas kisses me again before I can respond, though I have no idea what to say other than "please" and "thank you" right as James tugs my panties to the side and his finger slides deep inside my very wet pussy.

"Fuck," he breathes. "It's wet, Cas. She's so wet for us."

Hearing his words, feeling his finger pump leisurely in and out, as Cas teases his tongue against mine, has me swirling in a hot whirlpool of desire. I grip the front of Cas's linen shirt tightly, needing something to hold on to, to ground me.

Cas breaks away. I'm panting and rocking myself on to James's finger.

"That's our girl," Cas says. "So eager to be fucked, aren't you, our little adventurer?"

He makes that sound like an actual compliment.

A lot of people say adventurer to me in a way that suggests they really think I'm impulsive or can't make my mind up. That I wander because I can't settle.

But Cas says it in admiration. It sounds powerful. Which it is.

I *am* an adventurer, damn it, and I'm about to explore a whole new world of being fucked by two beautiful men.

I nod as Cas runs his thumb over my bottom lip. "God, yes." I squeeze my thighs tightly, trapping James's finger. "Fuck me so hard. Now."

James chuckles as he teases his finger out of my pussy and

over my clit, caressing the tight bud in a slow circle. "Not in front of Grayson's front door, sweetheart. You may think he doesn't want you, but trust me, he does."

The words snap me out of the sensual fog.

He's right. We're a mere two feet from Grayson's front door.

I can actually hear low voices from the interior of the apartment.

I had thought two nights ago when he carried me to bed he might...but no. He slept on the couch and yesterday he officially hired Pencil Skirt Kyle. She's probably there right now, behind that door.

It shouldn't matter.

It doesn't matter.

But I worry about her intentions and I worry about Evelyn and I worry that Grayson will invite her into his bed because it's convenient, and she's attractive.

I'm not normally a worrier, so worrying worries me.

I don't understand what it means.

I *do* know that a man like Grayson Ross is complicated and emotionally unavailable and I just don't do complicated.

This, with James and Cas, is deliciously uncomplicated.

That was my second question to them.

Won't this get messy?

They assured me it will be friends with benefits, no more than once a week while I'm in town. That we can all have fun because we respect each other and care about each other and we will openly communicate our needs and wants.

I one hundred percent trust James and Cas to stick to that.

"Then take me to your bed," I tell James. "Before I come on nothing more than your finger." He's still massaging my clit, and it's driving me insane in a very good way.

"We fucking can't have that," he growls, pulling his finger away and dropping my dress back down. "Cas, open the door."

"Already on it." Cas swings the door open and rests against it. "Get your tight little ass inside, sweet Caroline."

James gives me a little shove, even though I'm already walking through the door and I laugh softly at his eagerness.

My first question was where would Noah be tonight? They responded he is having a sleepover at James's parents' house. They assured me Papa and Mimi were thrilled to spend solo time with their one and only grandbaby.

"You were confident I would say yes," I had told them at dinner as I had suggestively licked crème brûlée off of my spoon. "If you arranged for babysitting."

"Hopeful," James had said.

"Prepared to present our very solid case," Cas had said, which had made me laugh.

Cas shuts the door behind us and cups my cheek. His touch is gentle, but commanding.

"I want every single inch of you," he says. "But first, I need to see my husband bury his head in your pussy and lick you until you come with his name on your lips."

"Is that right?"

"Yes." He nips my bottom lip. "It is. Now get to the bedroom so I can spread your legs for James."

Cas is in charge.

I glance over at James.

He knows it, and he likes it. He's got a full erection in his pants and he's kicking his shoes off.

I like it too, which surprises me a little. But I'm excited to experience something new.

Maybe next time I'll push back on Cas and have a little fun with him.

Next time.

I shiver.

I already know there is going to be a next time.

CHAPTER 16

James

CAROLINE SAID YES.

Which means this is mine and Cas's lucky night.

And hers, if I can brag a little. Cas is a great lover and I know what buttons to push on her, so together we can blow her fucking mind.

I take Caro's hand and lead her down the hall to our bedroom.

We waited until the end of dinner to ask her if she was interested in having sex with us and if she had said no, it still would have been a great night. Conversation flowed easily, with lots of laughs and reminiscing. She's the kind of friend that we can go years without seeing each other and just pick right back up where we left off.

Even kissing her again felt completely natural. It wasn't like trying to recapture being seventeen. It just felt…right.

Caroline and me. Now.

Add in my very fucking hot husband and I'm already rock solid and ready to take turns fucking them.

She gives me a sultry smile with a raised eyebrow. An amused *this-is-going-to-be-fun* look.

"Is he always this bossy?" she asks me over her shoulder, as Cas leads her to the bedroom, her hand in his.

"Yes. But trust me, by the end of the night, you'll be begging him to tell you what to do." I run my eyes over the soft curve of her ass in her cute little dress. I put my hand on the small of her back to encourage her to walk faster. I need her naked. Now.

"Begging isn't really my style," she says.

Cas stops with Caroline in front of our bed. He tugs down the zipper on the side of her dress and eyes me over her shoulder. "That sounds like a challenge, Husband. Doesn't it?"

"It sure does," I agree, stepping in behind Caroline as Cas kisses her.

I knead her ass greedily, crowding her so that I can watch their mouths moving together and hear the hitch of Caroline's breath as Cas forces her lips to part with the tip of his tongue. He's commanding, invading, and she's responding eagerly to him, in the same way I always do. Cas is a force.

He pulls you in, magnetically, and holds you there with his will.

In the past, I've enjoyed seeing him kiss other women, seeing the way they respond to him with trembling sighs and eager leans, but this is more than that. Watching the love of my life and my first love connect with such passion is incredible and I want more. I want to see their bare skin. I want to see their hands stroking each other in pleasure. I want to see them sucking and fucking each other.

But Cas promised me her pussy first and I want to taste her again for the first time in a decade. And show her my skills have improved with age.

I turn her head, breaking their kiss and take one of my own, her chin in my hand. She kisses me back eagerly, gripping my belt for balance. Then she breaks away and groans. "Why do we all still have clothes on?"

That makes me chuckle. "You were never known for your patience."

I step back so Cas can lift her dress up and over her shoulders.

He lifts it to his nose and inhales her scent as I strip down to my boxer briefs.

Then Cas says, "On the bed, sweet Caroline."

She obeys without a word.

"That's it," I tell her. "You're ready to be worshipped, aren't you?"

"I can't think of anything that sounds better."

Cas tugs down the little scrap of cotton covering her pussy and spreads her thighs wide. "For you, James. I know how much you want to taste Caroline again."

"I really fucking do," I breathe, gripping my cock tightly for a brief squeeze, then moving in between her legs.

Caroline is lying there, open for me, her hair tumbling across our bed, watching me with hooded eyes. She's lazily stroking her fingers along the front of Cas's pants, where his cock is hard and prominent. He undoes his button and zipper and pulls out his cock. Her eyes widen.

"Impressive, isn't it?" I chuckle.

"God, yes," she breathes. Her fingers dance lightly over his smooth skin, causing his cock to jump as he hardens even more.

"Wait until he's buried inside you."

"I'm tired of waiting." She lifts her hips in a blatant offering.

"Does that qualify as begging?" I ask Cas as I run my palms over her knees, then her thighs, edging closer and closer to her center.

"No," she says, not giving him time to respond. "Not even close."

"Hmm, I think she's right," Cas says easily. "That's still firmly impatient, but not begging."

"Then let's change that." I bury my head between her thighs and brush light kisses over her bare skin, up and down, skirting her pussy and across her pelvis, flicking my tongue very, very close to her clit but avoiding it.

She grips my hair, hard, and tries to guide me.

I resist, wanting the tease, and when she starts to rock her hips, seeking my tongue, I hold her down on the mattress tightly.

"James," she says, threateningly. "Stop it."

"Oh, you want me to stop?" I ask, pulling away entirely.

"What? No!" She glares at me. "Just do *more*."

I bend back down and kiss her clit, lightly, watching her. She jerks a little and gives a moan of frustration.

"I should have come in the hallway when I had the chance."

Now I'm thoroughly enjoying myself. I chuckle and blow on her clit as I massage her soft folds with my thumbs. Cas has shifted closer to her, his bobbing cock an inch from her lips.

"Open your mouth," he demands.

"Not until James does what he's supposed to do."

That makes me bite back a groan. Of course, Caroline would fucking negotiate. She knows who she is and what she wants.

"Fuck," Cas curses. He squeezes the base of his shaft and glances down at me. "Do it. Now. Give her what she wants."

Seeing him on edge too, his forearm muscles straining, his shoulders rigid, his jaw tense, is fucking incredible. He's still fully dressed and his nostrils are flaring and he wants Caroline to suck his dick this badly after this short of time that he's willing to let her wrest control from him.

I'm shocked and really fucking turned on.

I've only ever seen Cas lose control for me.

But this woman has gotten deep under both of our skin, and I understand his desperation.

I will also give my husband anything he wants in our bedroom.

This is an easy ask.

I bury my tongue in Caroline's slick pussy, closing my eyes to savor the taste of her, and the feel of her thighs beneath my fingers. She lets out a cry of pleasure.

"Yes, James!"

She immediately starts pumping herself against me, driving my tongue deeper inside her. I swirl my thumbs over her clit in an alternating massage and I get one last, "Fu—" from her before her exclamation is cut off.

When I glance up, I see my husband is sliding his cock between her open pink lips, drowning out her cry.

"Fuck, yes," I tell them. "Take him deep, Caro. All of him."

Cas is controlled, inching into her slowly as she moans around his length, her hand flailing out to grab his thigh—all while I stroke her over and over. Once I have the sexy visual of her mouth stretched fully, Cas easing in and out slowly—I flick my tongue back over her.

"God, this cunt tastes so good."

Then I just focus on her.

Plunging deep in and out, finding a rhythm, reading the response from her body. Her thighs start to tremble and she gets wetter, soaking my tongue with her hot, tangy pleasure. She's getting closer and closer, even if her cries are muffled around my husband's cock. I don't look up again, because I want her to break and she's almost there. Her hips are bucking, her heels shifting restlessly.

Swiping my tongue over her clit, I give a gentle suck on the tight bud while dragging my thumb through her pussy.

"That's it," Cas tells her. "You're going to come all over James, aren't you? With my cock buried in your throat. Do you want to come together, me and you? You can coat James and I'll coat you, sweet girl."

My skin is hot and tight at his words. I risk a glance up and groan when I see Caroline is nodding eagerly, her cheeks hollowed out as Cas thrusts hard in and out of her mouth. Her cheeks are stained pink, her chest rising and falling rapidly.

"I'm in if you are," I tell them both. I shove her knees up and out so I can access her tight little asshole.

Dragging my fingers along her slit, I press inside her ass, getting resistance. But I lap at her clit, and press on, feeling her body give way, opening for my finger. She jerks and moans in ecstasy.

"You love that, don't you?" Cas demands. "You love James destroying your pussy with his tongue."

I pump my finger harder while he's talking, sucking on her clit, before devouring her pussy as he talks.

Her response is to shatter.

Hot moisture bursts onto my tongue and lips and her muscles clamp down tightly on my finger.

Holy fuck.

Caroline just came all over me.

Cas gives a grunt. I can't stop what I'm doing, but I glance up over her pussy to see him gripping the back of her hair hard. He's holding her in place while he dumps cum down her throat.

Double holy fuck.

I ease back, shaking, wiping my chin. She soaked me everywhere.

Cas lets her go, and she collapses back on the mattress, swallowing and breathing hard.

His hand goes into his hair, then he pushes his glasses up the bridge of his nose.

"Fuck, Caroline," he murmurs.

Then he looks at me, his jaw locked. "Fuck her, James. Drive her into the mattress."

"Is that what you want, Caro?" I ask her, stripping off my briefs. "You want me to fuck you hard?"

"God, yes," she says, nodding eagerly, dragging her finger across her bottom lip to remove some of Cas's errant cum. She licks it off her finger.

My balls are tight, cock throbbing.

Cas tosses me a condom before stepping off the bed to finally undress.

"Is that begging?" he asks me, amused.

"No." I shake my head. "Not yet." I move between her legs and position myself right at her wet opening. "What do you want?"

"You."

"And when do you want it?"

"Now."

"Still not begging," Cas says, feigning disappointment.

He moves along the side of the bed and gives me a hard kiss. "Maybe start, then stop," he tells me with a wicked grin.

If I can.

Jesus.

Just edging her is damn near killing me.

Then she gives an unexpected, "James," and it sounds like a plea.

Her eyes are glassy.

But she clamps her hand over her mouth, like she realizes that was too close to begging and I take mercy on us both.

I thrust deep inside her pussy and just about destroy us both.

CHAPTER 17

Cas

CAROLINE AND JAMES moan simultaneously when he enters her cunt with a hard shove.

"That's it," I tell them both, so fucking turned on.

I always enjoy watching my husband take his pleasure with a woman. I love being able to stand back and see the flexing of his thigh muscles and his perfectly tight ass as he thrusts. To see his arms braced on either side of some soft and sweet female, her tits bouncing as he buries himself in her. I love seeing delicate fingers brush over his body, gripping his ass tightly, because I know how it feels. How powerful and sexy James is, but how considerate and loving and devotional he can be.

Seeing him pour that into a woman always gets me off. But this is even better. Because he loves Caroline. I've never seen him love anyone but me romantically and far from being jealous, it makes me love him even more. And feel like an intrinsic part of the connection that they share with each other.

Caroline has lost all semblance of control. She's not teasing or flirting now.

She's just taking him with soft cries of ecstasy, her legs slack and wide open, her hands gripping his biceps for support. She's staring into his eyes, but her gaze is unfocused, her skin flushed pink.

Sweet Caroline is going to come.

Not if I have anything to say about it.

Not yet.

I don't want this to be over too soon.

"Pull out, James," I order, stroking my cock, which has gotten rock hard again watching them. I roll a condom on.

"What?" Caroline turns to glare at me. "No! James, don't stop."

James gives a muttered, "Fuck," and one last stroke, but he does obey me and eases out of her wet heat.

She gives a groan of disappointment. "That was rude," she tells me.

I chuckle softly. "Don't you want two cocks at once? Isn't that why you're here?"

Blowing her hair out of her eyes, she nods. "Well. Yes. *But...*"

James has shifted to allow me room on the bed with them. I lay on my back, and with a firm grip, roll Caroline on top of me.

"Oh!" she says when her body makes contact with mine.

"But what?" I murmur, running my hands over her ass and kneading her soft curves. I love the feel of her chest against mine, but I need to taste her.

I ease her up so that I can lift my head and take a tight nipple between my lips. "Mmm. I love your nipples." I give the tight bud a little nip.

She gasps.

"Never mind," Caroline says, rocking her cunt against my cock. "You know what you're doing."

"That's fucking right." I give her ass a little smack as a punctuation point.

She gasps and there's a rush of moisture from her spread legs onto my rock solid cock.

Reaching around between us, I stroke her clit as I find James. We lock eyes as he comes up behind her. I give him a nod.

"Caro, have you been fucked up the ass before?" James asks, his voice tight.

She nods, her eyes hooded, her breasts bouncing a little as she rubs herself against me, teasing her little clit all on her own.

This woman. Fuck.

"Yes. But not a lot. And he was small."

James reaches over and pulls open our nightstand drawer. "Did you like it?"

"Yes." She sounds breathless, and she is questing more now, trying to reach between us and shift me so she can ride my cock.

I'm not inside her yet and the hint of her heat has me gritting my teeth. I want to pound into her with everything I've got, but not yet. I want to torture us both while James gets her ready to take his cock up her ass.

"Easy," I tell her, holding her hips. "Let James get you ready to take both of us."

"What did you like about it?" James asks her, squeezing lube onto his fingers and sliding his hand between her cheeks.

She shudders a little, which lets me know he's put a finger inside her.

"It just felt…good, in a surprising way. He couldn't really…fill my pussy, but he could my ass. He would put a vibrator inside me and fuck me from behind that way. It was…" she sucks in her breath. "Fun. *Oh, God, James.*"

I'm not jealous of the mystery man from her past with the small dick. If anything, I'm grateful he prepped her for us because, undoubtedly, James has more to offer than this past lover did. We need her to have been stretched at least a little.

"You like that, baby?" he asks her.

I can see his arm moving as he pumps his fingers in and out of her.

She's wiggling against me.

"You ready for my cock?" I ask.

She nods so eagerly I laugh softly.

Gripping her hips, I lift her slightly and seat her on me. She gives a soft shuddery moan.

My eyes briefly fall shut. Jesus, she's perfect. "Sweet Caroline. You have such a hot, tight pussy. The way you grip my cock…"

"Yes," she breathes. "I love you inside me, Cas. I feel so full."

"You're about to be filled even more." James runs his hands down over the back of her hair and pushes her forward. "Lean onto Cas."

She obediently puts her palms down on either side of my head and presses her chest against mine. I lift my hips to start to fuck her, slowly, leisurely, while reaching around and pulling her cheeks apart for James.

"Let me just test you, Caro," he says, moving in behind her. "Tell me if it's too much."

She's rocking onto me, eyes drifting closed. She jerks just a little and pauses when he pushes into her. Her mouth drops open on a soft sigh of wonderment.

"Okay?"

She nods. "Yes. So good."

"Open your eyes," I tell her, gripping her hips tightly. I'm holding back from pounding her the way I want to, but I'm still enjoying every single second. I want to watch her as my husband takes her ass.

When her eyes pop open, they're glassy. She's deep into her body, the pleasure, the sensation of being taken by two men at the same time. James and I have an alternating rhythm going, steady, but easy, neither of us taking her deeply.

"What do you think?" I ask. "How do you like being fucked by two men?"

"I think I have a new hobby."

That makes me laugh softly. "I think she needs more, James."

I can see how tense her arms are, how his teeth are gritted, and the vein in his neck is bulging. "Gladly," he responds.

Caroline tenses. "Relax, sweetheart." I run my finger over her lip, easing it into her mouth. "Suck on this."

She does, and her expression smooths out, her shoulders relaxing.

James grips the back of her hair, pushing her down onto me, and he fully buries himself in her. She bites my finger.

Then we're working together, both balls deep, fucking her frantically, stroking us all to sheer oblivion. Caroline is screaming with pleasure, her hair tumbling forward, her pussy a tight hot fist on my cock.

She's so tight and wet and I'm so close to the edge, but I hang on, wanting to watch her shatter.

When she does, it's wild and frantic, her hips bucking and her cries loud and triumphant.

"Yes, yes, yes!"

She's sobbing now, shuddering her way through a lengthy orgasm, and James swears. A second later, he pulls out and grips the base of his cock. I have a nice view of his cum spilling across the curve of her smooth ass.

I practically growl, squeezing her hips as I pound up hard into her, and come with such force I don't realize I'm holding my breath until I let it out in a hot expulsion.

Caroline is draped over me, hot and panting, making little whimpering sounds.

James falls beside us with a sigh and runs his fingers down her spine. He kisses the side of her head. "You okay, Caro?"

She nods, not moving. Her weight is deliciously heavy on me, and I turn my head to kiss James softly.

"I forgot to thank you for dinner," she mutters.

James laughs. "I think this was thank you enough, right, Cas?"

"Fuck yes it was." I give her ass a light smack. "I'm not sure I've ever been thanked so thoroughly."

CHAPTER 18

Grayson

"REMEMBER, she likes mashed bananas, but not banana baby food," Caroline says.

"Of course, I am –"

"She doesn't like barrettes in her hair. She prefers hats. But she'll tolerate that one bow with the clip on the back."

I pause, waiting to see if she's finished. She's only been here for a week, but she's acting as if she knows everything there is to know about my daughter.

And I think she does. There's been a huge change in both Caroline and Evelyn in the week that Caroline has been here. Evelyn smiles whenever she sees Caroline now and goes to her easily. I've seen how Caroline looks at Evelyn, too. She cares about my daughter—fuck, she even has me referring to Evelyn as 'my daughter' mentally. I don't know that yet. But it feels natural to think it. Dammit.

That's almost as big a red flag as finding Caroline acting protective of Evelyn with the nannies starting tomorrow a fucking turn-on.

"Oh, and I threw away that dark green romper that you had in her closet. She hates it. It's way too scratchy. And I was afraid they would just put it on her and not notice."

We are standing in the kitchen and Caroline is going over last-minute things with me before she leaves for the evening. It's her last day with us. She's already made two pages of notes and all of this is apparently the things she forgot to write down.

"Caroline," I say, waiting for her to straighten from where she's bent over, adding these things to yet another piece of paper.

She turns to face me.

"It will be okay."

The fact that I am comforting someone else about the situation surrounding Evelyn hits me as ridiculous. I am the last one to feel assured that everything is going to be okay. But I feel the need to send Caroline off with a smile.

Caroline blows out a breath. "You can call me anytime."

I want to call her. Actually, I don't want to let her go in the first place. And yes, in part, that is for Evelyn. The baby is going to miss her. I'm going to miss hearing Caroline's voice, her laughter, her singing out in the living room while I work. I'm going to miss seeing her every day. And I do worry about bringing yet more new people into Evelyn's life.

She's sleeping in the next room, looking like an angel when I laid her down, seemingly content and happy. But there is constant upheaval in her life and I feel lost as to how to change that.

"I can?" I ask about Caroline's offer to be available anytime. More for my sake than hers.

I cannot fuck the nanny. But if she's not the nanny…

"Of course. I can come over and help out whenever. I'm flexible. James will understand even if you need me during a class or something. If one of the nannies gets sick or something, I can fill in." She seems almost eager about that possibility.

"That would make you still kind of my nanny," I say, more for my sake than hers.

I cannot fuck the nanny.

"No, not really," Caroline says. "I'm just a friend, helping out now. You wouldn't have to pay me."

The money is, of course, the least of my concerns.

But that would make it cleaner. If I wasn't paying her, then fucking her wouldn't be complicated. It would just be…fucking.

But I can't fuck her. I can't risk it. What am I even thinking? I'm not sure there are enough condoms in the world to make me feel safe having sex again.

And as of right now, she is not my nanny, but she is still the gorgeous woman I've been hard for since I met her, and I probably should get her the hell out of my apartment.

"I…You've been a huge help to me and Evelyn."

"It's been fun. I'm glad you needed me."

If she only knew the ways I need her.

I cross to the refrigerator where I stored the flowers I bought her on my way back from the run I took on the beach this evening. I needed to pick up more diapers and formula too, so I took a run, stopped by the store, and saw the flowers in the shop window on my way back.

I turn and carry the bouquet to her. "Thank you so much. I know we upended your life this past week."

The frown lines on her forehead smooth and her expression softens as she takes the wildflowers from me. The bunch of yellow, peach, white, and purple flowers make her smile and that's all I needed to see.

"Thank you, Grayson. These are gorgeous." She lifts them to her nose.

"I considered something else. But something like a photo of Evelyn would just be something else to pack and move. I know when you travel a lot, you tend to keep physical possessions to a minimum. And that would have been presumptuous, actually."

I don't know if this woman who has known us for a week would even want a photo of Evelyn to keep.

But Caroline smiles. "I have *lots* of photos of Evelyn on my phone. *Lots*. Many with me in them, too. Several with James as well." She laughs. "If someone looks over my shoulder in a bistro as I'm flipping through them one day, they'll assume she's mine, I'm sure."

That makes something strange grab in my chest. And it's not entirely unpleasant.

I clear my throat. The idea of Caroline looking through photos of Evelyn while sipping coffee in a bistro somewhere around the world makes me strangely emotional. "I also thought about jewelry, but that seemed...intimate." My gaze drops to her mouth. I shouldn't have said that.

But I'd love to see her wearing a necklace around her pretty neck that I gave her.

The strange, hot surge of possessiveness surprises me.

She wets her lips. "Yeah. That would have seemed intimate."

"So, I settled for flowers."

"Well, everyone loves flowers." She lifts them again and inhales their scent. "And you remembered I said I love wildflowers best."

"Of course."

There's a pause—something hangs in the air between us—then she steps forward, wraps her arms around my waist and presses her cheek to my chest. "Thank you, Grayson."

I'm surprised by the hug, but my body reacts instinctively to having hers against it.

My arms go around her, and I pull her in fully, her body against mine. I love the feel of her in my arms. Her softness against my hardness. And I know she can feel my hardness, especially that behind my fly. My cock hardens almost instantly with her breasts pressed to my chest, her pelvis settled against mine, and her scent drifting up to my nose.

I drop my nose to her ear. "You really saved me, Caroline. Thank you so much for being here for me and Evelyn. "

"It was my pleasure," she says softly against my shirt front.

We stand there, holding each other for another few seconds, then she pulls back. But I don't let her go. She looks up at me. I study her gorgeous eyes, her nearly flawless skin, the copper, red, and gold strands in her hair, and finally the sweet shape of her mouth.

This is going to complicate everything. But…

"Fuck it," I mutter.

Then I kiss her.

The kiss turns hot and deep quickly.

Caroline moans and I quickly sweep my tongue into her mouth. I thread my fingers into her hair, holding her head and tipping it back. I turn her and press her into the wall, letting her feel exactly how hard my cock is, how much I want her, how good we make each other feel.

I hear the flowers drop to the floor, then feel her fingers sink into my hair, her fingernails scraping over my scalp.

That heats my blood and makes me growl. I slide one hand down her side, over the curve of her breast, then under her shirt and up to cup that sweet mound in my palm. I rub my thumb over her nipple and she whimpers into my mouth.

Her hands coast down my back and then start untucking my shirt from my waistband. She undoes my belt buckle, then her greedy, hot hands are under my shirt and against bare skin.

"Fuck, Caroline," I say against her jaw as I drag my mouth to her neck. "You feel so fucking good."

I dip my hand inside the cup of her bra, plucking and rolling her nipple, then palm her ass with my other hand. That tight, perfect ass I've been dreaming about biting, spanking, and gripping as I fuck her from behind.

My whole body feels like it's on fire. I lift her and she wraps her legs around my waist. I press her more firmly into the wall, rocking my cock against the sweet, soft spot between her thighs where I *need* to be.

She moans, then gasps, "Oh, God, Grayson," as she grips my shoulders tightly.

"I've wanted you from the very first day. I've fucked my hand so many times thinking of you."

She shivers and moans again. "God, I've thought of that moment more than I should have."

"While getting yourself off?" I lick down her neck, then bite gently.

"Yes."

"Does this sweet pussy need my cock, Caroline? Should we replay that scene but have it end the way we've both been imagining?"

"Yes. But..."

Something in her tone makes me pause in kissing my way back to her mouth. That hot fucking mouth I want around my cock more than I want my next breath.

"But?" I ask, pulling back to look into her eyes.

"That's...complicated."

I shake my head. Most of my blood is south of my belt, so I'm not totally clear-headed here, but I do remember that it's not complicated now. "Not anymore. You're not my nanny anymore."

"No. Right. Not because of that. But..." She bites her bottom lip.

I stare at it. I want to bite that bottom lip. I want to slide my cock past that bottom lip.

"I'm kind-of involved with Cas and James. I mean...we're sleeping together. And I guess we didn't talk about sleeping with other people. I mean, obviously *they* are. With each other. And this isn't a long-term or a serious thing. But I guess we didn't talk about anyone else while I'm here and it feels like I should at least tell them if I'm going to be doing this with someone else too."

She's rambling a little. She seems aware of that because she suddenly stops and presses her lips together.

I stare at her, my chest rising and falling as I breathe hard, forcing my mind to focus on something other than the fact my cock is *finally* pressed up against this woman's pussy. "What?"

"It's just for fun. Temporary while I'm in town. Obviously. But, yeah, we slept together. The three of us. And plan to again." She pauses, winces slightly, and says, "It was great," almost apologetically.

I let that sink in.

She slept with the guys next door.

She had a threesome with the guys next door.

Okay.

I blow out a breath. I slip my hand out of her shirt, letting go of the best breast I've handled in a very long time. I let her slide down the wall and make sure she's standing on her own, then step back. I shove a hand through my hair.

Finally, I say, "That's good."

She blinks up at me. "It is?"

"Definitely."

"Oh." She frowns, as if confused.

"I can't do this," I tell her. I take a step back as if to emphasize the point. To both of us. "I let this go too far as it is. I've wanted you since day one. I was serious about that. But I can't get involved."

"Oh," she says again.

Fuck, I sound like a dumbass. We both know if she hadn't said that about James and Cas, I'd be buried balls deep right now.

My cock pulses, and I silently curse.

Fuck, I want her.

But I Can. Not. Do. This.

"I know this feels like I'm running very hot, then cold. Being an asshole, or whatever. And I *do* want you. I just can't."

God, she looks good freshly kissed and driven against the wall. Her lips are plumper and pinker, her hair is mussed, she's breathing a little hard, and her nipples are poking against the front of her shirt, beckoning me.

I want to suck on her nipples so badly.

I could turn her, bend her over my couch, and fuck her good and hard, just once. Get it out of my system. Get just one taste of her. Feel her gorgeous pussy around my cock just once.

But once would never be enough.

And once is all it could take to wreck my life.

Okay, wreck my life even more.

It's not like you have to screw a woman four times to get her pregnant. I shove my hand through my hair again.

"I'm really sorry, Caroline," I say. "I just have to be more careful now. I've got Evelyn. And she's taught me that even one tiny screw up can change the lives of multiple people. My life has been turned upside down—hers is a confusing, chaotic mess. It's affected my business, it's even affected my parents and my sister. And everything else in my life. I just can't risk casual sex. Especially right now, when my life feels like a train barreling down the tracks with no brakes."

Caroline frowns. "I'm not looking for a long-term relationship. The last thing I want is to get pregnant or have someone misinterpret sex for something more serious."

I nod. "I believe you and I respect that. But as I've learned, things can still happen. The only way for me to be in total control of my life and Evelyn's is to do whatever I can to mitigate even potential complications."

She does not say, "*Oh now I'm a complication? Well, fuck you,*" like many other women would. Instead, she nods. "I get it. That makes sense."

It does. It really does. But I wish she could honestly say, "*Just fuck me, Grayson, I can make it all better.*"

"I think I'm just gonna go," she says.

I nod. "Okay."

She bends and gathers the flowers she dropped, cradling them against her chest. She walks to the door and I cannot help but let my gaze drop to that gorgeous ass as she sashays her way across my living room.

She opens the door, then turns back and says, "Maybe I'll see you around."

Then she steps out the door, closing it behind her.

And all I can think is that yes, I probably will see her around. Because she's fucking the two men who live next door. And I can't escape the images of her sandwiched between James and Cas, them kissing, touching, and making her come right on the other side of my bedroom wall.

"Fuck."

Well, I brought that on myself. I kissed her first and got a taste of what I can never have. I am the one who said this couldn't happen. I am the one who's apparently decided to live like a monk, until when? Evelyn is eighteen? Or maybe I should just go get a vasectomy now so that I can live my life happily and at peace.

But what if I want to make another baby someday?

I stomp over to my couch and sink into the middle of it. Something hard jabs my ass and I shift to the side, pulling out a rattle. I toss it onto the coffee table.

I stare at my front door, replaying everything from the moment I finally kissed her, to how her breast felt in my hand, to the way her thighs squeezed me, to her confession about her and James and Cas.

Caroline is sleeping with Cas and James.

Great.

Those two assholes can't be happy just having each other?

But then I start to really think about it.

They get to experience amazing, hot, very dirty sex with Caroline Bell.

Lucky fuckers.

But even more, it's obviously casual, and temporary.

I can't help but imagine it. A little.

I don't create an entire scenario but...I bet the three of them are very hot together.

And when there are two men fucking one woman, only one of them can be in her pussy. The other still gets to bring her pleasure, enjoy touching her, kissing her, have their mouth and hands all over her. They also get to have her mouth and hands all over them. But there are plenty of other ways to enjoy and satisfy a sexual partner without risking a pregnancy.

I glance in the direction of James and Cas's apartment.

So those guys are open to having a little extra fun in their marital bedroom. And Caroline is obviously open to multiple partners.

I wonder how they all would feel about adding one more to their party of three.

CHAPTER 19
Caroline

"YOU'RE LATE."

I try to look contrite, but Fiona's lifted brow tells me I'm not pulling it off.

"It's all my fault," Cas says, coming up onto the porch behind me.

I'd just pushed the front door to Frannie and Fiona's house open when Fiona blocked my entrance.

I was supposed to be here for brunch thirty minutes ago. With James and Cas.

It's Saturday morning, which means I spent the night at their house last night just like a week ago.

And it was just as good, if not better, than the first time.

So was this morning.

Which is why we're late.

"Oh, I have no doubt it's at least partly your fault," Fiona tells him.

"Well, it's not my fault that Caroline can't be left alone in the shower," Cas says. "But it *is* my fault that her hair got wet, and she had to blow dry it before we left."

"Why can't she be left alone in your shower?" Frannie asks, coming up behind Fiona, who is still blocking our way.

Cas's arm slides around my waist, his big hand splaying over my stomach, and he pulls me back against him. I can only imagine the wicked grin he's giving them as he says, "Because she can't reach *all* the spots that need…rubbing…when she's naked and soaking wet."

Frannie's mouth drops open on a surprised 'oh'. Fiona's eyes narrow.

"If you know what I mean," Cas adds.

I smile.

"I'm very sure they know exactly what you mean," James says as he comes up beside his husband. "And they probably don't need to know all of that right before they eat." He hands Fiona the bowl of mixed fresh fruit and Frannie the mini quiches we brought as our contribution to brunch. The twins, obviously, supplied the baked goods. He gives them a charming smile. "We are very sorry we're late. That was very rude of us. Thanks for inviting Cas and me along for brunch this morning."

Fiona leans over to inspect the quiches, then says, "You're forgiven. This time. Get in here and start drinking mimosas with me. And James, tell me what you think of our new curtains. Caroline has terrible taste in home decor."

"Hey," I protest as we all file into the house. "That's only because I don't really live anywhere for long, so I don't think it really matters."

"What about me?" Cas asks.

Fiona looks over her shoulder at him. "I haven't known you long enough to know your taste." She gives him a little smile. "Though you do have great taste in women. And men."

He chuckles. "That I do."

Soon we're out on the back deck, plates loaded with scrumptious food, huge mugs filled with French press coffee and cream, the ocean breeze lifting our hair, and honestly, I feel amazing.

James is laughing at something Frannie just told him, and I flash back to high school. We all got along so great back then and had such a good time and I'm so happy to see that hasn't changed. Fiona and Frannie were thrilled with the idea that James and Cas would come to brunch. They haven't seen much of James since he moved back and they want to change that. James readily agreed that they needed to make more of a point of getting together.

High school was filled with movie nights, bonfires, summer afternoons on the boardwalk and working various jobs here in town. Everything from babysitting to lifeguarding to working at the ice cream shop. We had a great childhood here in Honeysuckle Harbor and seeing three of my best friends back together, as if no time has passed, makes me miss them more than I usually do.

I keep in touch with the triplets and James, but I haven't been with them as a group in years. And I suddenly wonder what Camille, and Brandon, and other friends from our class are doing.

"Frannie, this is amazing," Cas says, biting into another mini puff pastry. "You two could make a living baking," he teases.

She laughs. "I should consider that."

I watch as Cas licks a dollop of cream from his index finger.

I literally can't look away as his tongue flicks over his finger, then over his bottom lip.

Instantly my pussy flutters and I feel my heart rate kick up. Is my face hot?

Cas licks through the little puff then, parting the flaky pastry, capturing the rest of the cream.

Oh my God. My clit tingles and I feel as if his tongue is actually touching me. Like it did last night. And this morning. He's *so* good with his tongue. As happy as he is with his husband, it's clear Cas has either spent plenty of time with women, or he's just a natural.

I see his lips curl into a smile and my gaze bounces up to his eyes.

He's watching me watch him.

That last lick was all for my benefit.

He gives me a wink, as if he knows what I'm thinking about.

Then he licks his finger again. I shift on my seat. He knows exactly what I'm thinking about.

"You wanna go to your room?" he asks.

"Yes," I tell him honestly. It wouldn't take him more than a few minutes to…

Frannie snaps her fingers and points at us. "No. You're going to sit there like two normal people and eat breakfast."

I look around the table. Everyone caught our little exchange.

"We are two normal people," I protest with a laugh.

"No, you're two very hot people who are banging each other's brains out," she says with a frown.

Cas laughs. "Having hot, amazing sex isn't normal?"

Frannie sighs. "Not for all of us."

Fiona shakes her head and looks at me. "You're going to sit there like you're a lonely, single person who hasn't had sex in too many months to count. Like the other two women at this table."

I laugh. Until a week ago, I was definitely one of them.

"Aw, Fi," James says. "That's sad. You're too awesome to not be having hot, amazing sex." He looks at Frannie. "You both are."

Fiona nods. "I agree. But we work a lot and this is Honeysuckle Harbor. The options are few. There are a lot of tourists, but that can be a crapshoot."

"And kind of dangerous," Cas inserts. "You shouldn't be going home with or bringing home a bunch of strangers traveling through town."

Fiona leans in. "One. I only need *one*. I don't need a harem like *some* people." She glances at me.

Cas laughs. "It only takes *one* serial killer to be a problem."

Fiona sighs. "I know. That's exactly it." She looks at her sister. "We don't all get lucky enough to find hot, grumpy FBI agents who are very interested in our…pastries."

Cas looks at Frannie, eyebrows up. "Oh? Tell us more."

Frannie shakes her head. "There's nothing to tell."

But we're all watching her with interest.

She rolls her eyes. "So Ford's wife, Ivy, well, before she was his wife, was engaged to Brad Richardson. Do you remember him?" she asks James.

He nods. "I know who he is."

"So they were engaged, Brad got into some trouble, he bought a house here and gave it to Ivy, the Feds were investigating him so they came here to question Ivy, yada, yada, yada, Hunter came in for dinner a few times and..." She shrugs, and blushes. "He likes my desserts."

"I'll bet he does," Cas says.

"Not like that." Frannie shakes her head. "I *wish*. He hasn't asked me out or anything. He's kind of..."

"Gorgeous. Sexy. Big. Broody. Sexy. Intense. Sexy," Fiona offers.

"Quiet," Frannie finally says.

"Quiet?" James asks. "Like shy?"

"No," Frannie says, but she seems to have trouble coming up with the right word. "He just..." Her cheeks get pinker. "Seems to like watching me."

Cas whistles. "Nice."

"He needs to ask me out!" Frannie exclaims. "He can watch me all he wants up close and privately!"

"That's right," James says encouragingly. "Why don't *you* ask *him* out?"

"That's what I said!" Fiona tells them.

"That's not really my style," Frannie says.

"But lonely and horny and bored is?" Fiona asks.

They all laugh.

I sit just watching them all, probably grinning like an idiot. I love all of these people and love that they can be friends like this. Even after I leave, they can still get together for brunches and talk about their lives. James and Cas can give the girls pep talks when it comes to men and dating. They can even vet the men. Of course, Frannie and Fiona have their brother Ford for that too, but there are never too many people watching out. The girls can have James and Cas over for dinner parties and Oscar watch parties so they have a social life outside of dad-hood but more low-key than their nightlife in Philly.

It will be so good for them all.

And that sharp stab of envy I feel is nothing to worry about. I'll be fine. Totally fine.

I did wonder briefly if one of the twins could even fill my role with James and Cas. The casual, fun, sexy role of woman-in-the-middle.

But I don't think any of them would go for that.

The guys need something *very* casual. Not someone they'll run into all the time long term. This isn't a *relationship*. It's a friendship with very, very hot sex as a benefit. And the sex stuff is temporary.

The doorbell rings and Frannie and Fiona look at one another. They both shrug and then get up together and head inside.

"They're the best," Cas remarks as he reaches for more fruit.

"They really are. We need to hang out more often," James says.

See? They're already making future plans.

I love that.

And I'm jealous as hell. Of all of them. These four people are awesome and I'm going to miss them like crazy.

"Uh, care to explain *this*?" Fiona asks from behind me.

I turn to find Frannie carrying an enormous bouquet of flowers.

Wildflowers.

They are an exact replica of the ones Grayson gave me on my last day with Evelyn. Except this is twenty times bigger.

What the hell?

"Who sent those?" I ask.

"I'm asking *you*," Fiona says as she clears space on the smaller deck table and Frannie sets the flowers down.

"Me?"

"Did you guys send her flowers?" Frannie asks James and Cas.

They exchange a look.

"No," Cas says.

"Should we?" James asks. "Is there etiquette that we're unaware of?"

"We've never had brunch with the woman we're..." Cas says, trailing off.

"We've never seen the woman two weekends in a row," James points out.

"We've never hung out with her two best girlfriends, known her mom and dad, or taken her to Prom either," Cas says.

I start laughing.

They all look at me.

"There's no etiquette that you're messing up, trust me," I say, pushing up from my chair and going to the flowers. "And clearly these aren't from them," I tell the girls. I pull the card from between the leaves.

My heart is pounding. Because I'm ninety-nine percent sure I know who they are from. But I don't know why.

I pull the card out and read.

Caroline, I need to apologize. The other night did not go the way I intended. I know I should apologize for kissing you, but I'm not sorry for that. I've been wanting that since I met you. I will apologize for changing my mind like I did. I shouldn't have started something I couldn't finish. I just wanted you to know that Evelyn misses you. And I wish you the best. Grayson Ross

I read it again.

Then laugh.

Oh my God, he signed it with his last name.

As if I wouldn't know who he was if he just put "Grayson"? And even in this note, he's a little hot and cold. Not apologizing for kissing me, bringing that back to mind rather than just moving on and letting me forget about it, but then reminding me that he can't go any further than that.

Why can't he just let this go?

Evelyn misses me? What about him?

And now I'm wondering how things are going with the new nannies and is Evelyn frowning or smiling at them? And do I want her smiling or frowning?

I want her smiling.

Probably.

I want her to be happy, for sure.

But I want her to like me best.

"Argh!"

"Everything okay?"

I look up from the card, remembering that I'm at brunch. With four other people.

"Oh. Um." I glance down at the card. "Yeah."

"Who are those from, and what does that card say?" Fiona demands.

And I want to tell them. I need them to tell me that thinking about Grayson Ross is stupid and I need to just let it all go. And that I need to quit replaying that stupid kiss in my mind. Over and over and over again.

I'm having mind-blowing sex with James and Cas!

I do *not* need to be thinking about a *kiss* with *Grayson*. He doesn't want more. He doesn't even want to do *that* again.

"Grayson," I tell them, reclaiming my seat at the table. I pass the card to Frannie.

Fiona and James lean in to read it.

James looks up quickly. "You and Grayson kissed?"

Cas leans over and plucks the card from Fiona's fingers and reads it, then looks at me. "When did this happen?"

I sigh and tell them the whole story.

"He's messy," I finally conclude. "His life is messy. His feelings are messy. I do *not* want that."

Cas is watching me thoughtfully.

James is nodding.

Fiona and Frannie are studying the flowers.

James says, "Yes you do."

"Yes, I do what?"

"Want that."

"I don't!" I protest. "I'm here temporarily! I'm here to relax and have fun before I leave again." I sit back in my chair and cross my arms. "Besides, he doesn't want it. He won't have sex because it could be complicated."

James nods again.

Cas leans over and grabs a strawberry. "That doesn't mean you don't want it," he says casually, as he bites into it.

"And Grayson is clearly still thinking about you," Fiona points out.

"Well, it doesn't matter." I tuck the card into my pocket. "It's not going to happen."

And I mean that.

Mostly.

My phone buzzes. I pull it out and see it's a text from Grayson. "Speak of the frustrating man…"

I got the DNA results.

My heart drops into my stomach.

I wait for another text but another one doesn't follow the first.

What are they???

Three dots appear, then disappear.

Shit. Shit, shit, shit.

"Grayson got the DNA results and now he's not responding," I announce. "We need to make sure he's okay."

"Just call him," Fiona says.

I shake my head. "No. He needs support if this is bad news."

If Evie isn't his…I can't even go there in my head.

"Definitely," James says, leaping up.

Cas pulls out his car keys. "Let's go."

CHAPTER 20

Grayson

I'M PACING back and forth, my phone on the kitchen counter on speaker. "Mom, please, just bring Evelyn home."

"First you complain that I'm not babysitting your daughter enough, and now you're demanding I bring her home?"

Sighing, I rub my forehead and strive for patience. My mother and I get along, for the most part. The problem is, we're basically the same person. She is reacting exactly the way I would to an unreasonable demand, and I get it. I really do. It's also really fucking annoying.

"I didn't know I was going to get the DNA results today. I want Evie with me when I read them."

The package had arrived via FedEx this morning. For some reason, I had thought it would be something more innocuous, less weighty, like an email.

But no, it was an overnight express envelope that I had to sign for, which felt ominous and downright terrifying. What if this is actually a letter from a judge telling me I have to relinquish custody of Evelyn right this second because she's not mine?

I'll throw up if that happens. I can't let this innocent, intelligent baby get yanked away from me and sent God knows where to live with God knows who.

Being afraid is a new emotion for me and I fucking hate it.

"Evelyn can't read," my mother says. "And we're at the zoo in Charleston. She's having fun. The monkeys are making her laugh. They're making your father laugh too. He's been very bored since he retired."

She's redirecting me. It's a great tool that I've utilized many times in business.

I refuse to fall for it. "What time are you coming home?" I've already lost the war. Might as well attempt to win the battle. "She needs to be in bed by seven or she's impossible to put down."

I open my refrigerator, suddenly wanting a drink. I don't have anything at all. I know food delivery has come to Honeysuckle Harbor but has alcohol delivery reached here? It has to. There are tourists from April to October who may or may not have cars and who might want a cocktail in their beach rental. If there isn't alcohol delivery here, I should invest in that.

Now I'm just distracting myself, which apparently I need. I'm a bundle of fucking nerves and that damn envelope is mocking me on the counter.

"We'll be there by seven, I promise, Grayson. Your daughter is a delight, I have to say."

"*If* she's my daughter," I say glumly. "What if she's not?"

"She's your daughter. She looks just like you."

She does. "But we don't know for sure," I insist.

"For heaven's sake, just open the results. Call me back on Face-Time if you want to see Evelyn."

I slam the refrigerator closed again.

I had impulsively texted Caroline that I've gotten the results. I don't know why, not exactly.

Okay, that's a lie.

I know why.

Because she cares about Evelyn.

And I care about Caroline.

I'm also jealous of the fact that she's having what is clearly hot sex with James and Cas next door. I know that because I heard them last night. The bed was hitting the wall, rattling the toys on the bookshelf in my living room that rests against what must be their bedroom. I'm ashamed to admit I put my ear to the wall and heard male grunting and a very clear, "Yes, James, yes!" from Caroline.

Aside from a positive DNA test, I wanted nothing more last night than to be hearing her yell, "Yes, Grayson, yes!" while I was buried to the hilt in her wet pussy.

Instead, I spent another Friday night with a bottle of lotion, my hand, and dirty thoughts of Caroline.

What made it even worse was Kyle, the night nanny, caught me with my ear to the wall and asked if I was okay.

I wasn't okay.

I'm not okay.

I may never be okay again until I can fuck Caroline Bell.

Which I can't do because I can't risk an unplanned pregnancy and I fucked it up anyway by kissing her and then basically shoving her away.

Then sending her flowers as an apology, followed immediately by a cryptic text that I got the DNA results back.

Who the fuck does that?

Me.

The world's biggest idiot.

But it was torture last night thinking about Caroline coming hard at the hands—or cocks or tongues—of James and Cas. Not because she doesn't deserve the pleasure, because she does, but because it could have been me.

I also know she spent the night because I heard the three of them talking and laughing as they walked down the hallway this morning. When I glanced out my peephole, James had his arm around her and she was smiling ear to ear, the smile of a woman who has been well fucked. Cas was walking backward toward the elevator, like he couldn't resist looking at both of them, an easy grin on his face.

They were probably going to breakfast. After sex and sleeping draped all over each other and waking up to morning cuddles and kisses and…

"Grayson! Are you even listening?"

I have completely forgotten my mom is still on the phone.

"Mom—

I'm saved from having to defend myself by a knock on my door. Frowning, I glance toward it. It's noon and no one can access this floor unless they're buzzed in.

Or it's James or Cas.

Or Caroline, because I sent her a text that I had the DNA results. I should have texted again, but I called my mom right away, immediately wanting to have Evelyn back in my arms before I opened the envelope.

"I'll call you back, Mom, thanks. Bye."

I hit the end button on my screen and head to my door. A glance through the peephole shows that it is James and Cas. And Caroline.

She's in front, looking worried. Her brow is furrowed and her fist is raised to knock again. "Coming," I say, then regret that choice of words.

I open the door. "Hi."

"Grayson, are you okay? What did the results say?" Caroline rushes forward, forcing me to step back and let them all enter the apartment.

"I haven't opened them yet."

She stops and shoots me a look of censure. "What? Oh my God, you had me so worried! We bolted out of brunch when you didn't respond to me."

"Did you text me back? Sorry, I was on the phone with my mother."

"Where's Evelyn?" she demands.

"With my mother. At the zoo in Charleston."

James and Cas have strolled in casually behind Caroline. James looks concerned and Cas looks…shrewd. Like he can read me like a book. It's an uncomfortable feeling.

"I'm sorry I interrupted your brunch."

"We were just about ready to leave anyway," James says. "Why aren't you opening the results? Is it an email?"

I pick up the offensive overnight express letter from hell and wave it. "It's this. Doesn't this look like it's court documents? Like some judge is going to demand I surrender Evelyn to CPS?"

"How do you know it's DNA results?" Caroline asks.

"Because Andrea called me and told me to expect them this morning."

"Who is Andrea?" James asks, looking bewildered.

"His assistant," Caroline says for me. "Poor woman," she murmurs under her breath.

Well, that's not sounding good for Team Grayson.

It's also not inaccurate. Andrea has put up with a lot from me over the years.

"You know I'm a lawyer," Cas says.

I actually had no idea he was a lawyer. I barely know who I am at this point, I certainly have not taken the time to get to know my neighbors as well as I could have. "Of course," I lie. "So is this bad news?"

"No, I'm sure it's just the DNA results, like your assistant said. If it was CPS, there would be a social worker and law enforcement at your doorstep."

That makes my vision blur and the room momentarily goes black. I lean heavily against the nearest wall. "Fuck. Fuck, fuck, fuck."

Caroline walks over to me. "Hey. Look at me." Her voice is soft as she puts her hands on my shoulders. "It's going to be fine. Evelyn is yours. We all know that."

"But..." I stare down at her, losing myself in her green eyes. The confidence there instantly makes me feel better.

"Let's open it together," James says, reaching out to tap my shoulder. "It's all good, man. You'll see."

I nod, but it still takes everything in me to rip open the envelope. I pull a couple of pieces of paper out with a trembling hand.

Scanning it, my heart in my throat, I see "biological father" and then my name. Ninety-nine point nine percent certainty.

"Holy shit, it's me." Then my throat closes and I can't speak. I briefly close my eyes as Caroline gives me a loose hug. I wrap my arm around her back and pull her in tighter, breathing in her scent, appreciating her softness.

"That's awesome!" James says.

"May I see?" Cas asks, holding out his hand.

I pass over the documents and he quickly reads, obviously wanting to confirm for himself that's really what it says. "Congratulations," he says with a grin. "You're a father."

Caroline has stepped back, but she smiles directly at me and says softly, "He was already a father. Evelyn is a lucky little girl."

My throat has released, but now my heart squeezes.

Evelyn is my daughter. Officially. Forever.

I never knew I could feel this way about another human being.

I also never knew I could feel about a woman the way I do about Caroline.

But she's leaving Honeysuckle Harbor, *and* she's getting fucked by James and Cas.

"Thank you," I manage to say. I turn my gaze to James and Cas. "To all of you. Seriously, I appreciate all the help and support you've given me."

"What are neighbors for?" Cas says.

"We're happy to help any way we can," James adds.

"The flowers weren't necessary." Caroline takes the papers from Cas and reads them too.

It feels like she's doing it to avoid looking at me.

"The flowers were necessary." I go over to her and I take the papers away and set them down on the counter. "I was...am... fucking everything up."

Brushing her hair back off of her shoulder, because I can't resist the urge to touch her, I take in her delectable mouth. I want to kiss her so fucking bad. But I glance over at James and Cas. "Look, I know you guys have a thing going and I respect that."

"But you want Caroline too," James says when I don't continue.

I nod. "I do."

"She's free to do whatever she wants," Cas says. "We're adults. Friends having fun together."

"She clearly wants you, too," James adds with a grin. "It's pretty damn obvious."

Caroline isn't saying anything. She's just watching me, like she's waiting for me to do or say something.

I don't know if there is a right or wrong thing to say here, but I decide the hell with it.

"I want to have sex with you," I tell her.

She crosses her arms. Not a good sign. "I thought you can't have sex because you're worried about an unplanned pregnancy."

I lean in and take her mouth in a passionate kiss.

Then I say, "I was actually thinking that *all* of us could be together. That way I can find other ways to be…satisfied. And you would have *lots* of ways to be satisfied."

Her mouth falls open. Her eyes widen. Her breath hitches. "Oh."

I caress her bottom lip, suddenly very fucking turned on by the idea of getting to see her come apart as three men are giving her attention. "Would you like that, Caroline? Getting fucked in various ways by three men at once?"

She nods rapidly. Her cheeks are pink. "Yes. I mean, yes, if it's the three of you."

My cock hardens painfully. "Good girl." I turn back to James and Cas. "What do you think? Can I join you both in getting Caroline off?"

They exchange a glance between them before they both nod.

I'm caressing up her arms now, and I let my thumb brush over her tight nipple. She inhales sharply.

"If that's what Caro wants, I'm in," James says.

"It's a fuck yes from me," Cas says. He rubs his jaw and gives her a sinful smile. "Three holes, three guys. What do you think, sweet Caroline?"

"Can we do it now?" she asks.

I groan. "Fuck yes, baby."

Today is the best day I've ever had, and it's just getting started.

CHAPTER 21

Caroline

STANDING IN FRONT OF GRAYSON, I'm vaguely aware of the fact that I am never going to have better sex again in my life. Already the sex with Cas and James, I fear, has made it so I can never go back to sex with only one man. The one man I thought would possibly be an exception to that is standing in front of me right now. And he is practically vibrating with need.

I know he's wound up with a number of emotions, and lust is only one of them. But this heat between us has been building ever since we met, and now suddenly there are no barriers. I don't work for him, and he has just figured out a way to get past all of his concerns and fears about another unintended consequence to sex.

These three men are going to ruin me. But despite that, I step closer, slide my hand up Grayson's chest, up the side of his neck to his face.

"This is going to be so good," I tell him.

I watch his throat move as he swallows hard.

"What do you want, Caroline?" Grayson asks. "How do you want us to do this?"

Fuck, what a question. I shake my head. "Everything. All of it. There isn't anything the three of you can do that I don't want."

I see the breath he takes actually shudder through him.

I feel Cas move in behind me, his big hot hands resting on my hips.

"So let me just make sure I get this right," Cas says, making small circles on my hips. "You want to help us make Caroline come? Make her crazy? Make her scream? But you don't want to fuck this gorgeous woman's tight, perfect pussy, is that right?"

I feel like hot oil, warm and thick, is pouring through me. I stare up at Grayson— the heat reflected in his eyes.

"Oh I want to," he says. "I just can't."

"But *you* intend to come," Cas clarifies. "And make her come. No one will be left hanging."

"Absolutely no one will be left hanging," Grayson promises, his eyes still on me.

Cas hands slide up my sides to my neck and then into my hair. He begins gathering my hair into a ponytail, then holds it back in one fist. "Okay then. Caroline, let's show Grayson that he has nothing to worry about. That your pussy is only one amazing, hot, wet hole he can get lost in."

He nudges me, and I sink to my knees in front of Grayson.

I love being bossed around like this, and I have a feeling Grayson is going to be just as demanding, if not more than Cas is.

I rest my hands on Grayson's thighs. "Do you want my mouth, Grayson?" I ask.

He seems surprised and it's good that he finds out early that I'm not quiet and submissive in the bedroom.

Instead of answering, his hands go to his fly and he jerks the buttons open and the zipper down.

I swear my mouth starts watering as he pushes his underwear out of the way and I get another look, this time very up close, at his long, thick cock.

He grasps it in his fist, giving himself a long, hard jerk. "You've no idea how many times I've imagined you on your knees in front of me."

"Was there another man behind me holding my hair back?" I ask with a grin.

"No. But I don't fucking care about anything but having your lips wrapped around my cock." He leans in, rubbing the head of his cock over my bottom lip.

I flick my tongue out, swirling it over his tip, relishing the hot, salty taste of him.

"Before you get going, I need her naked," James says.

I pull back to look over at him and Grayson growls.

I grin up at him. "You don't want me naked?"

He blows out a breath. "Fuck, of course I want you naked. Hurry up," he tells James.

James chuckles. "Trust me. She sucks harder when her pussy is being played with."

Grayson's reaction to that is a half groan-half growl that makes my pussy clench. I find myself hauled to my feet before I can even begin to stand on my own.

James strips my dress off over my head, and Grayson immediately removes my bra and fills his hands with my breasts.

"I'm obsessed with your tits."

He cups, squeezes, and teases my nipples and I have to press my thighs together. My entire body feels like it's tingling. He lowers his head and takes one into his mouth, sucking hard while Cas strips my panties down my legs.

"Come here, pretty girl," James says, sweeping me into his arms, my elbow practically clocking Grayson in the chin.

James carries me to the couch and sets me down on my knees.

"Kneel over the arm of the sofa," he directs, moving in behind me. "Grayson, her mouth is all yours now. At least until you come down her throat."

Grayson moves to the end of the couch, and I rest my forearms on the padded arm, leaning over. He strokes his cock in front of me. "Open up for me, Caro."

It's the first time he's called me that nickname and a hot shiver goes through me.

I feel one of the other guys move in behind me and a hot hand smooths over my ass before dipping between my thighs. A thick finger slides through my slickness and I moan.

"Fuck, we've got her dripping," Cas says. "Reward her for being so wet and hot for us," Cas tells James.

"Please," I moan. I try to shift back against the finger teasing me.

I get a little slap on my ass for my effort.

"Suck on Grayson," Cas orders. "We'll take care of your pussy." He rubs the spot he swatted. "You know that."

I can't argue that they've done a very good job of taking care of me every other time.

I lean forward and run my tongue over the head of Grayson's cock. He growls and his hand goes to the back of my head, fingers tightening in my hair.

"How greedy are you for cock?" my grumpy ex-boss asks.

"For these three?" I ask. "I'll do anything."

Grayson slides his cock over my lips and into my mouth. I moan.

"Very good answer," he praises.

James lays down on the couch, his face between my legs. He grips my hips and pulls me down until my pussy is against his hungry mouth. Cas moves in next to us, playing with my nipples.

I'm in absolute heaven. My entire body is being wound tighter and tighter, and I know I'm already on the verge of an intense orgasm.

I'm glad I have Grayson's cock in my mouth or I could embarrass myself with the way they're going to make me scream.

And these three egos? They don't need that.

"Jesus, Caroline," Grayson grits out, his fingers tightening in my hair. "Fuck girl."

I love that I can make him sound like that. He's been wound tight, and he needs this release. I squeeze his thighs and take him deeper.

His breath hisses out and I feel James suck my clit harder.

Cas tweaks my nipple. "Good girl," he says gruffly. "Fuck, you look so good like this." His hand slides over my ass, then circles my back hole with his finger. "But James's tongue isn't quite enough, is it?"

I whimper and instinctively press back against his finger.

He chuckles, low and wicked. He circles faster, the tip of his finger teasing just inside. "I know. You need to be really filled up, don't you?"

James sucks harder and I feel a finger slide into my pussy.

Oh, God. Yes.

I take Grayson deeper and he groans.

I want to feel him come.

James adds another finger and my pussy clenches around him. "Fuck, Caroline. Yes," he says before sucking hard again.

Cas eases his finger fully inside, James thrusts his fingers deep, and I *need* Grayson to come.

I reach up, cup his balls, and suck hard.

"*Caroline.*" It sounds like he's talking through gritted teeth.

"Come for us, sweetheart," Cas says. "Let it go. We're just getting started."

Grayson's low voice rumbles. "Fuck, Caro. I'm going to come."

I want that. My hands on his thighs pull him closer and I bob my head faster.

"*Fuck,*" he grunts.

"Let her have it," Cas says. "She wants it. Don't you, Caro?" His finger works faster.

James groans beneath me as he feels my pussy tighten around his fingers. "That's it, yes, Caroline. Come on my face."

Grayson thrusts into my mouth again and then tenses. "*Dammit.*"

Then he's coming, emptying down my throat.

That sends me over the edge. I clench around James's fingers, coming hard.

"That's right," Cas urges, finger fucking my ass. "That's our girl."

My orgasm keeps rippling as Grayson pulls out of my mouth. I swallow, but it's too much to keep some from trickling down my chin as I have to gasp at the sensations rocking through my body.

Grayson takes my chin with his hand, his thumb swiping over the stickiness, watching my face as I cry out.

"Oh god, oh god, oh god!"

"Jesus, you're beautiful," he mutters.

I slump forward, my head on the arm of the couch, trying to take in a deep breath. James's and Cas's fingers slip from my body and I feel them stroking my back, legs and ass, caressing, petting, grounding me.

"Oh no, not done with you yet," Grayson says, reaching under my arms and pulling me over the arm of the sofa and against his body. "Thank you," he says against my mouth. "You're incredible."

"My pleasure." I instinctively wrap my arms and legs around him as he seals his mouth over mine. His hands cup my ass and our tongues tangle and I'm lost in the deep, hot kiss, only vaguely aware that we're moving.

Seconds later, Grayson lays me down on his bed. He stands back, his hot gaze tracking over my naked body.

"Now I need to see you filled up with cocks, Caroline."

My eyes widen. "Yo…you do?" My eyes go to his cock, now tucked back inside his still unzipped pants. He just came hard.

"So fucking badly," he says, adjusting himself. "Cas, James, get in here and fuck this woman."

"Yes, sir," Cas says with a grin, starting to undress.

James moves in next to him. "Gladly." He pulls his shirt over his head.

And the three men who are going to ruin me for all others stand at the bottom of the bed, watching me with hungry, yet oddly affectionate gazes.

CHAPTER 22

Grayson

THIS IS ABSOLUTELY PERFECT.

I'm finally getting my mouth and hands on this woman and Caroline is even more than I imagined. She's gorgeous, sexy, eager as hell.

And there's no tight knot of anxiety in my gut. I can let loose, enjoy her, give us both pleasure and not worry about a damned thing.

"You are so beautiful," James tells Caroline, climbing up the bed, naked, to brace himself over her, kissing her deeply.

She wraps her arms around his neck, arching into his body.

It's clear they've done this before. They're very comfortable and one of his hands moves over her, gliding down her side, squeezing her hip, then up again to cup her breast and tease her nipple as if he knows exactly how to touch her.

"Make room, you two," Cas says. "I need to fuck somebody." He smirks at me. "Should I take Caroline or James?"

I have no problem with two men fucking and assume that if we all do this together multiple times—which is absolutely my plan and I'll do what I can to make it theirs too—I'll see Cas and James together, but right now, I want to see Caroline come apart.

"I need to see her scream," I say.

"Can do," Cas says, turning that cocky smirk on the woman on the bed.

James is lying beside her now, his hand running over her body, absently teasing a nipple, then drifting down to play between her thighs.

She's breathing hard and wiggling on the duvet, but she seems to be just waiting for instruction.

"Perfect pussy or tight, sweet ass?" he asks James. "I'm happy anywhere that has Caroline seeing stars."

James grins down at her as he slides two fingers into her pussy. She parts her legs slightly and I feel my cock start to swell again despite coming down her throat just minutes ago.

She's even more gorgeous than I imagined and I want to feel her pussy around my cock so badly I almost can't breathe.

I've imagined Caroline naked. I've imagined fucking Caroline. Since finding out that she's sleeping with Cas and James, I've imagined them fucking her. But honestly, I did not imagine the three of us fucking her or them going from brunch to double penetration within an hour.

I love that about this woman. She's bold, and minute to minute is able to assess the situation and know exactly what she wants from it.

I don't even need to hear her say it to know that she wants all of this.

But I do *want* to hear it. If for no other reason than because it's hot as fuck.

I step close and run my hand over her silky hair, brushing it back from her flushed cheeks.

"Will you take both of their cocks, Caroline? Show me how gorgeous you are stretched around both of them? Will you scream for us?"

She makes a beautiful whimpering noise and nods. "God, yes."

I lean over and capture her lips in a deep, hot kiss, fucking her mouth with my tongue, the way I wish I could fuck her pussy with my cock.

As much as I would love to bury myself inside her, I never realized what a fucking turn on it could be to watch a woman come apart at the hands of another man.

I've never done this before. Not because I'm against it, just because I've never had the right combination of a woman and another man. Or men.

But now suddenly, in this moment, it's not only hot, but it feels completely right.

Being here with these three seems almost obvious.

It's clear that they have figured out how they fit best together and I just feel lucky as hell that they're letting me be a spectator. A spectator that gets to participate as much as I want to.

I lift my head and stare into her eyes. "You're incredible," I tell her sincerely. "Thank you for this."

She laughs breathlessly. "Right. This is all for you, Grayson. I'm getting nothing out of it."

I lean down and palm her breast, giving her nipple a tweak. "No need to be sassy."

"She can't help it," Cas says.

She looks past me to give him a sly smile. "You all act as if you want a sweet little submissive. But I think you like having someone who will push back. Because you like putting me in my place."

Low growls come from the two other men and Cas says, "Your place is pinned to this mattress by two enormous cocks right now, Caroline."

I love the shiver that goes through her.

"Show me how well you take them," I tell her.

She takes a deep breath. "I'm ready," she says, her eyes on one of the other men. I'm not sure which since I can't look away from her face.

I lean back as the other men shift around. James lies back on the mattress on his back and pulls Caroline over on top of him.

They're very comfortable manhandling her, and she doesn't seem to mind.

She laughs as he pulls her thighs across his body to straddle him.

"You know what you want, don't you?" she asks.

His big hands knead her ass as he positions her pussy against his cock. "Just you. The answer is always you."

At that, she leans in and kisses him, and damn, that almost seems romantic.

Cas climbs up on the mattress between James's legs behind Caroline.

"Feel free to reposition so you can see well," he tells me. He strokes his hand up and down her back. "Once we're deep, we'll probably forget you're even here. It's all about her at that point."

I nod. "As it should be."

Caroline lifts her head and gives a breathy moan. "I've been absolutely spoiled by these two. You're telling me all three of you are making me the center of attention? I might not survive."

"You want one of us to be a selfish asshole?" I ask. "I suppose you expected me to fill that role?"

She looks over at me. "I'm not going to shatter your tough-guy CEO ego by telling you that I don't think you're actually a selfish asshole at all, and I am fully comfortable being worshiped by the three of you."

Cas gives her ass a little slap. "That better not mean that you're not open to some role-playing at some point," he tells her. "I wouldn't mind seeing you in a pencil skirt, bent over my mahogany desk at the office."

James chuckles. "And how are you going to explain me and Grayson to your staff, even if you get Caroline to pretend to be interviewing for an assistant position?"

I tense in surprise for a moment. That almost sounds as if we're always all going to be doing this together. Do they think there's not going to be any more times that are just the three of them?

I like that more than I should.

Cas's grin is wicked as he smiles down at his husband. "We have conference rooms. There's no reason you can't all be interviewing to be my new assistant."

The innuendo dripping from his words is obvious and I'm... not bothered at all.

If I had ever imagined a group scenario, I would never have believed that I would be as intrigued by the male interactions as I am the female, but here I am. I'm not sure I'm turned on by Cas or James, but I'm not turned *off* by them either.

"Do I get to see you all in suits?" Caroline asks, wiggling her ass and causing James to groan as she grinds against his cock.

"As long as you let me do whatever I want with my tie," Cas teases.

I shift, my cock definitely recovering from my earlier orgasm in Caroline's mouth.

As I move, I realize Cas's hand is underneath Caroline. He's obviously working her back entrance, readying her for his cock there and my erection pulses.

I realize that while I've had plenty of sex and several very sexy partners, my sex life has been possibly fairly vanilla compared to the three people I'm in bed with right now.

"Oh my god, you guys, I'm ready," Caroline pants. "Please."

"You sure?" Cas asks. "You dripping? Hot? Need us?"

"Yes, *yes*," Caroline pants.

Cas withdraws his hand and picks up one of the condoms I just now notice on the duvet. He rips it open, then leans around, shifting Caroline slightly so he can roll the condom down his husband's cock.

James groans as Cas squeezes him, then positions his cock and moves Caroline over the top of it.

"Take him nice and deep, Caro," Cas tells her as he moves her down the length of James's cock.

Both Caroline and James groan and I see James's fingers dig into Caroline's hips.

"Fuck, Caroline, you always feel so fucking good," James tells her gruffly.

Caroline nods her head quickly. "I know. This is always so good."

And now I'm a little jealous that they've all done this so many times. Not because I resent them being together, but just because I've missed it. This is the hottest experience of my life. I adjust my cock, giving my hard-on a squeeze.

I shift closer to the end of the bed, needing to see her gorgeous pussy spread around James's cock.

Cas notices, of course, and, of course, doesn't let it go without comment. He gives me a wink. "Lean in if you need to."

It occurs to me that maybe I should be embarrassed by how eager I am to see this.

I am so into Caroline, nearly obsessed with her, yet I'm nearly drooling, watching two other men fuck her.

But it's how into it she is, I realize. Seeing how well they take care of her, how much they want her, how they are just as into her as I am.

She's a fucking goddess, and they realize it too.

I could never share her with anyone who didn't think she was every bit as incredible as I do. But I trust these men to fuck her well, care for her, and make this everything she needs and wants it to be.

"You're all putting on a great show," I tell them.

James chuckles. "You're welcome."

Caroline grins at me and I lean over and kiss her hard and hot.

"Just you wait," Cas says, rolling the second condom down his cock.

He moves in behind Caroline. "You ready for me, sweetheart?"

"Oh God," she breathes out.

Cas chuckles and again runs his big hand up and down her back. "You take us so well. Don't let Grayson think that this is any kind of hardship. You've definitely adjusted. And if you're a really good girl, and show him how much you love this, maybe he'll let you have his amazing cock in this pretty ass sometime."

Jesus.

Lust hit me hard.

I fucking want that.

"Oh, *God*," Caroline groans.

"You want that, don't you?" Cas asks.

She meets my gaze. And nods.

"Is this the first time you've taken two men at once?" I ask her, brushing her hair back from her face so I can see her more clearly. "I mean, with James and Cas, not today." It's clear they've already done this with the three of them.

She nods again. "Yeah. I've never been comfortable enough with two other men to do something like this with them. But James and Cas have certainly opened my eyes and I trust them completely."

I love that. It's not even about me. My cock's not involved and yet I love that these two men have earned her trust in this way.

"Whose name are you gonna scream?" I ask her, still holding her face. "When these two men make you come apart? How do you choose?"

"Well, she yells *oh God*," Cas says, rubbing the head of his cock over her back entrance. "So obviously it's me."

James thrusts up into her pussy. "Whatever you say."

Caroline just gasps.

"Here I come, pretty girl," Cas says, pressing against her ass.

Caroline takes a deep breath and reaches out and grasps my hand, squeezing hard.

"Relax, honey," James says, stroking his hands up and down her sides. "You can take this. Remember how good it felt? Relax and breathe."

She does, relaxing against his chest, taking a deep breath, letting her eyes slide shut. She still holds my hand, but her grip relaxes.

Then Cas presses into her.

They all groan. I even groan.

The sight is hot as fuck, and gorgeous at the same time.

"Oh. My. God," Caroline groans.

"You're perfect," I tell her.

"So fucking good," Cas says, his jaw tight.

Then they begin moving. They find an easy rhythm and soon Cas and James are fucking Caroline and each other at the same time.

For several minutes, it's just the sound of skin on skin, groans, gasps, and moans. I'm transfixed. My cock is aching and I finally can't help it. I'm not going to fuck her, I'm not going to use her mouth again, so I slip my hand into my pants and pull my cock out. Caroline notices and reaches for me. But I shake my head.

"Just let them take care of you."

"I can take care of you too," she says, her voice breathless.

"No. I want to watch you and them. I'm good."

She meets my gaze. "Okay, but don't come until you can come *on* me," she says, the words dirty, and yet somehow grabbing me in the chest.

The guys pick up the pace, and I see James's grip on her hips tighten.

"Fuck Caro, I'm going to come."

"Yes, James, fill me up," she tells him.

"Need you to come again," he tells her.

"I'm close," she promises.

Cas is thrusting into her from behind, his grip on her hips just below James's.

He somehow slides a hand in between all of them, and I imagine he's found her clit when she gasps, then cries out, coming hard.

The men are right behind her, first James, then Cas.

They just hold each other for a long moment before Cas pulls back. James rolls Caroline toward me, and I jerk my cock, coming over her pretty tits as she lies on the bed below me.

Then the room is filled with nothing but the sound of four people trying to catch their breaths.

Being the pros at this multi-person sex thing, after a couple of minutes, James and Cas move us all around so we're all lying on the bed together. Caroline is half draped over my lap, her legs tangled with James's. Cas lies on the other side of James, but his hand is resting on Caroline's back. James and Cas intertwine their fingers between them.

Caroline starts to drift off, and I find myself brushing her hair back from her face again.

"I'm going to take her into the shower," I tell them.

They nod.

James rolls toward Caroline and presses a kiss to her shoulder. "Hey honey, we actually need to go. We need to go pick up Noah."

She mumbles something softly, but I can't make it out.

"You'll make sure she gets home?" Cas asks me.

I frown. "Of course. Eventually. We'll shower. I'll feed her. Maybe we'll nap for a while. Evelyn won't be home for a few hours."

Cas nods, seeming pleased. "Good job on the aftercare."

"Aftercare?" I ask.

His hand is still rubbing up and down Caroline's back. "When you fuck a woman to near unconsciousness, you should absolutely take care of her after. Make sure she's okay—cuddle her a little, make sure she's good afterward."

I know what aftercare is. I'm actually offended. His comment just caught me off guard. "Of course I'll be sure she's good."

James and Cas both give me pleased smiles. "Good."

I get out of bed and lean over to sweep Caroline into my arms and start for the bathroom.

She nuzzles into my chest, and I feel a strange warmth expand behind my ribs.

"You've got this," Cas tells me, encouragingly.

Fuck, yeah I do. Taking care of Caroline actually feels easy.

Maybe too easy.

But if this is a red flag of some kind, I'm not going to think about it until later.

CHAPTER 23
Caroline

I WAKE up at nearly five. For a moment, I'm disoriented, but then the scent hits me. Grayson's scent.

I roll over and bury my face in his pillow, breathing deep and squealing into the Egyptian cotton pillow case that feels like heaven against my skin.

We had sex.

Hot, dirty, I-want-so-much-more-of-that sex.

With James and Cas.

I would have never guessed Grayson Ross would be the type to share and honestly to stand back as much as he did and still enjoy it, but he did.

There's no way he faked that he liked it.

When he carried me into the bathroom and stepped into the huge glass encased shower with me—all four of us could have easily fit—he couldn't keep his hands off me or stop saying how amazing it was and how hot it was and he wanted to keep doing that. With the guys.

God, it was so good.

My body is still tingling and I'm a little sore and yet if the three of them climbed into this bed with me right now, I'd be ready to go again.

But I'm alone.

I sit up as I realize it fully.

I'm totally alone. I went from three lovers to napping alone.

I remember James and Cas needing to leave to pick up Noah. But I also remember falling asleep against Grayson's chest.

I look down.

I'm wearing the T-shirt Grayson pulled over my head after we showered. And I don't have panties on.

Huh.

I smile.

I want more with the four of us, but I wonder what kind of fun Grayson and I could get up to, just the two of us.

He's adamant about not fucking me but...there's a lot of other stuff we can do.

My stomach growls as I swing my legs over the side of the mattress.

I also need some food.

I pull the bedroom door open and step into Grayson's living room. The sun is shining in through the big window and it's quiet in the apartment, but I find him immediately.

He's on the couch.

And he's not alone.

So much for more sexy times.

But I don't mind.

I feel my soft smile and pause a moment, taking in the sight.

Grayson's sitting holding Evelyn.

And just staring at her.

She's fast asleep, looking like an angel.

I'm sure the zoo with her grandma wore her out.

But Grayson is looking at her now as if he's never seen her before.

I almost feel as if I'm intruding. But my panties are laying in the middle of the floor near the couch. I have to go out there.

I take a breath and step further into the living room. "Are you okay?" I ask softly.

He looks up. He gives me a smile that makes my stomach flip.

"Very okay," he answers. He looks back down at the little girl, who is now *officially* his daughter.

"I can't believe there was a time when I didn't want her."

My heart squeezes. "That's a natural reaction. It was a surprise, Grayson. It's not like she was planned."

"I know. And I haven't had her for very long. But now I can't imagine not having her. And it hit me when my mom brought her back and I saw her for the first time, knowing for sure she's mine. I don't know what I would've done if she wasn't."

I stop and pick up my panties, pulling them on before facing him. He gives me a little smirk and says, "I wish I could tell you to should just leave those off."

I just shake my head, then move to sit next to him on the couch. "Well, now you don't have to worry about if she's not yours. It's official. And congratulations." I reach over and squeeze his hand. "You're a good dad, Grayson."

Something flickers in his gaze, but he simply says, "If you get points for trying, then I guess I'm doing all right."

I smile. "You always get points for trying."

His gaze drops to my mouth. "This afternoon was amazing," he tells me.

He's already told me this. Repeatedly.

"I agree," I tell him. Also again. "And I hope it's the first of many afternoons like that."

"It is," he says simply.

And Grayson Ross does often get his way, so I have no reason not to believe him.

Evelyn squirms a little and her face wrinkles. My stomach growls at the same time.

Her eyes pop open, and she looks up at Grayson. Her brow furrows, as if whatever woke her up is still irritating her, but then she registers who is holding her and her little mouth curls into a grin.

God, these two are adorable.

"Hey, sweet girl," Grayson greets her. "You had a big day at the zoo."

"Did she come home asleep?" I ask.

"Fell asleep in the car, I guess. Didn't stir when they brought her in."

At the sound of my voice, Evelyn looks over at me. Then she gives me a big smile and my heart swells. "Hey, Evie."

She reaches a chubby hand out toward me, and I give her my finger. She wraps her hand around it and squeezes, clearly not intending to let me go.

"Thank you for being so good to her," he says.

"She's hard not to love." It's true. This little girl has stolen my whole heart.

My stomach growls again and Grayson chuckles.

"Why don't I make both of you something to eat? I have some leftover Primavera pasta. How does that sound?"

I smile at Evie. "I don't know about you, but that sounds amazing to me." I meet his gaze. "And since you definitely helped me work up this appetite, it's only fair you feed me."

I love the sexy grin that spreads across his face. He shifts Evelyn toward me and I hold out my arms. She comes to me easily and I'm surprised to feel the sting of tears at the back of my eyes.

I feel like I had longer than a week with her, and the fact that she's so comfortable with me, even after having the other nannies in her life now, touches me.

"I'll be right back," Grayson says, stretching up from the couch. "The pasta just needs heating up. Wine?"

I nod. "Sure."

Then the smell hits me. "Grayson," I groan.

He just grins from the doorway to the kitchen. "What?"

"I could heat up the pasta while *you* change the diaper."

He laughs and disappears into the kitchen. "You don't know which container it is."

I looked down at Evie. "Your dad is trouble, you know that?"

We meet back at the coffee table, me with a cleaned up Evelyn and Grayson with a bowl of baby food and two plates of pasta.

He puts her into her jumper and pulls her up to the coffee table and we all sit around eating and talking.

Seeing Grayson sitting on the floor to eat should be a surprise, but after this afternoon with him, I realized there's nothing that could surprise me about Grayson Ross now. There are layers to this man and he's not as uptight and set in his ways as I thought.

Either that or I'm getting to him. Or Evelyn is making him more laid-back. Or maybe it's Honeysuckle Harbor.

Perhaps a combination of all of those things.

Whatever it is, I like it.

Except that a more easy-going, smiling Grayson Ross is even more devastating to my libido than the growly, bossy Grayson Ross I first got to know and developed a crush on.

After we eat, we play with Evelyn until bath time, then give her the bath together. We fall into the routine easily without even asking one another what we're doing. We put her down for bed, then settle back on the couch together. We're sitting with my bare legs draped over his lap, a throw blanket over them, so I don't get cold, though with his hand sliding up and down from ankle to midthigh, overheating is a much more likely scenario.

I think about giving him a rundown of all the ways we could have fun that don't involve him putting his cock into my pussy and I am right on the verge of being that blunt about it when the front door to his apartment swings open.

Startled, I look over and sit up straighter when Kyle walks in.

The night nanny draws up short, clearly just as surprised to see us on the couch together.

"Oh, hi," she greets, closing the door behind her.

"Hi," I say, suddenly *very* aware that I'm pantless.

I look at Grayson. He doesn't seem surprised to see her.

Right. It's night time. Kyle is the night nanny. She doesn't have Saturday nights off.

And it is Saturday night.

How did I not think of this?

I immediately get up, wrapping the throw blanket around me.

"I…" I realize I don't actually need to explain anything to her, which is good because this is exactly what it looks like.

Grayson and I slept together.

Except…it was so much more than that.

And I don't want to explain any of that.

Even if I could.

I bend, pick up my dress, and head into Grayson's bedroom.

I've just pulled my dress over my head when the door opens and Grayson comes in.

"What are you doing?" he asks.

"Getting dressed and going home."

"You're leaving?"

"Yes. It's almost eleven, Grayson." Time really does fly when you're having fun.

And we were really having fun.

Even when we were dressed.

Dammit.

"Do you have a curfew?" he asks.

I roll my eyes. "We're not having a sleepover. Not with your nanny here. And probably not anyway."

"Why not?"

I'm feeling kind of stupid, actually. I got caught up in spending the evening with him and Evelyn. Was sex on my mind? Sure. After all the time I've been lusting after him, the chemistry that's been building between us, and the afternoon we spent, it would be ridiculous if I wasn't thinking about sex.

But I'd also been caught up in just being with him. Dinner, playing with Evelyn, putting her to bed, cuddling, and talking on the couch.

And all of that is dangerous. And stupid.

"Because this is casual," I answer, for his sake and mine. "And it's temporary. So I'm gonna go. And I will see you next weekend."

I pull the bedroom door open, but it's stopped abruptly by his hand. He shuts it again.

He is very much in my personal space as he stares down at me. "What do you mean next weekend?"

"Unless you're busy and have plans. But that's what James and Cas and I have arranged. We'll spend each weekend together while I'm here in town. But that's it. We all have a normal life during the week. Cas is going to work and sometimes getting home late. They both have to get to bed at a decent hour to get up to go to work. This is casual. Weekends only."

Grayson studies my face for so long that I am dying to know what all is going through his head. Obviously, several things. Options maybe. Possible suggestions he's considering.

But finally, he gives me a single nod. "Okay."

"So you're in? For more of this? The four of us?" *Please say yes.*

It's *really* dangerous how much I want him to say yes.

"Definitely."

Thank you.

"And weekends will work? You can make arrangements for Evelyn?"

"Yes."

"Great."

"But I'll be making overnight arrangements. You'll be spending the night. With me anyway."

I blow out a breath.

He's complicating this.

But I want that.

And...fuck. I nod. "Okay."

"But weekends only," I reiterate.

We need rules. We need guidelines. And we all need to remember what this is.

But as he walks me to the front door and says goodbye to me and we both hesitate as if we're considering kissing each other goodbye and then decide not to, it is clear that we are already fucking up.

At least I am.

Casual. Casual. Casual. I keep repeating the word to myself all the way back to the beach house.

And I still don't think it's completely sunk in when I get there.

CHAPTER 24

James

"THIS IS NOT A GOOD IDEA." I eye my husband warily. "You don't know anything about shucking oysters, babe."

Cas shrugs, confident he can do anything, which truth be told, he usually can. "What could go wrong?"

"You could stab yourself with the knife, for one thing. Have you had a tetanus shot?"

"James has a point," my mother says, sitting next to me and Caroline, holding Noah. "You should be careful, Cas." She stands up and makes sure Noah's beach hat is covering his head. "I'm going to go change Noah's diaper."

"Thanks, Mom."

Caroline has Evie on her lap so that both babies are safely under the giant beach umbrella. It's not a super hot day, but the Carolina sun, even in late September, is still no joke.

"I'll go with you, Miss Becky. I think Evelyn needs a change, too."

"We can just run on into the girls' house. The babies could use some air conditioning for a minute. We'll be right back, you two." She gives me and Cas a finger waggle.

"You're going to miss my rise to greatness," Cas tells Caroline, his voice just ever-so-slightly suggestive, given the presence of my mother.

"Oh, I'm sure I'll catch your rise to greatness later," Caro quips back.

The teasing innuendos between them have me fighting the urge to moan. I shift in my beach chair. Their vibe together never fails to turn me on.

Caroline and my mother disappear across the sand toward the street.

We're all having a beach day arranged by Frannie and Fiona, probably the last of the season, culminating in a bonfire tonight that we probably won't be able to attend because of the babies, but I'm glad we've carved out time to spend with our friends and family.

It's a boisterous crowd of about fifty people, with heaping platters of food, coolers bursting with lemonade, sweet tea, soda, and beer. There is upbeat music playing from someone's speaker, and apparently, there is a spontaneous oyster shucking contest about to commence.

Cas bends down and gives me a kiss. "I appreciate your concern, but I'd prefer you have faith in me."

"It's not about faith," I protest. "It's that you're going up against guys who have been shucking their whole lives. You'll get competitive, I know you will, and you'll go faster than you should."

He cups my cheeks. "I want you to think I'm hot."

That makes me lean forward and nip at his bottom lip. "I already think you're incredibly hot. You don't need to prove that to me." I sink back into my chair. "And this isn't about me. You just want to beat Grayson."

He nods. "That is true. Can you blame me?"

"No. Grayson does need to be put in place. He got a little greedy with Caro's pussy last night."

Cas grins. "I think we all get a little greedy with Caroline's hot little pussy."

"There's no lie there." Just the thought of her naked, writhing as I sink inside her has my shorts tenting. Cas brushes his hand over my thigh, making the problem worse.

The four of us have been together twice now, and it's been incredible. I don't want to compare it to being alone with my husband, because they're amazing for completely different reasons. But it has surprised me how much I enjoy having Grayson join us and it's not just because I love to watch Caroline shattering at the hands of three men all working on pleasuring her together. Though I really do fucking love to see that.

It's also because I like Grayson more than I expected to. He can be funny and charming and his love for Evelyn is palpable. I respect him. Being with the three of us is helping him relax, and I'm enjoying seeing that transformation. His shoulders aren't so tense now and his apartment isn't in a nationally declared state of emergency. He also is showering regularly, which is a good sign, even though like last night he showered with Caroline.

I'm a little jealous of their relationship. I haven't admitted that to Cas. Definitely not to Caroline. We all agreed this was supposed to be temporary. Just a little very-fucking-hot fun between four adults.

Only it doesn't feel that way to me.

I'm catching feelings for Caro. Or maybe feelings I've always had are just reigniting. I don't know. I just know that spending time with her, in and out of bed, makes me really damn happy.

But I need to talk to my husband about it. I don't hide anything from him. Though he knows me well enough that he probably already suspects it.

And will help me through my disappointment when she jets off to her next teaching assignment.

Or when she and Grayson decide they want to be an exclusive couple and our foursome is finished.

I have nothing to base that on.

But it's in the back of my mind.

If that does happen, I have the world's most supportive

husband and an adorable baby, who we're raising in my hometown surrounded by friends and family, so it's all good.

Better than good. It's fucking amazing.

I lace my fingers through Cas's. "Better hold your hand while you still have five fingers," I tell him.

He laughs. "I'm going to dazzle you with my skills—watch."

There are long tables set up under half a dozen tents with all the food on display, but they've cleared one off for this friendly competition.

"Points off if there's salt left in the oyster!" Sam Reed yells out.

The elderly man is wearing a button that declares "JUDGE" on it.

"Where the hell did he get that button?" I ask, amused.

"Oh, he got it online about five years ago," Camille, who I went to high school with, says, standing by the table eating from a paper cup filled with fruit. "I think he carries it around in his beach bag, just in case he needs it."

"That is very Honeysuckle Harbor." I scan the crowd standing around. "Who is competing?"

"Ford, Harrison, Grayson, your Cas." She gestures to my husband, who gives her a little bow with a smile. "Fiona, John Beauregard, Bud Hawkins, Mary Eunice."

"You can still change your mind," I tell Cas, even knowing he will sever an artery before he gives up.

"Fuck that."

"Yeah. Fuck that!" Camille says with a grin.

A hand comes out of nowhere and slaps her arm, causing her to drop a grape. "Watch your mouth, Camille."

It's her grandmother, who is in her seventies and still as feisty as I remember from childhood.

"He said it first!" She points straight to Cas with a smirk.

"Then you watch your mouth too." Cas is treated to an affectionate arm smack and a smile.

"Cas, this is Mary Eunice. Ma'am, this is my husband, Cas."

Cas's eyebrows shoot up. "You're in the competition?"

"You bet your boots I am. I'm not as strong as I used to be, but I have fun giving them a little scare."

"It's a pleasure to meet you."

"You'd better get in the lineup," I tell Cas. "They're already prepping."

Sam is yelling out more rules. "No blood in the oyster or you're disqualified!"

"Jesus," Cas murmurs.

"Told you."

But he squares his shoulders and takes a spot next to Grayson, who claps him on the shoulder.

"Try to keep up with me, Cas."

There's good natured smack talk and nudging going on as the oysters are brought out. I look up at the house, seeking Caroline. I know she'll want to see this.

"So, uh, what's going on with you?" Camille asks, flicking her tongue over a piece of melon. "You and Caro seem *very* close."

"It's great to see her again," I agree, striving for casual.

This was what Cas and I were trying to avoid—the Honeysuckle Harbor rumor mill. But it seems it is turning already.

"No one cares, you know. Ford and Harrison paved the way for you when they brought Ivy and Liam here from L.A. This crowd is a 'you-do-you-boo' crowd, you know that."

"I don't know what you're talking about."

"Okay. Don't share the juicy bits with me then."

"Where are Ivy and Liam? I was hoping to see them." I do want to say hi but I no longer remember to who when I see Caro pop out of the twins' house, Evelyn on her hip, a big smile on her face.

She's wearing a sundress today and her skin is glowing, and her eyes are bright. She has the look of a woman who has been fucked regularly by three men. I could drink in the sight of her all damn day.

She also looks good with a baby.

Grayson's baby.

That thought makes my chest tighten.

I wave to her. "Come on, before you miss all the shucking fun."

Caroline laughs. "Shucking fun? I definitely don't want to miss that!" she calls back.

My mother doesn't come out of the house but it doesn't worry me. She's very fond of air conditioning and it probably isn't a bad thing for Noah to be inside for a bit. I appreciate how much help my parents have been to me and Cas since we moved here.

Though I'm a little surprised my father isn't in the oyster contest. Glancing around, I see he's helping build the bonfire for later. If there's a fence to paint, a grill to clean, or a pile of wood to stack, he's always on it.

Caro comes up between me and Camille and leans briefly against my shoulder. "Who should I root for? I'm thinking I should cheer on Fiona."

"Girl power!" Camille says. "I'm familially obligated to root for my grandmother."

"I have to root for Cas."

"Oh, no, poor Grayson." Caroline bounces Evelyn on her hip. "You need to cheer for Daddy!" She raises Evelyn's arms up and down. "Go Daddy! You can do it!"

Grayson hears her and shifts his attention to them. His gaze is steely, intense. Electric. "Well, I have to win now," he says. "I have two beautiful ladies cheering me on."

It's probably too much for being in public, but I flick Caroline's hair off of her shoulder. "You weren't a lady last night," I murmur in her ear.

She gives a soft laugh. "I seem to remember saying 'please' and 'thank you.'"

My dick hardens uncomfortably. "You're such a good girl."

Grayson is watching us, his expression unreadable.

Cas looks like he wants to devour us both.

But then Sam Reed counts down, and the competition is on.

My husband has no idea what he's doing but he just dives in, grabbing an oyster and shoving the knife between the shells. When nothing happens, he glances at Grayson to emulate his movements.

"You've got this, Cas!" I call out in encouragement.

He's jabbing the knife repeatedly, making me wince. "Oh God, I can't look," I tell Caroline.

She squeezes my arm. "I'll tell you if I see blood. Look at the other end of the table. Fiona is killing it."

I take her advice and scan the row of contestants. Fiona is very efficiently working on her third oyster. Bud seems to be pulling ahead, but otherwise everyone seems evenly matched. Ford looks like he was born shucking oysters, which he probably was, and Grayson is holding his own. When I dare to look, I see my overly confident husband is struggling but refusing to wave the white flag. He is now beating his first oyster on the table.

"He's trying," Caroline says with a snort. "And at least he looks good doing it."

Cas has definitely turned some heads in town with his tall, muscular build and his tattoos.

"Go, Cas!" Caroline cheers.

He raises his knife in acknowledgement.

I get that feeling again—that maybe what Cas and I have been looking for when we bring women into our marriage is... Caroline.

Is it a crazy thought?

Probably.

That doesn't stop me from having it, though.

Which is why I wrap my arm around Caro and give her a side hug. She just laughs, still watching the contest. Camille gives me a knowing look.

"What?" I ask her.

"Nothing. Just seeing what everyone is seeing." She waves her hand. "Everyone here has excellent eyesight."

I have no response to that, so I just watch Sam call time.

"Time! Two minutes are up! Gotta check things over."

It's clear Bud has stomped the competition, followed by Ford, then Fiona. Grayson pulls a respectable fourth. Cas is last, with zero opened oysters.

"Bud's got it with nine!"

Everyone claps and the contestants all lift an oyster and drop it back and swallow.

My poor husband is left standing there, oyster-less. But he's smiling and laughing good-naturedly.

Grayson hands him an oyster. "Here. You can have one of mine." Then he picks up another from his ice pile.

They tap their oysters together. "Cheers," Cas says.

When they lift their respective shells to their lips at the same time, they lock eyes.

Is that…was there…sexual tension?

I look over at Caro. She's watching them too—her eyes narrowed a little.

Though I'm not sure why I'm surprised. They have been sharing Caroline. We've all been really fucking up close and personal with each other. That creates intimacy, intended or not.

Cas is coming over to me.

"Next year, babe," I tell him. "Good effort."

"It was an absolutely fucking terrible effort. But I have a new goal. I'm going to practice at home."

Caroline takes Evelyn over to Grayson, who dries his hands off with a towel before taking Evie with a big smile.

"You seem like you're in a good mood," I say. "Enjoying a day off finally? You work so hard for me and Noah. I hope you know how much I appreciate that."

"I'm happy to. I have the hottest stay-at-home dad in town as my husband." Cas kisses me. "And what's not to love about spending a day with family and friends? Plus, I have an adorable baby, and I'm having enormous amounts of casual sex. I'm literally living the dream."

"Casual?" I ask.

"Well, not with you, obviously. But with Caroline, yes, of course."

"Cas! Come here—we're taking a picture of the contestants!" Fiona yells.

"Someone has to stand in last place," Grayson says.

Cas groans, but he dutifully goes over.

Camille is watching me, her lips pursed.

"What?" I ask, again. "Why is your face so loud today?"

She laughs, but then she mimics zipping her lips shut. "I'm not saying a word."

"You just said five."

"James, you always were so cute."

CHAPTER 25

Cas

"I'M GOING to need extra attention tonight," I tell James. "After that public humiliation I just endured."

He laughs, but he gives me a sympathetic shoulder squeeze. "Your overconfidence is your greatest weakness. But I will give you all the attention you need and deserve."

"What I need and what I deserve are both the same thing," I tell him with a smirk. We're seated in our beach chairs, enjoying the light breeze off of the ocean, the many people at this gathering all talking and laughing and milling around behind us.

I quickly learned when we moved here that when Southerners say "it's just a few people" and "It's just thrown together" they are not telling the truth. Or maybe my idea of a few people and theirs is just very different. But I love my adopted hometown and the people here. It's made my transition from the city to a slow-paced beach town easier. James has always worried that I wouldn't feel a part of his world, but Honeysuckle Harbor has embraced me as one of their own.

Even after my lack of shucking skills.

James laughs and lifts an oyster to his lips. He's brought a tin of oysters on ice down for us to eat.

The gesture reminds me of Grayson locking eyes with me

earlier. It wasn't sexual tension between us, exactly—it was more of a moment where we both realized even if the two of us aren't personally involved, we are engaged in a sexual relationship with the same person. At the same time.

It's, well, intimate. A shared experience.

Because in spite of what any of us think, you can't live next door to each other, share the same friends, raise your babies side by side, and it *not* get personal.

Even if I insisted to James it's casual.

I can see that it's not for him.

I'm not even sure it is for me anymore either and that's concerning. That isn't what any of us agreed to. It's not what we signed up for. It's not practical or smart and yet the three of us guys have fucked Caroline together twice and now we're spending the day at a picnic. This is starting to feel like a relationship beyond the bedroom, and I need to know where my husband stands.

The truth is, I already know where he stands.

He's falling in love with Caroline all over again. Not just nostalgia for the teen relationship they had and a healthy dose of lust, but real feelings for her as an adult.

Which I understand. She's fun, she's carefree, she's intelligent, and she's compassionate.

But James and I need to have a conversation and figure out together what we do about this.

"Where's Caroline?" I ask James, knowing full well he'll know exactly where she is.

"She's with Grayson and Evelyn and his parents." James puts down his oyster shell and wipes his fingers on a napkin. His eyes scan the beach, seeking them out.

They're sitting on a blanket on the sand, Caroline with her legs crossed, Grayson casually flopped on his side, Evelyn between them. His family is surrounding them.

"Caro loves Evie," James adds.

"Maybe we should let Caroline and Grayson have a night to

themselves tonight." It's my way of testing the waters.

Frankly, I think Grayson and Caroline would enjoy it as well. There is something brewing between them that also isn't strictly casual sex. This is all getting more complicated than I intended.

James sits up straighter at my suggestion. "You think they want to be alone?"

"I think it's possible. And I would like to be alone with you." Not because I'm feeling insecure. Far from it. I know what James and I have. But because it's starting to feel like we have to return to neutral and all give each other time to process what this is and where it's going.

Or if it's going anywhere.

"Listen, I need to talk to you," James says.

"About?"

"About Caroline. You know I always want to be honest with you." James reaches over and laces my fingers through his. "I'm falling in love with Caroline."

"I know," I tell him simply. "I have to admit, I should have seen this coming. You're a very bighearted man and she's special to you. I understand that."

"I know she's leaving, so it doesn't mean anything for the future, but I wanted you to know what I'm feeling."

"I appreciate you being honest." I squeeze his hand, my chest tight as I take in the troubled expression on his face. God, I love this man with my whole heart and fucking soul. "And of course it means something. And if it means something to you, it means something to me. We're a team. So tell me...what do you need from me? Do you want to see more of Caroline? Or less? I don't want you to be heartbroken when she leaves."

"I think it's inevitable I'm going to be heartbroken when she leaves. But I don't want to see less of her. I want to soak up as much time with her as possible while she's still here, if that's okay with you."

Throughout our entire relationship, James has always been giving and supportive and generous with me. With his attention and love, and his habit of leaving me little notes at night on the bathroom mirror so I find them when I'm getting ready for work. He cooks for me. He cleans our apartment, and he raises our son and he never, ever resents my long hours at work. He worries about my acclimation to South Carolina, and that I miss my family, and he always encourages me to do video calls and send gifts to my sister's kids, and to plan on trips back to the Netherlands.

He deserves to love and be loved to his fullest capacity.

"It's more than okay with me. I want you to be happy and Caroline makes you happy."

James lifts our entwined fingers and kisses my knuckles. "You make me happy."

"I know." I don't doubt that and I never will. "But love can be multiplied."

I suddenly know what needs to happen. I don't want to comfort my husband through a heartbreak. I want him to have everything he wants and then some, complicated or not. I want to give him the entire world, and if that includes Caroline Bell, then I will move mountains to make it happen.

James sighs. "I love you so damn much."

"I love you too. With everything inside me." I reach over and steal one of his oysters.

After a few seconds, James says, "I wish there wasn't an expiration date looming over our time with Caro."

"I know. Maybe she'll change her mind?" I probably shouldn't get his hopes up. Or hell, my own hopes. I'm really enjoying what we've got going on.

James shrugs. "I don't know. I certainly don't want to talk her into anything. She loves teaching."

"There are schools here."

"Yeah, but..." James glances over at Grayson. "What about Grayson and Caroline? Is there something more going on there?"

"I have no idea. Possibly. Should we ask him?"

It's obvious to me what needs to happen. I'm a logical person and this is a problem with a very simple solution.

James frowns. "What do you mean? I don't know if that's our place…"

"Get Grayson over here." I smile at him. "Just trust me. Don't let Caroline come over. I want the three of us to talk without her."

I relax and take a sip of my red wine, frowning a little at the plastic goblet. No glass on the beach is an excellent rule, but it does absolutely nothing for my expensive cabernet.

James returns with Grayson in tow, who has his phone to his ear and is nodding.

"Okay, I understand. I heard you, Andrea. I said I'll be there."

Grayson sighs as he sinks into a free beach chair after ending his call. "Is there a beer in this cooler?" He flips up the lid.

James sits down on the opposite side of Grayson. "Should be. Help yourself. Business call?"

"Yes." Grayson fishes around in the cooler and pulls out a lager. He tries to twist it off, but nothing happens. He puts the cold bottle to his forehead. "There is a crisis with a deal we're doing in midtown. The developer got raided by the Feds and now I have to be back in New York on Monday to see what the hell is going on and mop things up if necessary."

"It must be hard running a business remotely," I say. "How is that going?"

"It's okay. Not disastrous, but not easy either." Grayson shrugs. "I don't know."

James fishes a bottle opener out of our beach bag and hands it to him. "You've taken on a lot, Grayson. I'm impressed with how you're managing it all, seriously."

"Thanks. You both have been a big help. Having two nannies is a lifesaver as well." He takes the cap off of the bottle. "Caroline has been there for me too, obviously. I couldn't have done this without her after Rose quit."

His voice softens when he mentions Caroline.

It's the perfect segue. "Speaking of Caroline," I say. "I'm just going to come right out and ask—are you falling in love with her?"

Grayson chokes on his beer. "Jesus, Cas."

"He's very direct," James says. "It's because he's Dutch. He doesn't know you need to dance around the subject endlessly with lots of hints and convoluted sayings for advice to be a true Southerner."

"It was definitely an adjustment," I say. "I still don't fully understand "might could" in its intended use."

"It just means that it's a possibility but nothing definite," James says. "What's so hard about that?"

"Then just say it's a possibility," I argue. "Don't say 'might could make it to the barbecue on Saturday.' Say that you can't commit."

James shakes his head. "You don't get it."

"I really don't. But anyway, back to Grayson and Caroline. How do you feel?"

Grayson wipes his mouth. "I guess you could say I've been sowing my oats on Saturday night and praying for crop failure on Sunday." He can barely get the sentence out before he's full on smirking.

James laughs. "I know the feeling."

I glare at both of them. I just want to know if he wants more with Caroline or not, and he's talking in riddles to mess with me. "What the fuck does that mean?"

"It means, yes, I have feelings, but I'm worried about what happens after all the sex. Caroline is leaving in less than a month."

"Are you in love with her?"

"There he goes again," Grayson says to James. "Just bold as can be."

I sip my wine and wait for them. I'm not going to drag them to the obvious conclusion.

James knows me well enough to understand that, and he steps in. "Cas and I have been talking. We know Caroline is planning to leave and if that's what she wants, we will respect that. But I think we've all gone way past casual. We're all catching feelings and developing friendships and hell, blending our families. How do you feel about that?"

Grayson's eyebrows lift. "What, like the four of us, long-term? In a relationship? I mean, hell, yeah, would be my first thought. I don't want Caroline to leave at all. *Ever*. Followed by, that would be the solution to all my problems, frankly. I respect and like both of you. I'm falling for Caroline. I trust you guys with my daughter. I'm very fond of your son. It would make my life easier and more fulfilling to not do this single dad thing alone. Or single."

I nod. This kind of logic I understand. Grayson thinks with both his heart and his head. Oh, and his dick. Which aligns with my approach to life.

"That's what we want too." James looks at me for confirmation.

I nod. "Exactly."

Grayson lets out a breath. "But what does Caroline want?"

"I don't know. But I think we need to spend time with her that isn't just about sex. One on one time with her, each of us. Show her this goes beyond sex for the two of you."

"And you?" Grayson asks.

I'm not sure exactly how to answer that. "I like her," I say simply. "This isn't something I anticipated, but I'm fully on board with this moving in a direction we never anticipated."

I am, because of James. And because of Caroline. And Grayson.

This isn't really about me, which for a man who likes to get what he wants, that might seem confusing, but it's cut and dry to me. I want this for a variety of reasons, and so I'm going to do my best to make sure the people I care about are happy.

"Where is she right now?" I ask.

"She's with my daughter. Because she loves her." Grayson's jaw tenses. "I'm not going to use that to my advantage though, however tempting."

"Of course not. Caro wouldn't be with you for that reason

anyway," James says. "She's independent and knows her own mind."

"So just…show, but not tell, her what we could be? Together and one on one?" Grayson asks. He looks thoughtful.

"Yes. Like I said, if she wants to leave, we wish her well."

"We have to let her come to that conclusion on her own," James says. "I know her. She's a free spirit. It has to be her idea to stay in Honeysuckle Harbor."

Grayson chuckles. "I agree with that. She does know her own mind." He sips his beer. "Hell, that's half the reason I'm falling in love with her."

I don't think he even realizes what he's said aloud.

"Just so we're clear—no sex when any of us are alone with her."

"No sex," Grayson says. "Agreed."

"No sex." James nods.

"I should take her and Evelyn with me to New York on Monday," Grayson says, sitting up straighter. "That would be a great way to spend time together. I'll have meetings, but we can do some sightseeing. I definitely don't want to leave Evelyn home with the nannies. They're too new to her, and I could take one of them to New York, but I'd much rather spend the time with Caroline."

"That's perfect." I raise my plastic wine glass. "All in."

James shakes his head and raises his own beer. "All in."

"I'm not sure exactly what I'm agreeing to," Grayson says. "But what the hell? I'm in."

CHAPTER 26
Caroline

"WOW, LITTLE RICH GIRL," I say to Evelyn as I sway with her in front of the enormous windows in Grayson's living room. "Nice view to grow up looking at."

Grayson's penthouse apartment overlooks Central Park.

I wouldn't say I'm surprised by that exactly, but I didn't give any thought to where he lived before we walked in here this morning.

I knew he was rich, but I haven't really thought about it. I know Grayson as the barely-holding-it-together guy living back in Honeysuckle Harbor and trying to get his life figured out. I know him as the broody, sexy man who can make my panties wet with a single look. I know him as the amazing lover who can blow my mind even without actually fucking me. I know him as Evelyn's in-over-his-head and yet still incredibly sweet, protective, and in love with his baby girl new dad.

But he's rich. Like really rich.

He flew us here first class. We rode from the airport in a car with Grayson's personal driver. We brought the elevator to the top floor of this building, where he strode straight into the bedroom to change before heading to the office.

I was gawking at the expensive leather furniture, the incredible artwork on the walls, the high ceiling, the plush carpet, the chef's kitchen, and this view with the breathtaking view of the autumn colors exploding in Central Park when he walked back out of the bedroom adjusting his tie.

My mouth had instantly gone dry.

Maybe it's because I've only seen him in joggers and T-shirts, jeans and T-shirts, and once in jeans and a button-down.

But damn.

That wasn't Grayson, single dad, next door.

That was Mr. Ross, CEO.

And seeing him in a suit did all kinds of things to me. Hot, tingly, wet things.

I hadn't realized I had a thing for hot boss types.

But I also almost immediately realized that I don't.

I just have a thing for Grayson. And what that suit does for him is make him feel like the old Grayson: In charge. Confident. Comfortable.

His stride had been purposeful. His spine had been straight. His smile had been genuine.

And that was what made him so incredibly hot.

Though custom-tailored Armani didn't hurt.

He'd come over to Evie and I, kissed both of us on the forehead, told us to be good girls, and that he'd see us later, then left in a little cloud of cologne and confidence that had made my knees weak.

Evelyn kicks her legs, looking down at the park now, and I laugh. "Maybe we should go down and take a walk after your nap," I tell her.

I hope she takes her late morning nap. She'd been wide-eyed and interested at the airport and on the plane, interested in all the commotion and people—until anyone, including the nice older woman in the airport and the flight attendants, tried to interact with her or get her to smile. Then she'd scowl at them in her typical grumpy-baby way. She had, however, fallen asleep in

Grayson's arms about fifteen minutes into the flight and stayed asleep until he'd stood to deplane.

Of course, the gorgeous millionaire holding his adorable baby girl had led to us getting extra attention throughout the flight from two of the female flight attendants and one male.

So I'd adopted Evelyn's scowl-first-ask-questions-later habit. Grayson isn't mine, but he doesn't need to be collecting phone numbers from the flight crew. He's got a baby now. When he returns to New York, he's going to need to be a little more careful and choosy about the people he sleeps with and when.

That got me frowning even more.

Is Grayson going to return to New York with Evelyn full time? I know he went home to Honeysuckle Harbor because he was drowning and thought his family would help.

And they have.

But he's also getting so good at this. He's definitely figuring this dad-thing out.

Plus, obviously, he's figured out that he can hire around-the-clock help.

He could come back to New York full time. He could raise Evelyn here.

That thought makes me sad for some reason.

Honeysuckle Harbor isn't perfect, but it was a great place to grow up. And

Evelyn's grandparents and aunt, uncle, and cousins are there.

Plus, Grayson has friends there.

I'm sure he has friends in New York too. But not friends like James, Cas, and Ford and Harrison.

Evelyn makes a little growly sound and pats my face with her hand. I look at her, realizing that I'm scowling. She scowls up at me and pats my face again.

"What, baby girl?" I ask her.

"Uh," she says, patting me.

I smile. "You're so funny."

Then she smiles in return, and I realize that she didn't like me frowning.

"Oh, really? Miss Grumpy Girl? I'm not supposed to be frowny, though?" I laugh and bring her in so I can nuzzle her neck.

That makes her giggle.

God, I love her.

I sigh as I pull back and look at her. "I don't want you to be a big city girl with only nannies," I tell her. "You need to see Grandma and Grandpa. And Noah and James and Cas."

I feel my heart squeeze. Damn. Not only will Grayson's family do a great job helping with Evelyn, but so will James and Cas. They're so amazing, and I want them in Grayson and Evelyn's life.

Evie pats my face again and I realize I'm frowning again.

I make myself smile. She smiles back at me.

"It's none of my business," I tell her.

But I feel like it's my business. And that's probably not a good thing. Because I'm going to say something about it to Grayson and overstep.

Dammit.

"I don't even know what I'm doing here right now," I tell the little girl. "I mean, am I here as your nanny? Your daddy's friend? Or..."

Or what? What else is there?

He needed someone to come along to New York. He didn't want to bring one of the other nannies. None of them have agreed to a full twenty-four-hour—or more—long shift. He didn't ask any of them about doing that if needed.

Maybe he should have, but again, Grayson's just recently gotten organized.

He didn't want to try to hire someone here. That would have been ridiculous.

He should have left her in Honeysuckle Harbor with his

parents, but he wanted to see how she'd do on the plane. Or so he said.

I didn't want him to bring one of the other nannies either, so I'd easily agreed to come along.

But now that we're here, it feels…not weird, just a little confusing, I guess.

My phone rings and I gratefully pull it from my pocket. Distraction. That's exactly what I need.

"Hello?"

"Is this Caroline?"

I don't recognize this woman's voice. "It is."

"Caroline, this is Andrea. I'm Mr. Ross's executive assistant."

"Uh, hi." Is Grayson okay?

"I'm going to be sending the company car over for you and Evelyn," Andrea says

"Mr. Ross would like you to join him at the office for lunch."

I frown. Grayson said nothing about lunch at the office. "Oh, I don't think that's right," I start. "He didn't—"

"He just decided," Andrea interjects.

"Oh."

"I can't believe Evelyn is in town with him and he didn't think he should bring her over here," Andrea said. "I swear that man doesn't think. I was here when she was initially dropped off, you know."

I look down at Evelyn. "I didn't, actually. I—"

"Yes. So obviously I need to see her. I'm so glad things are going well, but I want to get my eyes on her."

"Well, I can assure you—"

"The car will be there in fifteen minutes."

I stop. Clearly, I'm not going to get out of this. Andrea works for Grayson. She'd have to be pretty headstrong to do that job, I suppose.

"And it would be very good for Felicity to see Grayson with his daughter and girlfriend," Andrea goes on.

Girlfriend? Hang on. But Andrea obviously got my number

from Grayson, and I don't know what he told her about me. Maybe he used the word girlfriend to make things...easier? Maybe that's a simpler explanation for some reason than calling me the nanny. Maybe if he's moving back to New York, it's easier to explain a break-up than firing a nanny when he arrives here without me in a couple of months.

I don't know if that makes sense, but explaining that I'm the woman who was Evie's nanny for a week but I'm now just the woman he's casually fucking with two other men, temporarily, isn't really a quick, easy explanation either.

"Who's Felicity?" I finally ask.

"He hasn't told you?"

I want to ask why Andrea thinks Grayson would have told me but...

Well, fuck it. "Why would he have told me?"

"I just assumed he'd fill you in on her since he's coming back to the office. Not that you have any reason to worry."

Worry?

"Maybe there's a reason he doesn't want me to know," I suggest. Maybe Andrea shouldn't tell me whatever this is.

Andrea scoffs. "There's no reason his girlfriend shouldn't know. It would be only because he has no feelings or intentions toward her, but you and I both know that a determined woman could still make things awkward and difficult for you. I want you to know about her so that you don't listen to anything she says about her and Grayson."

Ah. It all clicks into place instantly.

Felicity wants Grayson.

It sounds like Grayson doesn't feel the same way, but Andrea's right. Felicity could still try to cause trouble between me and Grayson.

If there was a me and Grayson.

Still, without even seeing Felicity, I feel a niggle of jealousy and...possessiveness.

I'm not Grayson's girlfriend. No, really. Not long-term.

But he's mine for now. Kind of. At least for while we're doing this thing we're doing with James and Cas.

We're just having fun, but we're really having fun. It's not just sex. It's friendship. It's mutual support for all the guys as new dads. It's a reunion between the three of us who share Honeysuckle Harbor as home. It's establishing a new, hopefully lasting friendship between the guys.

And I can definitely see them all being people I want to see when I'm home between jobs.

Hell, I can see them being people I stay in touch with while I travel.

I can imagine texting with them, sending selfies while I'm sight-seeing, asking about how their days were.

I better be getting photos and updates on Evelyn and Noah.

So yeah, while we're doing this friends-with-hot-as-fuck bene-fits thing, Grayson is mine and Felicity can just back off.

"Okay, so Evelyn and I need to make an appearance so Felicity will leave Grayson alone?" I clarify with Andrea.

"Please," Andrea says. "Grayson never dates people who work for him. Ever. But Felicity thinks he's going to make an exception for her. It's starting to become very annoying and make other people in the office uncomfortable."

"And you're sure he's not interested?" I ask.

Andrea laughs. "Very. Even if she didn't work for him."

Okay. Andrea probably knows him well. She sees him every day and I'm guessing they put in long hours.

"He's very picky," Andrea adds.

Stupidly, I feel my ego inflate a bit. He really likes me. Yes, he likes sex with me, but he also trusts me with his daughter, in his personal space, seeing him at his worst, and I can make him laugh.

He could have had me as a helper with Evelyn without ever opening up or letting me closer, but he did open up.

And he really likes me naked.

"Then shouldn't Grayson just put his foot down?" I ask. But

I'm already headed for the bedroom and my suitcase to find something else to wear.

"Yes. He's told her he doesn't date people in the office. But he doesn't want to be firmer because she's very good at her job and he doesn't want her to leave and he doesn't want things to be awkward between them. He's sure he can handle it." Andrea lowers her voice. "He's actually a little oblivious to a lot of it."

I grin. I can see that. I'm sure Grayson is totally in charge and on top of everything with the business, but interpersonally? Yeah, I can see him missing some things.

"Despite how it might seem, he's actually a nice guy," Andrea says. "And while he'll take the head off of a fellow CEO or competitor, he treats his employees very well, with a lot of respect."

I smile. Of course, he's a nice guy. Or he *can be* a nice guy. "I guess it's better he misses a few flirtations versus being a prick."

"Yes. Except this woman needs to cool it. So this is perfect. You and Evelyn here should make the point perfectly."

I think about that.

No matter how Grayson and my relationship would be defined, or all the details around it, we are friends. I can help him out.

I don't want some woman harassing him. And I don't want some pushy woman thinking she can cozy up to Evelyn to get close to Grayson.

"We'll be there soon," I tell Andrea.

"Great. I can't wait to meet the woman Grayson can't stop talking about."

My eyebrows lift. "He's been talking about me?"

Andrea laughs. "He's said your name even more than Evelyn's and he has talked about her even more than the stock reports, the operations report from the Seattle office, or the new marketing director in Chicago. And those were his favorite topics just a few weeks ago."

I smile. "Oh."

"See you soon," Andrea says.

We disconnect and I prop Evelyn up on the bed. "Okay baby girl, we need to find something to wear. Something that says 'I'm not worried because I know exactly how my man feels about me' even though I don't really know."

The thing is, I might be getting an inkling of how Grayson might feel about me.

And if it's what it sounds like, that is going to make things really complicated.

CHAPTER 27
Grayson

"MR. ROSS, there's someone here to see you."

I swivel my chair toward the conference room door where my executive assistant Andrea is poking her head in. I smile. Andrea knows better than to interrupt me during this meeting unless it's really important.

Since I've been gone for several weeks, this meeting is really big.

But this interruption *is* important. Caroline and Evelyn are here. And I can't deny the way my heart trips, knowing they're in the office.

Andrea suggested they come in for lunch and I readily agreed.

So readily that she gave me a knowing smirk.

The funny thing is, typically I would have called her on that smirk. I would have denied that I was eager to see them.

But I am eager to see them.

I'm eager to show them off.

Why would I deny that?

And yes, I'm even willing to admit that it's *them*—not just my adorable baby girl who is officially mine and who Andrea cannot wait to see again, but the gorgeous woman who has traveled to New York with me.

Caroline hasn't asked if she is my employee on this trip. I would happily pay her for her time with Evelyn, but I am aware that makes things a little weird between us, considering I referred to her as my girlfriend to Andrea without even thinking.

I can't have sex with her while we're in New York because I promised Cas and James, but she is definitely here as more than a nanny.

"Okay, everyone, that wraps it up." I close the folder in front of me and push back from the table.

"Wait, we haven't finished the agenda," Felicity protests from next to me on my right-hand side.

"The rest can be an email," I say. I almost laugh. I like in-person meetings better than emails and everyone in here knows that. At least when I'm leading the meeting. I actually hate sitting through meetings when other people are in charge. I have never uttered the words that I just did before in my life.

Everyone around the table takes note of that. But no one else is smiling. They're looking at me as if concerned for my mental health.

"I have a lunch date," I tell them. "I don't want to keep my girlfriend and daughter waiting."

I see Felicity hesitate in gathering her papers.

I'm not stupid. I am very aware of the fact that Felicity would like something romantic to happen between the two of us.

I am also aware of the fact that, on paper, Felicity probably seems like a great match for me.

However, not only do I never date or fuck employees—and I do not want to lose her as an employee—I am not attracted to Felicity.

She is objectively an attractive woman, but she doesn't do it for me.

I haven't thought about it in any more depth than that. And now that I've met Caroline, I simply know that Felicity isn't Caroline. There was no instant chemistry, connection, or desire to know her better.

I don't need to understand it any further than that.

I stand and start for the door.

"Can I walk with you to your office?" Felicity asks. "I have a couple of questions about the project in Nashville."

"Of course."

Felicity is very good at her job. I will always be available to my vice presidents when they need to discuss business matters with me.

I open the conference room door and stand to the side, waiting for her to step out into the hallway in front of me.

She passes very close to me, the sleeve of her white silk button-down blouse brushing against my stomach.

I fall into step next to her.

"The office has been very different without you here," Felicity says. "We've missed you."

"That's nice to hear. I'd like to think that I add something when I'm here. But everything has been running very well without me physically in the office. That pleases me."

It's true. It's nice to be back. This is my comfort zone and I've fallen back into my habits here easily. But...

I'm not sure it's completely my comfort zone anymore.

I'm noticing stupid things like my dress shoes pinch a little and the air feels a little stale inside the building and I'm missing the smell of baby shampoo.

"Nashville has run into a couple of snags. They're a little behind on their timeline. I think you and I should go for a site visit. I think it would help them if you were in the office. Show them that you're invested in what they're doing."

"Isn't my name on the company and CEO as my title a pretty good indication that I'm *invested* in this project?" I ask dryly.

She smiles. "I mean *emotionally* invested. That you're involved in the details. That it's not just a line item for you. It will motivate them."

I wouldn't say it's just a line item, but I also wouldn't say I'm *emotionally* invested. The Nashville project is business. It's how I make money. It's part of my company. It's not my life. "And what would you be there for, then?" I ask.

This whole being a cheerleader and motivating people is literally Felicity's job.

I know exactly what she's thinking she'd be there for—to warm the other side of my hotel bed.

That's not going to happen.

"I'm a great motivator," she says, beaming up at me. "You know that. I can talk anyone into anything."

Almost anyone.

"Then you don't need me along," I say, stopping outside my office door. It's shut but not latched and I can hear Caroline talking to Evelyn through the crack.

"Your daddy's desk is so big, isn't it? He does such important work there." She pauses. "Or maybe he's trying to compensate for something." She chuckles softly. "Though I guess I know he's not compensating for *that*."

I want to laugh. And I should scold her for talking about things like that with my daughter.

But I should be focusing on what my junior vice president is telling me.

"They'll appreciate it," Felicity says, ending her mini-monologue about why I should go to Nashville.

"I don't think so," I tell her simply. I don't need to give her reasons. I'm the boss.

"Grayson," she says, reaching out and putting her hand on my forearm.

She, wisely, only calls me Grayson when it's just the two of us speaking privately, but I'd really rather she continue to call me Mr. Ross.

"I just think if you'd spend a few days there with me, it would not only be good for the local office, but it will give me a chance to really show you what I can do. We've never done a site visit together and I'm really eager to show you all of my ideas about how we can move forward."

Uh, huh?

"Felicity, I—"

The door beside us suddenly swings open, and Caroline and Evelyn are there, smiling brightly.

Well, Caroline is smiling. Evelyn is scowling. At Felicity.

"Hi!" Caroline greets. "I heard your voice." She looks from me to Felicity. "Hi, I'm Caroline. I'm Grayson's girlfriend." She extends the hand not holding Evelyn.

She looks amazing.

And as opposite of Felicity as she possibly could.

Felicity is a blonde who wears pencil skirts, blouses, and high heels—like the navy blue and white she has on today—gets French manicures, and her hair is always sleek and perfect.

The gorgeous redhead holding my daughter is in jeans, a bright yellow V-neck T-shirt, and canvas sneakers. Her hair is loose and looks like she's recently pulled her fingers through it. She's got little or maybe no makeup on. And she's stunning. She's clearly not trying to impress anyone. She's confident in who she is and, I hope, how I feel about her regardless of how she dresses or does her hair.

Caroline goes on. "I just wanted to pop my head out and let you know that Nashville isn't going to work for us."

Felicity looks a little surprised. I'm surprised, but amused. I decide to let Caroline take the lead here.

"Traveling a lot with Evelyn isn't really a good plan. We want her to get used to flying, of course. But it's better for us to go back-and-forth between New York and Honeysuckle Harbor, where Grayson has apartments and she can feel more settled."

Felicity nods. "Of course. Don't feel that you have to come along. Grayson and I can handle the trip without you."

Caroline gives her a cool smile. "I don't feel that I *have* to come along. But I know Grayson would want me to be there. Evelyn too. He prefers spending time with us over anything else. If we're not there, I know he won't want to be gone. And he certainly won't be at his best." She looks up at me and smiles, moving closer and leaning into my arm. I move that arm so it's wrapped around her, my hand resting on her hip. "He'll be distracted and crabby without us." She smiles at Felicity again. "But it's so wonderful that Grayson is so good at hiring excellent people. So that you can handle this trip on your own."

Felicity's eyes narrow slightly, but her smile stays in place. "Well, Grayson and I can discuss it further later."

I decide this is the perfect opportunity to make things very clear to Felicity, thanks to Caroline.

"There's nothing further to discuss, Felicity," I say. "It's exactly as Caroline said. I will only be making trips that one or both of my girls can accompany me on. I am certain you can handle Nashville without me."

Before Felicity can respond, Caroline raises her voice slightly. "Andrea, we're ready for you to take Evelyn for a few minutes."

Andrea suddenly appears with us and reaches for my baby girl. "Wonderful. Come here, sweet thing," she says to Evelyn.

To my surprise, Evelyn goes to her easily with a smile.

"We'll just be a little bit," Caroline tells Andrea. "We'll come find you when…we're done."

That pause makes my eyebrows arch.

"Of course," Andrea says. "Take your time." She gives us a smile, then turns and heads toward her desk with Evelyn.

Caroline looks up at me, loops her arms through mine, and turns, tugging me through my office door. "Nice to meet you, Felicity," she says.

It occurs to me that I did not introduce the two of them.

Caroline shuts the door on Felicity before my junior VP can say a word.

Then Caroline locks my door with an audible click.

She pulls me away from the door toward my desk.

"What was that?" I ask with a grin.

"Just establishing some boundaries," Caroline says.

"You mean staking your claim?"

She smiles and lifts a shoulder. "Andrea filled me in on the fact that Felicity has a hard time getting the message that you're not interested. I thought I might as well help you out while I was here. Do you think I made that clear enough that you're not available?"

"I do." I fucking love that she did that. Not because I needed the help but because she was willing to be that help.

"I hope that all her fantasies about you and your desk are completely ruined by thoughts of what I'm doing to you on it right now."

"You're not doing anything to be on it right now," I point out, my hands settling on her hips and walking her backward toward the desk. "But we could easily rectify that."

She gives me a playful smile. "Well, I suppose that depends if I'm here this weekend as your nanny or your friend with benefits."

She's definitely not here as my nanny and she's so much more than my friend with benefits, but we're not ready for that conversation and the guys and I agreed not to spook her.

Still, I say, "Definitely not the nanny." I lift my hands and cup her face. "You're really hot when you're jealous."

She scoffs. "I'm not jealous. I know you don't have feelings for Felicity. She's totally not your type."

I laugh. "Actually, she's very much my type. Until I met you."

"Then why haven't you fucked her?"

"She works for me. I don't fuck my employees. As you know. Personally."

Caroline studies me. "I think it's more than that."

I run my thumbs along her jaw bone on either side. She's right, but I'm curious if she knows why exactly. How well does Caroline Bell know me? "What do you think it is?"

"I think you liked women like Felicity before because they liked the Grayson Ross you were before. You like that side of yourself. The take-charge CEO, who always makes the right decision and is perfect, put together, organized and on top of things. You liked that they liked that side of you." She pauses. "But you like me because I like the side of you that you had forgotten. Or maybe you didn't even really know him. The Honeysuckle Harbor side, the in-over-his-head dad. The one who doesn't always have the answers. The one who maybe messes up a little bit sometimes. The one who needs help, but who has finally learned how to ask for it. The one who is a little more laid-back, who smiles more easily, who likes to have a beer on the beach, who has friends and family and roots." She reaches up and plays with the knot on my necktie. "And as absolutely hot as you are in this suit, I know and very much like the Grayson Ross who wears blue jeans and T-shirts with baby spit up on them, and who some-times forgets to brush his hair, and who spills baby food on his couch, and gets baby poop down the front of him, and will still smile and hold his baby daughter with hearts in his eyes."

I stare down at her, my heart pounding in my chest.

I would never have articulated all of that in that way, but she's exactly right.

Caroline is my type because she really knows *me*. The Grayson Ross who does business in this office and conducts meetings in that conference room down the hall is certainly part of me, but he's not the real me.

I didn't know the real me until Evelyn came into my life and I went back to Honeysuckle Harbor.

Not only is that the real me, but I really like that Grayson.

So of course I love the woman who likes that side of me. The woman who's helped me find and appreciate that side of me.

Felicity would be horrified if she saw the way I spend most of my mornings, or if I ever answered my door in a T-shirt with baby food stains, or if she walked into my apartment after Evelyn had a diaper explosion.

"Am I close?" Caroline asks.

And if I'm not mistaken, there's a little bit of hope and maybe a tiny bit of fear in her eyes.

Is she worried that I'll say no? Does she want me to like her for all of those reasons? Does she want to be right about all of this?

And if so, what does that mean?

Well, I guess we're going to find out.

"One hundred percent," I say.

Her smile is bright, and she says simply, "Thank God."

Then I have to kiss her.

I lower my head and seal my mouth over hers.

The kiss turns hot quickly, and I pick her up and put her on the edge of my desk, stepping between her knees. She opens her legs for me and her hands go to my waist, her fingers tucking into my belt loops, holding me close.

I slide my hands from her hips up under the hem of her shirt, dragging my fingertips over her bare skin up to her breasts. I cup them, running my thumbs over the stiff nipples, eliciting a moan.

I pull the cups down so that I can palm her bare breasts and pluck at her nipples. I'm still obsessed with her tits and assume I always will be.

Needing to see and taste them, I quickly strip her shirt off over her head and toss it toward my office door. I stare down at her while playing with her pretty nipples, watching her chest move up and down as she breathes hard. I dip my knees and take one nipple in my mouth, swirling around the tip with my tongue, then sucking hard.

"Grayson!" she gasps.

"God, I love hearing my name on your lips," I say roughly against her breast.

"Fuck me on your desk," she pleads. "I want you to think of me every time you're in here."

"Yes," I say, my cock hardening. I want that too. I want her bent over, spread open, taking my cock so that I can think about it every single time I sit down for a conference call.

I want to fuck her here before Cas has a chance to fuck her on *his* desk.

I want…

Fuck.

Cas.

James.

Our foursome.

She reaches up and starts undoing my tie and I jerk back, sucking in air.

I stare down at her, then close my eyes with a groan. She's so fucking hot and I want her so much and I'm half in love with her and she's half-naked on my desk.

Goddammit.

I run a hand over my face. "Fuck, Caroline."

She reaches for me, pulling me close by my belt loops. "Yes," she says. "Do that. Fuck Caroline."

But I shake my head and step back. "I can't. Sweetheart, fuck. I want to. So much. But I can't."

She frowns. "What do you mean, you can't?" She glances toward the door. "I'm pretty sure Andrea knows what we're doing. She'll keep Evelyn. It won't take that long." She gives me a mischievous smile.

"No. I really can't."

She blows out a breath. "Grayson, *please*. I know the whole accidental pregnancy thing is scary, but I promise we can—"

"I promised the guys."

She stops. Then frowns again. "The guys? Do you mean James and Cas?"

I nod. "Yes. The only guys I'm discussing sex with you with."

"Well, that's good. But what do you mean, you promised the guys?"

"I told them we wouldn't have sex without them."

She sits up a little straighter and pulls her bra up over her breasts.

"Oh." That seems to sink in. "You all discussed…rules? Like you all decided, this would just always be a foursome. Never just you and me?"

"Yes. Just like they won't be having sex with you without me."

She seems to think that over for a moment, then shakes her head. "Well, I appreciate that we are committing to this and that we're communicating and establishing boundaries but, I don't really love that you all are having that conversation without me."

Yeah, that's fair. "You're right. We should've included you. You just weren't there. And we were discussing things, including this trip. This conversation just happened right before we left for New York."

She scoots off the desk and goes to retrieve her shirt, pulling it on and smoothing the front, then running her fingers through her hair. "Okay. But going forward, nobody makes rules about sex without everyone there."

"That seems like a good rule." I smile. "That we just made without them."

She finally smiles. "Right. Okay, but seriously, we need to talk when we get back."

"Okay."

She seems to still be thinking things over. "So the rule is, it's the four of us or nothing?"

"Yes."

"Does that include oral and hands and fingers? Just no cocks? Or is it everything?"

I groan. "Honey, you're killing me. Even hearing you talk about it all makes me hard."

She lifts a brow. "I don't care. You helped get us to this state, knowing that you were going to pull back."

I nod. "Fine. We didn't discuss specifics. We just said no sex."

She puts a hand on her hip. "But you and I aren't having pussy-cock sex, anyway."

My cock reacts to her saying those words like I'm a horny thirteen-year-old. I have to adjust myself and I give her a stern look.

She doesn't care. "So really what you mean is no orgasms without the other two present," she says.

"I suppose so, yes."

"Does that include phone sex? Like what if we called them and included them? Or we could get on a video call with them. They could have sex at the same time. Would that count?"

I actually growl now. That would be really hot. "We didn't discuss specifics, Caroline."

"So we could do that. Torture them a little for having the conversation without me."

I grin in spite of the fact that my dick is hard enough to drive nails. "You have a bit of a mean streak."

"I know. You should warn the others."

I laugh. "Noted. But, this phone sex plan. What if they refuse? We get all worked up and ready to do a show for them and they say no?"

"Then *I* would do a show for all of you. Just me and my vibrator. Torture *all* of you for coming up with this idea without including me. Because I would have thought of all of these contingencies and we'd be clear about tonight."

I'm picturing her on my bed back at the apartment already. Fuck. We could do that. James and Cas would not end that phone call.

I clear my throat, trying to sound firm yet hoping she pushes that idea. "We need to discuss this stuff when we're all together."

She sighs. "You're right. So, what are we doing about sleeping arrangements tonight?"

"I really want you in my bed," I tell her honestly. "Can we sleep together? Hold each other without it being too torturous?"

She studies me, her expression softening. "Yes. I mean, it might be a little torturous, but I would like to sleep with you, too."

"We'll make it through," I say with a wink.

She laughs lightly.

"What?" I ask.

"I'm just thinking, after I leave, I am so calling you all, and using my vibrator on a video call. And I am guessing that, even if we haven't discussed it ahead of time or if it breaks some rule you all set, you're all going to answer the call."

See? She knows us well.

I narrow my eyes. "We are going to discuss this mean streak of yours when we get home to Honeysuckle Harbor," I promise her.

She suddenly gives me a soft smile that is full of affection. "I love that you call Honeysuckle Harbor home," she says. "I'm glad that's home now and New York is just a place for business trips."

And fuck, just like that my heart squeezes hard.

I have a lot of difficult decisions to make, and they're all pressing in on me at once.

Like where am I going to live and raise Evelyn? What am I going to do about future trips with her and my need to have a nanny along when Caroline isn't here?

And what am I going to do about the fact that I'm pretty sure I'm falling in love with this gorgeous, amazing woman who swept into my life, made it so much better, and who doesn't want to be tied down?

CHAPTER 28

Cas

"HOP ON." I gesture to my motorcycle.

"If I had a nickel for every time a guy has said that to me," Caroline says with a flirty smile.

I laugh. "Then I would say you have terrible taste in men. Except I know that's not true." I pop a helmet onto her head and lean in to do the strap. "You're going to look very hot riding on my bike."

"Too bad you won't be able to see me." Her voice is breezy, her smile relaxed and casual.

Caroline and Grayson arrived back from New York on Tuesday evening, and immediately Caroline had suggested the four of us get together for a glass of wine at our place. I had hoped it was for unexpected weekday sex, but it had been to discuss us making rules for our foursome on Saturday without involving her.

It wasn't that I didn't see her point—she definitely needs to be involved in discussing how we all engage in this relationship—it's just that there hadn't been time before she and Grayson left for New York to loop her in and hear her thoughts on the subject. Yet it also seemed if she and Grayson were alone, they were going to end up in bed together, and that might complicate things for all of us.

She was right that we needed to clear the air and make sure we're all on the same page. It wasn't a confrontation or anything like that, and she wasn't upset. It was four adults having a rational conversation, and I was grateful that was how it played out. Not that any of us are irrational, but James has big feelings and Grayson likes to get his way. I do as well, if I'm being honest. I do love to hammer home a point with logic and facts. It's why I became a lawyer.

The conclusion we all mutually drew is that no solo sex rule means just that—no solo sex. There are no loopholes or workarounds or walking the line.

Obviously, James and I are different. We're married, we can have all the sex we want. But none of us guys can fuck Caroline alone.

I'm a little surprised that we were even having that conversation.

I had been certain that when she and Grayson jetted off to New York and played happy little family and spent the night in a hotel together, Grayson would have tossed our impromptu rules out the window, fucked her, and they would have recognized what I can see brewing between them.

They're falling in love with each other.

Grayson admitted it without even realizing he had at the beach picnic.

Hell, maybe that's exactly why he agreed to not fuck her alone. If he does, he'll drown in his growing feelings and we all know she's leaving in just a few weeks.

Caroline hasn't said a word about her feelings for any of us, not even last night when she was discussing our foursome. For someone with a big heart, who seems to be an open book, she doesn't indicate she wants anything more than casual from us.

Which I should take at face value. Caroline is an honest woman.

That leaves me with one conclusion—she hasn't admitted to herself yet that she is falling for both Grayson and James.

It's been obvious to me since the beginning that she isn't just attracted to Grayson physically. It started out flirty and I think she felt compassion for him, having had fatherhood dropped on him so unexpectedly. He's risen to the occasion, and she respects that and cares for him and they've bonded over Evelyn. Her eyes go soft when she looks at Grayson. Her smiles are different, deeper. Like when she looks at James.

Me? Not so much.

We have seen each other naked. I've been inside of her. I've done dirty, intimate things to her, and she has to me, but I wouldn't say that we *know* each other.

This is the first time we've even been alone together.

And this only came about because she doesn't have a car and needs to go to Charleston for a banking appointment.

I intend to take advantage of it, though, to get to know her a little better.

"I won't be able to see you, but I'll be able to feel your thighs squeezing mine and your tits draped all over my back and that has its own particular charms." No sex is one thing, but there are no rules against innuendoes.

"How do you know I'll be clinging to your back?" she asks as I climb on my bike.

"Because I like to go fast."

"This is the sole reason you moved to the States, isn't it?" She gestures to me on the bike. "You can't look this sexy on a moped."

That makes me laugh. "Maybe not the sole reason but definitely in the top five."

She climbs on behind me and lightly wraps her arms around my waist. "You'll have to give me the full list when we get there."

It's an easy ride to Charleston. The tourist traffic is winding down for the season and the weather is perfect. Slightly overcast, dry, little to no wind, and temperature in the low seventies. I don't usually ride my bike to work because the weather is unpredictable. I can't arrive at the office soaking wet or rumpled to hell and back, so this is a treat.

I also never have someone riding with me and I'm keenly aware of Caroline tucked up behind me, her legs clamped against mine, her pussy bumping my ass. She is holding onto me, but she's not leaning against my back, probably just to prove a point. She can be a little stubborn. It's something she and Grayson have in common.

My motorcycle gives me a sense of freedom. It's why I love it. I have a logical mind, but I also tend to overthink. I can go in circles in my own brain and being out on the road with the roar of the engine drowns out my thoughts. The gym does the same for me. Pushing myself physically grounds me in the here and now instead of the cerebral.

I don't sense that Caroline is that way at all. She lives in the moment. Not that she doesn't have plans, because she clearly does, but that she appreciates where she is right now. Not looking back, not looking forward, just being. I like that about her.

It's how James is as well, and I can see that is part of why they were drawn to each other as teens. They're both outgoing and fun loving and confident without being remotely arrogant.

"That was incredible," Caroline exclaims when we park in front of the bank and she pulls her helmet off. "Cas, I can see why you love riding. It feels so powerful."

"Unlike a moped." I take the helmet from her and smile.

She laughs. "Definitely not. Mopeds are convenient but a little whiny."

To my surprise, the smile falls off of her face when she looks at the building in front of us.

It's classic revival, with dominating columns and an austere presence.

She is taking deep breaths and looks like she's bracing herself to enter.

Caroline isn't in her usual uniform of leggings and a crop top today either. She's wearing black linen pants, a color I don't really associate with her, and a pale green lightweight sweater, a purse across her shoulder. I told her to wear close toed shoes and so she's wearing striped sneakers. It's not a dressy outfit, but different from what I associate her with.

"Is everything okay?" I ask.

I'm wearing jeans and a button-down shirt. My plan is to take Caroline back home and then change and go into the office. I'll just work an extra hour or two tonight. Or hell, maybe I won't for once. I certainly dedicate enough hours of my life to my law firm.

"What?" Caroline shrugs. "Oh, I'm fine. I guess."

She doesn't elaborate as I lock up our helmets and my bike, so I press just a little. "Are you nervous about this banking appointment?"

I don't know anything about Caroline's financial situation. She doesn't act like she's concerned about money, but she did step in as Grayson's interim nanny and she's teaching classes at the baby gym. Maybe that's out of necessity.

"No, the appointment is fine. I need to open an account in Colombia before I arrive there and I didn't think the branch in Honeysuckle Harbor would be familiar with doing a foreign wire transfer."

"Probably true." We're just standing on the sidewalk. I decide to wait for her to start up the stairs first. Something's on her mind and causing her to hesitate—that's clear.

Maybe she's having second thoughts about going to Colombia.

Caroline reaches out and touches the leaves on a plant that is inside the giant concrete planter boxes lining either side of the imposing bank.

"I love plants," she says. "I tell myself I'm not going to get any when I move and then I can't resist and start collecting them again. Then when I leave, I have to rehome them. But I can't stop myself. This is a purple coneflower. It's super common all over the country and it's hardy as hell, but look at how pretty it is. I'm surprised it's here though, because they're pollinators and attract bees."

I'm not sure what to say, so I decide to just listen. She's leading me somewhere and I want to let her take me there.

Then it comes out in a rush of words when she's still running a finger over the velvety petals of a flower.

"My dad used to work here. He was a senior personal banker. He used to bring me here to show me around. He died when I was fourteen. Heart attack in his office, actually."

"I'm so sorry. I had no idea you had lost your father."

"Thanks. I just have both good and bad memories here, you know? But I don't want the bad ones—knowing he passed away here—to steal away the good ones."

"I understand that. My dad died when I was twenty-one in a car accident. I was away at university."

Caroline's head whips around, and she locks eyes with me. "Oh God, Cas, I'm so sorry. So you really do understand."

"I do." I reach out and take her hand, leading her to one of several benches. "Let's sit for a minute. Tell me about your dad, about the good memories. Just the good ones."

"His name is, was, Robert and everyone called him Rob. He was tall and intelligent—he read books so fast—but he also loved food and traveling and making dad jokes. So many dad jokes. When he would bring me to the bank, he would appoint me his assistant for the hour or two I was here and would have me get him coffee. I would work so hard to get the cream and sugar ratio just right and then he would tell his co-workers I had a fine eye for details. Honestly, Cas, that coffee was the color of biscuit mix —I had so much milk in it. I don't even know how he drank it with a straight face."

"Because that's what dads do." I give her a smile. "Put family photos on their desk and clap loudly at dance recitals and brag unabashedly about their kids. My father was the same way. He was quiet, but he was warm and loving. He used to twirl my mother around the kitchen and pat her ass, which was mortifying to us as kids, but now is a positive memory of being shown what a loving marriage was like."

Caroline squeezes my hand. "That sounds lovely. How is your mother doing?"

"She's okay. She has a full life with friends and family and my sister's children. She skis and is a cyclist, and much like you, loves a good plant to nurture. How is your mother? Were your parents still married?"

She nods. "Yes, they were. She's actually remarried and lives in Florida a few minutes from my sister, who has two kids. I saw them before I came here, but her love is a little smothering. She wants me to be all in on her husband and call him my stepdad, but I don't really know him. I'm sure he's a nice guy, but he's her husband, not my stepfather. I've met him all of a handful of times and I was twenty-five when they got married. I don't like that she pushes a relationship."

"Have you told her that?"

"Yes, and she just tells me I have to accept that she's married. I accept it. That doesn't mean her choice of a husband is some kind of replacement to my father when I'm a grown woman. It's like she wants to erase him and it pisses me off."

"That is a perfectly reasonable response. So you stay away."

Caroline suddenly grins. "I don't travel because of her—that's my own passion and desire—but it's a bonus not to live in the same country. For right now, anyway." Then she stands up. "We'd better go in or I'll be late. Thanks for listening, Cas."

"I'm sorry we share this in common, but it does make me feel less alone in my own grief, and I hope you feel the same way."

"I do."

When I stand up, I reach out and brush her hair back off of her cheek tenderly. I give her a soft, barely there kiss because it feels right and natural. Then I pull her into my arms and hug her. She hugs me back, hard.

"Noah is a very lucky little boy," she murmurs into my chest. "You and James are great parents."

That makes my chest tighten. "I love that little guy with all my heart. I can suffer the heat and bugs to give him a life surrounded by friends and family."

"You still haven't told me how you wound up in the US."

"Ah, we'll have to save that for another day. It's nothing exciting and we don't want you to be late."

She pulls back and eyes me. "I feel like there is an exciting story there. A sordid tale of lust and greed and betrayal."

I laugh. "Not even close. My father's sister married an American man, and I came to visit them in Philadelphia and wound up staying."

She wrinkles her nose. "You need to polish that story up because that isn't exciting at all."

"It only became exciting when I met James, who is the love of my life."

"God, that's so adorable." She puts her hand in mine and swings them back and forth as we walk up the steps. "And baby makes three."

"Yes."

But as we hold hands like a couple of kids or an actual couple, I feel a strange tug in my chest.

This is way more complicated than I ever expected it to be.

And I'm not sure if that's what any of us need in our lives.

CHAPTER 29

James

"CAN I HOLD NOAH?" Grayson asks. "I feel a little weird not having a baby in my arms right now. Is this how women feel without a purse?"

Cas lifts his eyebrows. "I have no idea how women feel about their purses." But he passes our son over to Grayson.

I laugh. I'm holding Evelyn on our couch, bouncing her up and down on my thighs and making faces at her. She's been chuckling and grinning, drool rolling down her round chin. She's a very adorable baby, even when she's making Grayson's notorious frown.

Grayson settles Noah into his arms in the cradle position. "Hey there, little man," he coos, pacing back and forth in front of the couch. "Look at how tiny you are compared to Evie."

We're in our apartment because Grayson said he needed to speak to us. I don't know what that means, but it definitely feels important. Grayson looks like he's been up half the night, which can't be because of Evelyn because it's Thursday and I know for a fact he has the night nanny there Tuesday through Saturday. Given that my parents take Noah on Saturday nights, it's allowed us our foursome fun in our place the last couple of Saturdays.

"It sucks that Caro is gone this weekend," I say, my thoughts now on sliding my tongue up between her smooth thighs and burying it deep inside her pussy.

"She's having a girls' weekend with the twins," Cas says. "She's entitled to do whatever she wants with her weekend."

I frown at my husband. I wonder if he realizes how sharp his comment sounds. He's been acting a little off since he got home yesterday after taking Caro to Charleston. It doesn't seem like he's upset or anything—he's just…pensive.

He's clearly working something out in his head and I know Cas well enough to know that it's best to let him get where he's going on his own instead of trying to pry.

"Of course she's entitled to do whatever she wants with her weekend," I say. "I'm just going to miss our time with her, that's all. She's only here for a few more weeks."

It's a reality I don't like to think about. I love Caro and I love having her back in my life. It feels like we've just started something amazing and now it's ending.

"She'll be here in a minute," Grayson says, surprising me.

"What? You invited her over too? What's going on?"

He's not looking at me, but down at Noah in his arms. "I need to talk to all of you. Together."

"That sounds ominous," I joke. "Kind of like Evelyn's expression right now."

Grayson's daughter is scowling at him hard core.

That gets Grayson's attention. He smiles at his daughter. "Hi, sweetie. What's wrong?"

"I think she's jealous that you're holding Noah," Cas says. Cas, who just got home from work, tugs at the knot of his tie to undo it.

"Maybe she's picking up on the vibe," I say. "Both you and Grayson look like you have a lot simmering under the surface."

"Me?" Cas asks, sounding surprised. "I don't have a vibe."

Grayson sighs, swiping at his phone. "Caroline is downstairs at the front door. I just buzzed her in. Shit, this is so fucking hard."

"What is hard? What is going on?" I ask, bewildered.

Cas levels me with a hard stare and stands up to go to the door. He opens it before Caroline can even knock and he freaks me out by giving her a hug. Cas isn't a hugger. She doesn't look startled, though. She hugs him back tightly, and when he releases her, she squeezes his forearm.

What the fuck happened at the bank in Charleston?

Also, why is Grayson clearing his throat repeatedly?

"What the hell is going on?" I ask.

"We all need to talk," Grayson says.

He already said that and I'm starting to get concerned. "Is this like the kind of summons my mother gives where we all think it's super important and then she just wants to tell us that she broke my grandmother's big bowl? Or is this like of the "I'm getting investigated by the IRS?" variety?"

Or worse. Oh, my God. What if it's about Evelyn's custody?

Caroline drops her little body bag on the coffee table and sits down next to Grayson, her eyebrows raised.

"This isn't about Evelyn's mother, is it?" I ask, instinctively holding her tighter against my chest. I'll be sick if someone tries to take this little girl away from her father.

"No, no, it's not that." Grayson shakes his head. "I wouldn't be sitting here all fucking calm like this if that was the case. I'd be screaming at a lawyer on the phone. And it's not the IRS. And I didn't break an heirloom bowl, and no one has cancer. Just chill, James."

I instantly felt relieved.

"This is about me and Caroline and the four of us having sex."

Not relieved anymore.

"What about it?" Cas takes Noah from Grayson. Just swoops in and takes our son.

Without a baby to hold, Grayson looks like he doesn't know what to do with his hands. He claps them on his knees.

There's a pause, where it feels like we're all holding a collective breath.

Then Grayson blurts out, "I need to remove myself from our arrangement."

I hear the words, but I wasn't expecting them at all. We all wait for him to expand on that bomb he just dropped, but he doesn't say anything else. He just swallows hard.

"Why?" I demand when no one else does.

Cas is frowning. Caroline looks caught off guard. Some of the color has drained from her face and she's tensed up slightly.

"Because..." He turns toward Caroline. "When we were in New York, I loved telling everyone in the office you were my girlfriend."

"You told everyone she's your girlfriend?" Cas asks.

Caro nods. "Yes. To get Felicity off of his back. She's been aggressive in her pursuit of Grayson."

"Exactly. And I loved it. Not because it sent a strong message to Felicity, but because I wanted it to be *real*. I wanted you to be territorial because I'm yours and your mine and we're together, raising Evelyn." Grayson takes her hand and massages her knuckles with his thumb. His voice softens. "I'm in love with you, Caroline. Completely and totally in love with you."

Caroline's mouth drifts apart on a soft sigh. "Oh. I..."

"No, don't say anything." He stops her. "That's why I'm breaking things off. We all agreed this was casual, this was temporary. I want to respect that and I would love, absolutely love, to share this last week or two in bed with you all, but I can't because I'm in too deep. Way too fucking deep. It would just be...painful."

"I see," Caro says softly.

"You do?" I ask. "Because I don't."

Evelyn gives a shriek, like she doesn't understand what the hell is happening either.

"Are you sure this isn't you mistaking what you're feeling for me?" Caroline asks. "You've been through a really tumultuous time and I..."

Grayson doesn't let her finish. The softness on his face evaporates. "No. Oh my God, are you kidding me? Do you know how often I've told a woman I've been in love with her? I don't. I'm not that guy. I know what I'm feeling, for fuck's sake. So I'm out."

He suddenly stands up and stalks over to me. He holds his hands out for his daughter. "I have this little girl now and she's been through a lot. She was dumped at my office like she doesn't matter and she's already had so much change and new nannies and all of you being around. I can't be dicking around with who she gets attached to and I can't…" His voice cracks. "I *cannot* fuck this up. She is my priority. She has to be."

Caroline nods. "Of course not. I understand." She stands up, and I can see her hands are trembling a little and her face is pale. "I never meant to…I never thought that…"

"That I would fall in love with you?" Grayson asks.

She nods again.

He gives a soft laugh. "Sweetheart, the real question is, how could I not? You're *everything*. Adventurous and caring and intelligent. You see joy in everything and everyone. How could I not fall in love with you?"

There are tears in her eyes. *"Grayson."*

My chest is tight with emotion. Grayson is right. He really sees Caro. He gets her.

I understand exactly how he feels because I'm in love with her, too.

My heart is going to break when she leaves and yet, I have a husband and a son and I have an incredible life. That's the rub, though. It doesn't mean I don't love Caroline and I see what Grayson is doing—he's protecting himself as much as he can, even though it's already too late to stop what he's feeling.

Maybe it's more he's attempting to protect Evelyn.

But unlike Grayson, I want to steal every minute I can with Caro before she leaves.

"This was always what we planned," Caroline tells Grayson softly. "The four of us until I leave."

"I know. But plans change." Grayson bends down and strokes her cheek, kisses her softly. "I didn't plan on falling in love."

Evelyn grips Caroline's hair and stares at the two of them with big, solemn eyes.

It's intimate and heartfelt, and I feel like a spectator.

"Do you two need a minute?" I ask, gesturing to Cas that we should take Noah and go into our bedroom.

But Grayson shakes his head. "No. This was about all of us. And I'm leaving." He takes a step back and runs his free hand through his hair. "Jesus fuck. This is hard. Maybe…in a few years, when you're done with your assignment, we can circle back to this."

"Circle back? You tell me you're in love with me and then that we can circle back to that in a few years? This isn't a business merger we're discussing."

He winces and then tries to cover it up.

That was a poor choice of wording.

"Of course not. I just meant…if you…if there's a time…" But then he just stops speaking.

Caroline shakes her head, looking bewildered as she runs a finger down the soft skin of Evelyn's arm. "Bye, baby girl." Then she lifts her gaze to Grayson. "Bye, Grayson. Take care of yourself."

It doesn't escape my attention that she doesn't say that she loves him.

He pauses, like he's realized that very thing and is waiting for her to declare her love and jump into his arms, but she doesn't do anything.

I feel terrible for him. I also feel like his face right now is exactly what mine is going to look like in two weeks when Caro leaves—heartbroken but resigned.

When the door closes behind him, tears fill Caroline's eyes. She puts her hand on her throat. "I honestly didn't see that coming."

"Come here." Cas opens his arms, and she goes right into them.

Well, fuck me.

I didn't see that coming either.

CHAPTER 30

Caroline

GRAYSON ROSS IS in love with me.

That is the most bizarre thing I've ever heard.

The broody, grumpy billionaire turned sudden single dad has fallen in love with me.

No way.

Except Grayson doesn't say things he doesn't mean.

He is intense and blunt and sincere.

Holy shit. I step out of Cas's arms and blink the tears out of my eyes. Then I look at James and Cas.

Cas is wearing a strange expression. He doesn't look nearly as surprised as I think he should. This is a stunning revelation, isn't it? Then I look at James. He looks a little pained.

"So, that was weird," I say.

Cas shakes his head with a rueful smile. "Weird? Not the word I would use."

"Why don't you seem shocked? Did he tell you about this or something?"

"No. He waited until you got here," Cas says. "But I'm not shocked because it's not shocking."

"Grayson thinks he's in love with me," I say. "That doesn't surprise you?"

Cas looks over at James. "No, that's not shocking."

I frown, looking from one of them to the other. "Yes it is," I insist. "It's ridiculous. We are just messing around. This is just sex."

But my mind almost immediately rejects that. I know it's not just sex. I already had thoughts like that in New York. I know that we all have more affectionate feelings for each other than just lust or chemistry. But it's because we're all nice people. We enjoy one another. I've seen them as dads. We have Honeysuckle Harbor in common. I've seen the three of them establish a friendship. I've seen Grayson and James with their families and with all three of them with other people in town. They are great guys. Of course, I feel more for them than just wanting to fuck their brains out. And they've been extremely good to me. They treat me so well. They seem to truly care about me and have been not only giving in the bedroom, but supportive and caring about learning about my career and passions and understanding my love of travel and my desire to go to my next assignment.

We're friends.

Friends with very fun benefits.

"You guys have to talk to him," I finally say. "Convince him that he's mixed up. Grayson probably hasn't had a friendship with a woman before. He's getting mixed up in feeling things for me other than passion, but he just defaults to thinking that's love or something."

But James is shaking his head. "We're not gonna talk him out of being in love with you, Caroline."

I frown at him. "Why not? He's ruining everything. We have such a great thing going. The sex is amazing. But we're also having such a good time. And he needs us. He's settling in so well to being a dad, but he needs our friendship. He needs our support. It's more than just sex."

James sighs. "It is. That's what he just told you."

I shake my head, frustrated. "No. There's a lot between lust and love."

"Of course there is. But in this case, Grayson knows exactly how he feels."

"You actually think he's in love with me?" I demand.

James stretches up from where he's sitting and takes a few steps until he's standing in front of me. The look in his eyes is intense.

"Yes, I think he's in love with you. In fact, I have absolutely no trouble believing that at all."

I frown. "What are you talking about?"

"I am certain Grayson is in love with you because I'm also in love with you. Caroline, what we're doing is so much bigger. I know it started out as one thing, but it's turned into more."

I feel tears welling up again. My gaze moves from James to Cas.

James's husband doesn't seem shocked or upset by James's sudden declaration to me.

"Cas?" I ask. I need him to make sense of this.

He lifts a shoulder. "It all turned into love, Caroline. None of us expected it. None of us planned it. But James has been in love with you for years. The chance to have you back in his life, back in *our* lives, has been amazing. Our foursome has been amazing.'

My eyes go back to James's. "Why didn't you say anything? This complicates everything."

"That's precisely why I didn't say anything. I wanted every second with you I could get."

"I'm leaving," I say. Dammit, these men are making this unnecessarily hard.

"I know. We all know. We would never try to talk you out of that. If you want to stay, we want you. I think our foursome could be amazing. I think this could be a long-term thing. Something all four of us actually really need. But none of us are going to beg you to stay. You just need to know what you can have if you do."

I look at Cas again. "This is crazy."

He shakes his head. "It makes a ton of sense. You're amazing, we're all amazing, we work together better than any of us could've ever imagined. If you stay, the four of us can be something special. But, like James said, we wouldn't ask you to give up your dreams. If your job is still your dream, then you have to go. But if your dream has changed, you need to know what else there is."

I shake my head and step back from James, unable to think clearly when I'm so close to him. "So what about us? The three of us started out without Grayson. We can't just keep going for the last two weeks I'm here?"

James smiles at me sadly. "Is that really what you want?"

I think about stepping up to him, grabbing him, and kissing him.

But I can't.

I just stand staring at him.

It's Cas that finally says, "We're a foursome now. If one of us is missing, we don't work."

"Do you really feel that way?" It's strange to me that these men have fallen so completely into the idea of including another man in this thing that started out well between the three of us.

Cas nods. "We didn't know what we were missing before Grayson came along. But he completed the picture. We're better with him. If the three of us try to go on, it's going to feel like something is missing and you know it. Besides, we can't do that to him. It would hurt Grayson, no matter what he says."

Fuck. I cross my arms over my stomach and squeeze. He's right. And I want all of them. But it's not just my body that wants them.

And I need to get out of here.

"I have to go," I say, my voice choked.

They don't seem surprised by that either.

"Let us drive you home," Cas says, heading for the side table where he keeps his keys.

But I'm already at the door. I yank it open. "No. I need to just...go."

They don't try to stop me again, and a minute later, I step out onto the sidewalk in front of their building. I glance at the front of the building, and the window that looks into James's studio with the big Daddy and Me class sign in the window. I feel like all the oxygen has been sucked out of my lungs.

I start walking toward Frannie and Fiona's beach house. I feel like I'm moving through a fog. Nothing is quite clear. The sounds around me sound muted, the sights are hazy. But I know it's my brain, and the emotional swirl rather than real life.

I don't know what to do with all of these feelings. I'm normally a very even-keel person and I definitely wasn't expecting tonight to include emotions beyond lust, pleasure, and enjoyment.

What am I feeling? I think I'm a little shocked. I know I'm sad.

So, my situationship ended. I knew that was going to happen. Just because I didn't expect it to happen tonight doesn't mean I need to act like the world is ending. This was never going to be a long-term thing.

It's not like I broke up with my boyfriends. From the beginning, we knew this was going to end when I left. So we're two weeks ahead of schedule, so what?

I stop at the corner and take a deep breath. *You're fine,* I tell myself. *You don't have to feel this crushing sense of loss. You and James and Cas are still going to be friends. And you can be friends with Grayson, eventually, too.*

No, Grayson Ross doesn't seem like the type to be friends with his exes. *But you're not his ex,* I remind myself. *He wasn't your boyfriend. He was just a guy. You had some really hot, dirty sex with a few times.*

But even as I think the words, they don't sit right. Grayson was more than that.

Probably because of Evelyn, I tell myself. *You got attached to his little girl. You felt more bonded because you helped him out at a very vulnerable point in his life. You're going to miss Evelyn, not Grayson.*

I take a deep breath. Yeah, that sounds good. I call up my rideshare app and see if there are any cars in the immediate area.

It looks like I can have someone pick me up in two minutes and take me to Raw.

I think I want to go out. I was supposed to be busy tonight, and that fell through because Grayson ruined it.

That doesn't mean I can't have any fun, though.

I think about asking James and Cas to join me at Raw for a drink. As friends. I can show them I'm fine and that we can immediately go back to being just friends. We can go out. Casually. As fucking *friends*.

Then I shake my head. No, not fucking friends. Just friends.

But the car pulls up just then before I make a decision about texting James. So I get into the car by myself.

Honeysuckle Harbor is small enough that the drive to the restaurant doesn't take long. I am walking through the front doors, trying to paste on a smile just a few minutes later.

"Hi," I say to the hostess at the front. "Can I just sit up at the bar? And I'd love it if you could tell Frannie and Fiona that Caroline is here."

The hostess is looking at me with wide eyes.

"Okay," she says.

I frown. Why is she acting weird? "Is something wrong?" I ask.

"Um–" She starts

But just then a tall, broad shouldered man approaches me quickly. "Ma'am, are you okay? Can I help?"

I look up at him. He's really big. "I'm fine," I tell him, confused. "What's going on?"

Of course I just lied. I'm not fine. I am brokenhearted. I'm confused. I'm…mourning. I actually feel like I'm mourning.

I need to get it together. This is not the appropriate reaction to what happened tonight. I am a grown ass woman. I cannot be flipping out about this.

Frannie suddenly comes rushing forward. "Oh my God, Caroline, are you all right?"

Why does everyone keep asking me that? Maybe because the answer is no.

"I've had kind of a bad night," I tell her truthfully. "But how do you all know that? Why do you keep asking me that?"

"Ma'am, where are you coming from?" the big man asks me.

That's a weird question. And I'm not sure how to answer it. I am coming from James and Cas's apartment.

"I thought you were with the guys tonight," Frannie says.

"I was." And then I am horrified because I burst into tears.

Frannie's eyes widen, the big man's brows slammed together, and suddenly Fiona is with us as well.

"Oh my God, what is going on? Caroline, what happened to you?"

"We broke up," I say. "Which is stupid, because we weren't really together. Not like that. Not like a breakup type of together."

Through my tears, I see Frannie and Fiona exchange a look.

"Ma'am, I have some questions—"

"Cool it Agent Intense," Frannie says. "We've got this."

Agent? Oh, this guy must be the FBI agent that comes in here a lot.

Wait, I have an FBI agent worried about me? Why?

"Come on," Fiona says, tugging me toward the women's restroom just off the lobby.

With Fiona in front of me and Frannie behind, they escort me into the restroom. The minute I face the mirror, I see why everyone seems so concerned.

I'm a mess.

My makeup is streaked, which could be explained by the crying I've been doing, but my hair is wet and hanging in limp strands around my face, my clothes are soaked and sticking to me, and I look dazed and confused and upset.

Well, I understand that last part. I *feel* dazed and confused and upset.

I frown at my reflection. "Why am I all wet?"

Frannie and Fiona look at each other again and then look at me in the mirror.

"Maybe because it's pouring rain outside?" Fiona asks. "You didn't walk here, did you?"

It's raining outside? How did I not notice that? Okay, I might be a little more rattled than I thought.

"I started to walk back to your house from Cas and James's. But then I decided to come here, so I got a ride."

"So you did walk for a while in the rain," Frannie says, grabbing one of the expensive paper towels, which is actually just as soft as an actual cloth towel, and starts dabbing at my face.

Fiona starts pulling her fingers through my hair, straightening the wet tangles.

I nod. "I guess I did."

Frannie wipes my smeared mascara off my face, and Fiona pulls my hair back into a loose ponytail. She reaches into her own hair, pulls the ponytail holder loose and wraps it around my hair. "I have more in my purse," she tells me before I can ask.

"We also have some restaurant T-shirts in the storeroom," Frannie says. "I'll have someone grab you one."

"You're gonna have to sit in your wet jeans, though," Fiona says.

Honestly, I don't care. I'm still not feeling any of it.

"The guys broke it off tonight," I tell them.

They both move around to face me.

"I'm sorry, honey," Fiona says.

"That really sucks," Frannie says. "Why? You're still here for two more weeks."

"Well, Grayson broke it off because he's..." The wave of sadness hits me again and my eyes well up with tears.

Fiona frown. "Shit. You are not a crier. What happened?"

"Grayson's in love with me."

Frannie's eyes widen. "He's *in love* with you? He said that?"

I nod.

"And he broke it off because of that?"

I nod and lift the tissue that Fiona hands me to my nose. "He said it's too complicated. That his feelings are making it impossible to keep this casual. That since I'm leaving, he needs to break it off now instead of dragging it out."

Frannie blows out a breath. "Fuck."

I sniff. "He knows I'm leaving. He understands that and everything, but he thinks more time together will just make that harder."

Frannie nods. "He's probably not wrong."

I nod. "I know. But then, with James and Cas, it just felt weird. Like...wrong, somehow, if it's not all four of us." I swipe the tears that are falling that I can't seem to stop. "James has feelings for me, too. And Cas, I mean, we're definitely friends. It's probably a little more than that. They're fine with me being a part of their relationship. That's kind of huge."

The girls both nod. "Really huge, I'd say," Frannie says.

I take a deep breath and try to stop the tears. "I just didn't want to be alone at your house. But I'm sorry I'm a mess."

Frannie frowns and shakes her head. "I'm so glad you came down here."

"For sure," Fiona says. "This is definitely the place for you. This definitely calls for liquor and pastries."

Ten minutes later, I am slightly more composed, seated at the bar, with a Kahlúa and cream in front of me and a plate with a variety of pastries sitting on the bar in front of me.

Harrison, a co-owner of Raw, is bartending tonight and his girlfriend Ivy and her husband Ford are seated next to me at the bar. On their other side is Liam, Harrison's husband.

As I bite into a small lemon tart, that is absolute perfection, I study them. There is so much love and easy affection between the four of them that I am consumed with jealousy.

Ford and Ivy are married, as are Harrison and Liam, but they live as a foursome. They are absolutely a committed unit that is clearly bound by friendship, love, and loyalty.

They're making it work. In real life, right in front of me, in Honeysuckle Harbor.

It's possible.

But they all live here. There aren't kids in the picture.

Right. Their situation is not my situation. It's not the same.

Still, I'm jealous as fuck, and I want what Ivy has.

I pause with my coffee-flavored liqueur half-way to my mouth.

Oh. Shit.

That's not good.

You mean the sex. You just mean the sex. You're really, really going to miss the hot foursome sex.

Sure I am. *Of course* I am.

But…that's not what I mean.

"Hey Harrison?" I ask.

He turns away from flirting with his wife—okay, she's not *technically* his wife, but…oh, hell, she's pretty much his wife—and gives me a grin. "Yeah?"

"I'm going to need another drink."

"You got it." He starts to reach for the Kahlúa.

I shake my head. "Oh, no. It's going to need to be *way* stronger than that."

CHAPTER 31

Cas

"YOU BETTER BE NAKED," I tell James as I set my glasses on the nightstand, strip off my pajama pants, and pull back the sheets to slide into bed with him.

"Feel for yourself," he says with a smile. "Is Noah finally asleep? I can't see the monitor from here."

I pause, and grab the tablet to prop it next to James, knowing if he can't see our son sleeping peacefully in his crib on the screen, he would be distracted with every little sound, real or imagined. The way he loves our son is incredible, so I never dismiss his fretting.

Once I'm under the comforter, I snuggle up against him and find he is very much naked and very much sporting a hard cock.

"Babe, I've been thinking about you all day," I murmur, stroking over his cock with a light touch that I know will drive him crazy. I give him a hard, demanding kiss and pull back to stare at his handsome face. "It's been years since we fucked."

"It was yesterday," he says dryly. He cups my cheeks and kisses me back, sliding his tongue between my lips.

He shifts his foot and calf over my leg so that his cock is pressed against mine and I give a low moan of approval. The kiss heats up and I grip his tight ass, the result of all his years of hard work in the gym.

I love these moments with him, in our quiet apartment, the only sound our mouths moving together, our heated breath.

Noah lets out a startled sound. We both jump. Then our baby goes full throttle.

It's not a cry that indicates he'll settle right back down. It sounds like he's scared or has gas, or maybe both.

"Shit." We fall apart.

"I'll get him," James says. "You don't have your glasses on."

"I can put them back on," I protest. "It's not like it's hard."

But James is already out of bed and padding across the floor, pulling on a pair of joggers. Noah has only been sleeping in the small room next to ours for a few weeks and it's been hard for James. He prefers him close by. I do too, but I also prefer fucking my husband in our bed any and every way I please, and that includes being able to moan or talk dirty if I want. Silent sex is only hot if it's a choice, not a necessity.

With a sigh, I roll onto my back and stroke my cock a little so I don't lose my erection and have to start all over.

But James returns almost immediately, with Noah in his arms.

"Babe," I say. "We talked about this. You can't bring him into bed with us every time he cries."

Though I have to admit, he does look pitiful in the glow of our soft lamp. His cheeks are damp from tears, his lashes wet. He has a snot bubble forming, and he's shuddering like he just endured something terrible and Daddy rescued him.

"I know. Just five minutes, then I'll rock him back to sleep."

James can't be firm. This is something we've already figured out. I've been relegated to the role of firm father and while I don't necessarily love that, it does suit my personality better than it does James. Noah is going to be very well loved, if a little indulged. But hey, James can't say no to me either, so I'm not complaining.

"Let me hold him," I say, reaching out to take Noah. "I don't want him to always associate me with being the hard ass."

"I like you being the hard ass. With both of us." James gives me a grin as he passes over Noah and sinks back into bed with a sigh.

"He's probably just pissed you make him wear this bag thing," I say, settling Noah against my chest, my back against the headboard. "There's no freedom of movement."

"I'm not going over all the reasons why a sleep sack is appropriate for a four-month-old." James rolls onto his side and props his head up with his hand, running a hand down over Noah's back.

"Please don't. I've heard it all before." I kiss the top of Noah's head. "Now that we've been interrupted, this is a great opportunity to talk about what happened earlier tonight. How are you feeling about all of it?"

James sighs. "Well. I didn't want Caroline to cut things short with us, that's for sure. I also didn't realize Grayson's feelings were that strong—that he felt like he had to end it. I knew that he was falling in love—hell, it was obvious. So I guess I assumed he'd want every minute with her before she left. I know I do. But I totally get where he's coming from when it comes to Evelyn, though. He has a huge responsibility to his daughter."

I knew that was what he would say, and I agree with all of it. I just don't think that either Grayson or James, who is also in love with Caroline, are seeing the big picture. "You're in love with her, too."

He nods. "Yes. I do love her. Like I told her. I've always loved her."

"And you're in love with her and you miss her already and are going to miss her even more when she's officially left the country. I just want you to know it's okay to feel that way."

"You care about her, too."

"I do. I really care about her. She's an amazing person. A great friend, and an incredible lover, an excellent nurturer to both of our kids." To lighten the mood, I add, "She has great tits, too, by the way. That needs to be said."

James laughs, but his heart isn't in it. "I just want…more. But I feel selfish even saying that."

"Selfish toward me or selfish toward her?"

"Both. I don't want you to think this isn't enough." He reaches out and strokes his fingers over my bare shoulder. "You're enough."

"I know that. None of these things are mutually exclusive. That's what I wish everyone could understand. We can all love each other and be together or love each other and not be together. But let's be honest, together is better."

James is quiet for a second. "So you would be fine with us being a foursome in a permanent, serious relationship?"

"Yes. Absolutely. Raising our kids together, the whole thing. We all bring something different to the relationship and to parenting and to each other. But I don't want any old foursome. I just want *this* foursome. It's either the four of us or it's you and me."

"But this isn't what Caroline wants."

I shrug. "Let's give her space. I don't think she's even had time to wrap her head around Grayson declaring his love for her, and then breaking up with her thirty seconds later. Or maybe it was breaking up with her and then telling her he loved her after. At any rate, it was kind of a one-two punch."

James snorts. "That was very Grayson Reed, wasn't it?"

"It's called let-me-be-vulnerable-and-then-make-sure-I'm-not-immediately."

"I get the feeling Grayson has never been in love before now."

"Which is tragic." I smooth a hand over Noah's head—who is, of course, sleeping peacefully because he's lying on my chest.

Not that I blame him. We're not meant to be alone. None of us are.

"Caroline has had her mother try to force a relationship with her stepfather on her and she resents it. We need to let her come around to this on her own."

"What if she doesn't?"

"She will." I'm certain of it. "She loves all of us, too. She just hasn't acknowledged it yet."

"I hope you're right."

I smile at him. "Never doubt me."

"I don't," he says softly. "I never have. Now let me put Noah back to bed so I can show you how much I appreciate you."

I lean over and kiss him. "I like the sound of that."

CHAPTER 32

Grayson

I LOVE NEW YORK CITY.

I love my job.

I love my apartment.

I love my daughter.

And I am absolutely fucking miserable in New York City, doing my job, living in my apartment, with my daughter.

And my misery has nothing to do with any of those things.

I had to leave Honeysuckle Harbor. I couldn't risk running into Caroline. And I couldn't deal with seeing her around every single corner, whether she was actually there or not. Everything in my apartment reminds me of her. Everything around town reminds me of her. Seeing James and Cas reminds me of her.

But now that I've run away to New York City, I've realized that just being alive reminds me of her. I can't even escape her when I'm unconscious. I dream of her.

So the fact that Evelyn and I are living in New York, and my daytime nanny agreed to accompany me here for a week, hasn't made anything better.

I'm miserable.

I don't know how my daughter is doing. Probably fine. The perpetually scowling baby girl is hard to read. Evelyn still frowns at ninety percent of the people, activities, and locations around her.

And Jane cries once a day.

Not Evelyn, who really doesn't cry much.

No, Jane, the nanny.

But that's not unusual or reserved for New York. That was a daily occurrence even before boarding that plane and, honestly, I'm surprised she agreed to come with us.

The crying is always my fault, but it's always an accident. At this point, it's become a routine and neither of us actually gets that upset about it. I usually say something brusquely—i.e., in my usual tone—or *don't* say something I should, and she tears up for a few minutes.

But we both realize this is just how the other person is wired and we've somehow learned to move past it.

I keep waiting for her to quit and I even asked her if she feels that she needs to move onto another job.

She's assured me that she knows she is overly emotional and that she takes things the wrong way and not to worry about it. She thinks this is a learning experience. Well…okay.

We're practically to the point where if she didn't cry, I would think something was wrong.

So, for the most part, everything in New York is fine.

Things at work are great. Felicity has backed off, all of our projects are on target, and I'm back in my comfort zone.

At least I should feel that this is my comfort zone.

But I'm in love for the first time in my life and the woman who has inspired that is in Honeysuckle Harbor, the place where I have felt more comfortable, more myself in years. And I am very aware of the ticking clock that is marching ever closer to the day she gets on a plane and goes to Colombia.

I was hoping I could just survive 'til that point. If I could stay in New York, until Caroline was gone, I could return to Honeysuckle Harbor, find a house where I could finally put down roots, and raise Evelyn close to my family and my friends.

Because yes, this trip back to New York has shown me that my true friends are in Honeysuckle Harbor. My friends here in New York have called to ask me to go to basketball games, to go out for dinner, and I've even had an invitation to the theater.

All things that I did before and enjoyed with people I saw often and truly liked.

But now none of that sounds as good as a bonfire on the beach with Cas and James and Harrison and Ford and everyone else.

Or even just a beer on the balcony of our building, the sounds of downtown Honeysuckle Harbor drifting up on the salt-tinged evening air.

I want to be back there so much I ache with it.

And I want Caroline so much that it's physically painful.

"Oh, and I embezzled seven million dollars and slept with the entire IT department, all seventeen of them. At the same time."

I focus on Andrea, who is seated across my desk from me.

She's been going over my emails for the past few minutes and I realize I have zoned out.

"Who is that email from?" I ask.

"No email. That was me. Confessing."

"That you've been embezzling from the company and having orgies?"

She nods. "Finally, you've listened to something I said."

I sigh. Honestly, if someone wanted to embezzle from the company, Andrea would probably be the best bet for pulling it off. And I wouldn't even be that angry. She's probably earned at least seven million for putting up with extra bullshit from me over the years.

"I'm sorry. I'm a little distracted."

"No shit. I wonder why that is."

I frown. "There is no way you know what that's about. You know me well, but you can't read my mind."

"Actually, I think I can, but I don't need to read your mind to know what this is about, Grayson."

I lean forward, linking my fingers on top of my desk and

regard her across the wide stretch of polished wood. "Enlighten me."

"You're in love with Caroline and you broke up."

"Why would you think that?"

"Because the last time you were in town, she was here with you and I've never seen you happier. This time she's not with you and you're fucking miserable. And distracted. Two things you never are."

"I'm widely regarded as a grumpy asshole."

"Grumpy and asshole are not synonymous with miserable. I think you've always kind of enjoyed being a grumpy asshole, actually. You're sad, Grayson," she tells me, her expression almost pathetic. "You miss her. So I have to ask why you're here without her."

"It's complicated."

Then she has the audacity to laugh. "Complicated? You're a grown ass man with more money than you could ever spend. What's complicated that you can't solve?"

"I have a daughter. Caroline is about to leave for a job that will take her to Colombia. There are two other men who I think are in love with her as well. If we were to pursue a relationship, it would be a polycule."

She nods. "You have a daughter who adores Caroline and vice versa. Airplanes do fly to and from Colombia. And two other people mean even more people to love your daughter, and this woman that you love, and more people to fill your life." She shrugs. "So I ask again, what's complicated? You're an adult who already doesn't really care what people think of him. You know what you want. Just go get it."

"I know what I want. It might not be what *they* want."

She frowns and leans in. "*Might* not? Are you telling me you didn't even ask?"

I think about her question, then shift on my seat. "I'm saying that I told her how I felt and she said goodbye to me and Evelyn."

There is a stabbing pain near my heart remembering Caroline's soft goodbye.

"And had you at any point prior to that, given her any indication, this is how you felt? Or did you just drop it on her like you did the shareholders about the acquisition of four new properties that cost them nearly one billion dollars last year?"

"They were *very* grateful to me by the end of the year."

"Yes. You always know best, don't you?"

Kind of. At least, I thought so.

I don't answer. Which gives Andrea her answer.

She nods. "You have this way of assuming that you know what other people think. And doing whatever the hell you want to and expecting everyone else to catch up, eventually. Maybe she just needed a couple of minutes. Did you ask her how she feels?"

"We had an agreement. Hot sex while she was in town. I messed it up by catching feelings. I broke the terms of our agreement. That makes it null and void."

Andrea rolls her eyes. "She's not a business deal or a real estate acquisition, Grayson. She's a person. And these are *feelings*, not dollars or stocks. Besides, even in business, if you want an agreement to continue, but you no longer like the terms, you renegotiate."

"To renegotiate would mean to ask her to stay. I can't take Evelyn to Colombia. I want to settle down in Honeysuckle Harbor. I need stability for my daughter. I want to be closer to family and friends. I want a house, a yard, maybe a dog. Caroline is traveling the world. I don't need to negotiate. I already know our terms aren't compatible."

Andrea shakes her head as if very disappointed.

"You can't expect someone to consider a proposal if you don't even make one, Grayson. You've had people say no to you before. You'll survive. But she deserves the chance to consider all the options. You don't actually know what other opportunities she would entertain. Sometimes I wonder how you got this far in this business." Andrea stands and starts for the door. "Actually, I don't wonder. You're extremely good looking, you're a man, and you have a gigantic ego. That's how you got this far." But she pauses at the door and gives me a smirk. "But like all powerful men throughout history, I have a feeling that a woman is about to teach you a thing or two."

I frown, thinking that over. Then realize that I really hope she's right. "So what should I do?"

"Get your ass back to Honeysuckle Harbor before Caroline leaves."

CHAPTER 33

James

"I CAN'T BELIEVE you wouldn't let me make a sign," I tell my husband as we wait in the baggage claim area at the Charleston airport. "I love those signs."

"While I would have appreciated seeing the sheer mortification on Grayson's face if you were holding up a 'welcome home' sign, there wasn't time for an arts and crafts project this morning." Cas pushes up his glasses and gives me an amused smile.

He's right. But I still would have loved it. "There is always time for arts and crafts. I feel like Caroline would agree with me on this point."

The thought of Caro has me rubbing my jaw and shuffling on my feet a little, wishing things could be different. I miss her already and she hasn't even left the country yet. But it's been a whirlwind since Grayson ended his relationship with her, which abruptly halted all of our involvement. Caroline has been wrapping up all her final details before leaving the country, including spending two days down in Florida to see her mother. We've barely seen her and when we have, it's been brief and casual at the baby gym or at the coffee shop.

"I'm sure she would." Cas glances at his phone. "If she were here. Besides, Grayson was only gone a week. That hardly merits a welcome home sign."

"But he's made the decision to stay in Honeysuckle Harbor permanently. I think that's a big deal."

"You think everything is a big deal and a case for celebration and I love you for it." He leans over and gives me a quick kiss. "I know you miss her. I do too. I'm sorry, James."

I nod, a knot in my throat. Letting Caroline leave is just as hard as I imagined it would be. I fucking hate it. I've been torn between being respectful and just demanding she stay here with the three of us and the babies.

"She'd be happy here," I tell Cas stubbornly. "And very well fucked."

I realize I might have said that a little too loud when an older woman turns and scrutinizes me, her eyebrows lifting. She's dressed in a floral caftan and rolling a cherry red suitcase behind her.

I wince. "My apologies, ma'am."

But the corner of her mouth turns up. "She sounds like a lucky girl." She winks and moves past us.

I'm so stunned I almost laugh. But I can't because damn right Caro was a lucky girl. We all were lucky. Lucky to have found each other, lucky to have shared the time together we had, lucky to have fallen in love.

I shift on my heels again, restless. What are we doing? Why are we just letting this all end with a mere fucking whisper? It doesn't feel right.

"Grayson's flight has landed," Cas says, staring at his phone screen again. "I wonder how Evelyn handled flying commercial."

That makes me laugh, in spite of my general feelings of discontent about the way our foursome shook out.

"She's a baby. I don't think she's bougie just yet."

Grayson had cut his trip to New York short and could only secure a commercial flight in economy class, which is not something he's used to. At all. I have a feeling he's going to step off that plane frazzled as fuck.

When he had called me yesterday to tell us he had decided to make Honeysuckle Harbor his permanent home, we'd been thrilled. For him and for Evelyn, who is going to reap all the benefits of small town life on the coast, with lots of family and friends around. I'm glad for us too—we value Grayson's friendship, and I want Noah and Evelyn to grow up together.

I'm a little uncertain as to why he is jetting back so quickly after his decision, but he asked for a ride from the airport and said he needed to talk to us about something. I'm assuming he's going to want to vacate the apartment next door to us and move into a house closer to his parents, with more work from home options for him.

We left Noah at my parents' house so that Evelyn can ride in Noah's car seat. One of us probably should have stayed home with Noah because it's going to be a tight fit in the car, but we were both eager to help out Grayson. And okay, we were curious about what is actually going on in his head right now.

"I don't know," Cas says, wryly. "Evelyn is Grayson's daughter, after all. She's going to appreciate the finer things in life. I just hope she didn't fuss too much."

"He does have the nanny with him."

"Then I shouldn't be worried about Evelyn crying but Jane."

Cas and I exchange a look. Jane the nanny cries a lot. We've both witnessed it and it makes me feel bad for her. Cas thinks the nanny is overreacting.

True to form, Jane is wiping her eyes with the sleeve of her shirt as she comes down the escalator, sniffling and repeatedly lifting the strap of her overnight bag onto her shoulder. Grayson is behind her, holding Evelyn. Father and daughter are both scowling.

"That looks about right," Cas murmurs.

"I bet a sign would have cheered her up," I tell him.

Cas laughs and puts his arm around my waist. "You're probably right. Next time I'll just leave you to your poster board and markers."

"Thank you." I wave to the trio and Evelyn's scowl melts into a smile. She bounces up and down on Grayson's hip, practically launching herself out of his arms in my direction. "Hey guys!" I say, holding my hands out for Evie.

"Please, take her." Grayson does indeed look frazzled as fuck. His hair is sticking up, and he has dark circles under his eyes like he hasn't been sleeping in New York. His T-shirt has a food stain on the shoulder. "My daughter would not take a nap today. She's reached some level of slap happy delirium where all she wants to do is shriek at random intervals and then laugh at herself. Oh, and throw her pacifier at the other passengers. And smear food on me."

I cuddle Evelyn to my chest and kiss the top of her head. "Sounds about right for her age. Jane, you okay?"

The nanny nods, still sniffling.

Grayson shakes his head behind her. He actually looks sympathetic, reaching out and squeezing Jane's shoulder. "Some woman on the plane yelled at Jane for changing Evelyn's diaper. But come on, it's not like she could change it in the bathroom. Those are insanely small."

"Ouch," I say. "People don't even try to be understanding, do they?"

Jane shakes her head. "She waited until Grayson took the dirty diaper down to the flight attendant too to complain. She knew she could yell at me and make me feel bad, but she wasn't bold enough to do it with him there."

"That's terrible." Cas leans over and tickles Evelyn's belly, making faces at her.

"Do you need anything?" Grayson asks Jane. "A water? We can get you an ice cream on the way to your house."

"If it's okay, I'm just going to get an Uber," she says. "I'm tired."

"Sure, no problem. Let me order it for you." Grayson swipes on his phone, then strides over and retrieves his luggage.

By the time we exit the airport, Jane's car is waiting for her and Grayson gets her safely off. He gives a big sigh when he returns to us. "I wish I could teach that girl to be more sure of herself. It scares me for Evelyn. I want to raise a confident daughter."

I kiss Evelyn's cheek. "I think you're going to be great at instilling confidence in her."

We chat casually about New York and Grayson's business as we walk to Cas's SUV in the parking garage, but I have to admit, my curiosity is getting the better of me. Now that we don't have Jane with us, there's no reason we can't talk openly about the subject I know is on all of our minds—Caroline Bell.

"How have you been?" I ask Grayson from the passenger seat. He's in the back, next to the car seat. I turn around so I can see his expression.

"I'm miserable," he says shortly. "I fucked everything up with Caroline and then, ultimately, that fucked everything up for you two with her as well. I was trying to do the right thing…protect myself and protect Evelyn, but my timing was off."

"Your timing sucked ass," I tell him flatly. "You told Caro you can't see her anymore and that you love her practically in the same breath. The girl never had a chance to react."

Grayson sighs and runs his fingers through his hair as Cas pulls out of the parking garage. "I know. But be honest, did you really handle it any better?"

I'm a little fucking offended. "We handled it rationally."

"Exactly. Cas, be honest with me. Did you two hold back because you didn't want to influence Caroline's decision to leave or potentially to stay?"

"Of course. We wanted to respect her independence and not talk her into something she'll regret."

"But that's just it—none of us really told her *exactly* what we're offering her." Grayson leans forward to be closer to both me and Cas. "Not with the fierceness we feel in our hearts. Not with a 'I-will-fucking-love-you-until-the-day-you-die'. Not with a promise that what the four of us can have here and now, which is an abundance of love and laughter and 'tear-up-the-sheets' sex every night. Because we all got stuck in this bullshit narrative that it was casual. It was never casual. Not for me. It was different with Caroline from the first minute."

"It was for me too," Cas says. "We've shared women before in our marriage, and I never wanted to become friends with them. Cook for them. Hug them. I knew it was different almost immediately."

I stare at my husband. "Why didn't you say anything?"

Cas shrugs. "Because you were in love with her already. I knew that. You even knew that on some level, so it's not like I doubted you'd want to keep seeing her while she was here. But Grayson is right—we all agreed it was casual because Caroline was leaving."

"Blah, blah, fucking blah," Grayson says, flopping back into his seat.

That makes me laugh. "Excuse me?"

"I'm not putting up with this 'she's leaving' crap anymore. I'm going to tell her exactly how I feel and that I want her to stay and if she still leaves, at least I'll have tried. Are you with me?"

I'm already nodding. "Hell, yeah. I need to tell her how I feel. With more...*heat* this time. Not the polite version. Cas, how about you?"

"I think we need to at least be able to say we tried. Everyone is tired tonight. Let's meet at the gym tomorrow after the eleven a.m. class and figure out how we're going to approach Caroline."

Now I feel a spark of hope that we've got a shot. I nod again, vehemently. "Let's do this."

CHAPTER 34

Caroline

I STARE at my suitcase all packed in my bedroom at Fiona and Frannie's and resent the hell out of it. I've always loved the freedom of living my life out of a bag. I can just pack up and go on a moment's notice. Okay, not a moment's notice—I usually have friends to say goodbye to and plants to rehome.

But with a few days' notice.

I like that about my life.

Except leaving Honeysuckle Harbor this time sucks so much and my suitcase is symbolic of that. I give it a swift kick, which only serves to stub my toe.

"Ow. Damn it."

I'm not leaving until tomorrow, but I wanted to spend the day saying goodbye to my friends and taking one last stroll along the beach. Alone. Which is actually how I spend most of my time abroad. Sure, I make new friends and hang out, but a lot of my traveling is solo, and it's been an incredible adventure.

But now the thought of settling into a new apartment in Colombia, meeting the other teachers, the students, the parents, being the perennial new hire, learning a new city by myself feels...lonely.

As does a walk on the beach by myself.

Disgusted, I shove my feet into my sneakers and pull a sweatshirt on over my tank top and leggings and shove open the front door. I need to be around people.

The last week and a half has sucked.

I haven't seen Grayson. Not one time. Not even a 'oh-hey-look-at-us-bumping-into-each-other'. I had just, I don't know, assumed that would happen. It's a small town. I work in the baby gym underneath Grayson's freaking apartment. I get coffee where he does. I have the same friends as him. But nope. Not one glimpse of him or Evelyn.

It's been so frustrating that I would have even welcomed running into Kyle, the night nanny, just to confirm that Grayson is still alive.

James, who I have seen but just briefly at the gym, finally told me that Grayson is in New York taking care of some business.

It was a punch to the gut. He took Jane, the day nanny, with him. Instead of me.

Because he loves me.

How ironic is that?

Who tells someone they're in love with them and then breaks up with them in the next breath?

Grayson, that's who.

As I run down the porch steps, my heart squeezes at the thought of him. He's grumpy and infuriating...and warm and loving and unintentionally funny and wears a suit like nobody's business and is fiercely protective of his daughter.

I understand he's just trying to protect Evelyn by not continuing our foursome. And himself, too.

That doesn't mean I have to like it.

I hate it.

Like I hate my packed bag and the thought of leaving Fiona and Frannie.

Then there's James.

And Cas.

I hate the thought of leaving them even more than the girls.

And not because of the sex—though the sex was mind blowing—but because they're my best friends. My lovers. The ones who get me. Who love me.

Which means more than casual friends with benefits, and I should have realized that. Plus, I adore their son and Grayson's daughter. Jesus, we were blurring lines all over the place and not even noticing it because we were having so much fucking *fun*.

I miss that. So damn much.

I'm walking like I'm making a video advertising the benefits of speed walking and I don't even know why. I have no destination in mind. I just couldn't look at my offensive suitcase for another second. I shouldn't get a coffee. I'm too keyed up as it is. The twins are at work and I don't dare go into Raw and cry all over the pastries again.

I just head down the street because it feels like I can power walk my feelings away.

Because I'm starting to doubt that leaving Honeysuckle Harbor will actually make me happy.

I'm suspecting it might make me really fucking miserable, to be honest.

"Good morning, Caroline."

"Hello there, Caro."

"Beautiful day, isn't it?"

The trio of men who play chess outside the coffee shop all greet me. I pause and put my hands on my hips, catching my breath. I'm trying to be polite, but I'm also repeatedly craning my neck to see if I can see James in the gym. I need a James hug.

He's been normal-ish to me. A little awkward, sure, but not too bad. Cas has been polite, but reserved. No more hugs from him, it seems. Then again, I've only seen him once since we all ended our foursome.

"It's a day," I tell the older men.

Sam laughs. "Not a ringing endorsement. Where are you off to?"

"I have no idea," I say truthfully. "Where are any of us off to, anyway? Life is a journey, right? We don't know the final destination."

"I think it's the cemetery, actually," Walt says.

I blanch.

"Jesus," Sam says with a frown. "Don't scare the girl."

"Having a bit of a crisis?"

"Yes. A huge one. What do you do if someone loves you but you're leaving town?"

"Do you have to leave?" Sam asks.

"Yes. I mean, I accepted a job. But...no? I guess technically not."

"Then you don't leave."

Huh.

I glance over at the gym again and then the apartment windows above. "What is that?" I asked, instantly distracted. "Is that a For Rent sign in Grayson's apartment?"

"Huh?" They all turn and squint. "Looks that way."

"Oh my God. He's moving to New York! Bye, gentlemen!"

I need to talk to James.

When I'm in front of the gym a minute later, I draw up short before yanking open the front door.

James is in the gym with Noah.

But so is Grayson with Evelyn.

And Cas, who is there too, legs stretched out as he leans against the cubbies filled with toys.

They're all smiling and laughing.

They're sexy and masculine and so, so loving toward their children.

I take two steps backward.

Holy. Shit.

I'm in love with them. All of them.

Those five humans in that room are my world.

It's not this vast planet we live on. I don't need to explore it looking for anything or anyone anymore. Sure, vacations would be great. But I don't need to travel to find something, because everything I need in the whole world is right in front of me here in Honeysuckle Harbor.

My people.

Then you don't leave.

The words ring in my ears.

It's so obvious.

I push open the door with such force that it smacks against the door stop with a loud bang.

Three heads turn toward me. Actually five. Noah has jumped in his sleep and Evelyn swivels her head and starts crying.

"Caro, are you okay?" James asks, gawking at me as he scrambles to stand up with Noah.

Cas is watching me carefully, and Grayson's nostrils are flaring.

"No, I'm not okay!" I stand there for a second, breathing hard, looking at each of them. "I'm in love with you."

"Who?" Grayson asks, looking and sounding cautious.

"You. And James. And Cas. All of you. I can't leave. I'm not leaving."

Now Grayson is getting to his feet as well. "Caroline…"

James is in front of me now. "What about your job?" He's searching my face carefully.

"Fuck it. I can teach here." Now it all seems so obvious to me. I'm not sure why it took me a whole week and a half to figure it out. "I won't be happy unless I'm with all of you."

They're a little more reserved than I was expecting when I burst in here. I don't know what I was envisioning—maybe literal fireworks—but this felt underwhelming.

This must have been how Grayson felt when I just stared at him after he said he loved me.

"Are you sure?" Cas is also now getting to his feet.

"Yes. I'm one hundred percent sure. I love all of you and I want us to be together…if that's what you want," I finish, a little deflated.

But then, all at once, they all react.

James grins and presses a hard kiss on my lips. "Oh my God, I'm so happy to hear that. I love you so much, Caro. Yes, I want this. If the guys do, that is."

Grayson puts Evelyn down on the mat and scoops me up in his arms and twirls me around. "Hell, yes, that's what I want! I love you, baby."

Relieved, I laugh and hold on to him when he sets me down and I stumble a little, my face warm with emotion, heart racing.

I look past him. "Cas? How do you feel?"

Cas surprises me by cupping my cheeks gently and giving me a sweet, tender kiss. "Welcome home."

That makes me sigh, and tears form. "I'm ready to be home. All of you are my home."

Grayson has retrieved Evelyn from the floor and I run my hand over her hair, and then Noah's. "I love these two as well."

James squeezes my hand. "Let's go upstairs."

"Jane will be here in ten minutes," Grayson says. "She can watch Noah too."

My body warms. "Why?" I ask, slyly.

I'm fooling no one.

"So we can celebrate," Grayson says, crowding in on me from behind. He brushes my hair off of my shoulder and kisses the back of my neck. "By the way, we were here together plotting ways to convince you to stay."

I shiver.

"We were going to tell you we love you so fucking much," James says.

"And if that didn't work, we were going to use other powers of persuasion." Cas moves in on my side. "We're going to fuck you so hard and so long as punishment for torturing us for over a week."

Yes, please.

"Do what you think you need to do."

James, who isn't normally a growler, does just that. "Then get that sweet ass upstairs."

CHAPTER 35

Grayson

I HAVE NEVER NEEDED to fuck someone the way I need to fuck Caroline right now.

I thought I'd needed her before this, but it's nothing compared to my need for her now that we are in love, together, and committed.

I never thought I would have a long-term relationship like this. But this woman has come in and turned all of my previous ideas upside down.

"Thank God Jane agreed to take Noah too," Cas says. "We will pay her extra."

"Don't worry about that," I say. "I'll take care of it. Jane is fine. The babies are fine. Right now, it's just about the four of us."

The elevator doors swish open, and Caroline turns to say something to me.

But I bend, haul her over my shoulder, and stride toward Cas and James's apartment door.

Caroline laughs. "Eager?" she asks.

"For you? Always. And I swear, if I am not buried in your pussy in the next two minutes, I might die."

I feel her stiffen in surprise. "Do you mean–?"

Cas shoves the door open and I stride through it, straight to the bedroom. I dump Caroline on the bed and start stripping. "I mean, I am going to fuck you, my love. I'm going to be balls deep in your sweet, tight cunt and I'm going to fuck you hard, deep, and thoroughly."

Her eyes are wide, but it is certainly not with trepidation. She is just as eager. She scrambles up to her knees and starts unbuckling my belt and then undoing my pants.

I glance at the other men. "Sorry, I'm calling dibs on her pussy tonight."

James looks at me with eyebrows up. "I, for one, am looking forward to this. Grayson unleashed is going to be hot." He looks at our girlfriend. "I hope you're ready, Caroline."

She licks her lips and looks up at me with a mischievous grin.

"I'm not sure I am," she admits. "But I can't wait."

Cas moves to the edge of the bed and reaches for her. "Here, let me help." He strips her shirt over her head, her hands falling away from tugging my pants down only long enough for him to free her shirt and then her bra straps. Her hands immediately go back to my cock, shoving my silk briefs out of the way impatiently, then wrapping her fist around me.

Jesus, her touch is almost enough to send me off. I grit my teeth and toe off my shoes.

Cas moves in behind her on the bed, filling his hands with her breasts, tweaking her nipples, and making her moan.

James, on the other hand, is getting rid of his own clothes.

"I'm going to need you to suck my dick while Grayson fucks our girl," James tells Cas.

Cas gives him an amused look. "That's uncharacteristically bossy of you."

Caroline sucks in a breath as Cas's big hand slides down her stomach and into the front of her pants.

James's gaze is on Cas teasing Caroline. "The two loves of my life are making each other crazy," he says. "I'm about to explode here."

"Don't you dare come in Cas's mouth," Caroline tells James. "I want you to fill *me* up."

Three male groans fill the room.

"Jesus Christ, Caroline," James says, stroking his hard cock.

"What?" she asks, stroking my cock, then shifting to hands and knees to bring her mouth closer to the tip. "I know I can ask for whatever I want and get it from you three. And I'm feeling selfish tonight."

I catch her underneath her arms before her mouth touches my cock. "Almost anything, almost anytime."

Cas senses what I'm about to do and moves out of the way as I flip her onto her back. My hands go to her pants, and I strip them down her legs, taking her panties with them. "But right now, we're not doing the foreplay thing. I will do anything you want me to do to you all night long. *After* I've felt your perfect pussy around my cock and made us both come so hard we can't see straight."

A shiver goes through her as I toss her pants and panties to the floor. I spread her thighs and run my finger through her hot wetness. She's so ready for me. For us.

"Oh my God," she moans softly.

"Want me to use a condom?" I ask.

She shakes her head quickly. "No. I'm good. Are you sure, though?"

I move onto the bed between her legs, bracing my arms on either side of her head and staring down into her beautiful face.

"I'm sure. If we end up making a baby tonight, that will be amazing. If we don't, that's amazing too. Right now I just need to be inside you, skin to skin, showing you how much I love you."

Tears well in her eyes and I love the fact that she knows that even hot sex with no foreplay is actually very meaningful for me. I do intend to have children with this woman, if she wants them. Whether it's accidental or planned. I assume James and Cas want more children as well. However it happens, it will be perfect since the four of us are all together. We can do and handle anything.

"I'm not afraid of anything anymore," I tell her. "I've got the three of you. I've got Evelyn and Noah. Everything is perfect."

She smiles up at me with a soft smile, full of love. I've only seen that smile directed at the two children, and it wraps around my heart and squeezes. "Well, it's *almost* perfect," she says.

I give her a little frown. "Tell me how to make it perfect. I'll do anything."

She lifts her legs and wraps them around my waist, her heels digging into my ass, pulling me down. "Get inside me."

"That I can do," I tell her.

"Well then, please ma—"

I cut her off with a long, hard thrust.

My cock sliding into the hottest, tightest, wettest, most perfect pussy I have ever met is my idea of heaven. I have never felt anything as good as fucking Caroline Bell.

"*Fuck*, Caroline," I say on a low groan as her pussy tightens around me.

"Oh my God, Grayson, *yes*."

I haven't forgotten Cas and James and I am grateful they're willing to let me go first with no discussion and not even involving them in any foreplay.

But a glance to my right shows them locked in a steamy kiss, both naked, their hands roaming.

I pull back and thrust again and Caroline's cry grabs their attention. They both turn to watch.

"I believe you had a request," Cas says to James, going to his knees in front of his husband. "How's Caroline look being fucked hard?"

"I don't know, I think Grayson is holding back," James says. Then his breath hisses out as Cas takes his cock in his mouth. James's fingers go to Cas's head, tightening in his hair.

"You think she needs it harder?" I ask him, then look down at Caroline. "You need more, Caro?" I thrust hard, and she gasps.

"God, you feel good," she tells me.

"She says she feels good," I tell James with a smirk.

"Maybe it's just that I can't see her gorgeous pussy stretched around your cock," James says, thrusting into Cas's mouth as I thrust into Caroline.

Caroline makes the most beautiful moaning noise and I lean over and take her mouth in a deep kiss, sliding my tongue against hers, slow and deep, moving my hips with the same rhythm. When I lift my head, I ask her, "What do you say Caro, do you want to show your other men how gorgeous you look taking my cock?"

She bites her bottom lip and I pull out slowly, then slide back in slowly. "Use your words, gorgeous."

She nods. "Anything you guys want."

I give James a look. We all know that Caroline actually holds all the power, but it's sweet when she makes it sound like she's willing to take orders.

"What do you think? Should we test her?"

"Ride him for us, Caroline," James says. "I want to see your whole body as Grayson fucks you."

Cas actually pulls off James's cock long enough to say, "Fuck yes. That."

I scoop my hands under her ass and roll to my back, taking her with me. She sits up to straddle me, but I have a better idea. "Let's show them everything," I tell her, giving her nipple a little suck and then grasping her hips and turning her so that she's facing away from me.

"God, that's gorgeous," James growls in approval.

Now Caroline is straddling me, facing James while his cock is down Cas's throat.

Lucky bastard. He really does have the best of both worlds.

Caroline braces her palms on my thighs, lifts her sweet ass, then lowers herself, taking me deep. I grip her hips. "That's right. Fuck me, Caroline."

She takes that seriously, moving up and down.

I can't see James and Cas now, but I hear James tell her, "Your tits look perfect, bouncing like that while you fuck him."

I feel how his words affect her when her pussy clenches around my cock.

"Remember, Cas doesn't get your come," Caroline says, her voice breathy.

"You look so good, and then you talk dirty like that and you expect me to hold back?" James asks.

"I want you to fuck me, James," she tells him. "I want Grayson to fill me up and then I want you to fuck me right after. I want Cas to take you at the same time."

Cas and James both groan And I feel myself climb even closer to orgasm.

"Dirty girl," I say, my voice gruff. "You better start working your clit. You have to come before I do."

She immediately sits up a little higher, her hand going between her thighs.

"Fuck, Cas," James says. "You gotta watch this."

I assume Cas pulls off of James's cock because I hear him say, "You're the hottest fucking thing Caro."

She's moving faster on me, one hand working her clit, and from behind I can tell her other hand goes to one breast, playing with her nipple.

"God, I'm gonna come," she says.

The graceful arch of her back, the way her hair sways against her shoulder blades, the way her hot pussy grips me, is all absolute perfection.

"You better," I tell her, giving her ass another little slap. "I want to empty my balls in you."

That seems to help because a moment later, she gasps my name and her pussy clamps down on me.

"Grayson! Oh my God, *Grayson!*"

Then she's coming, and I let myself go. I grip her hips and thrust up into her rapidly. I assume the view from the front is hot, her tits bouncing, her thighs open, her pussy stretched wide.

"Caroline!" I shout as I erupt. I come hard, filling my woman with my seed and, for just a brief moment, I actually hope I do get her pregnant.

The thought passes quickly. There's plenty of time for that and God knows we have our hands full with the babies we've got, but it is a primal instinct to claim Caroline this way the first time I actually fuck her and do it bare.

"Spread those gorgeous legs for me," James says roughly. Caroline moves off me and lies back on the bed right next to me. She spreads her legs, her hand playing in her pussy and I prop up, not wanting to miss the filthy view of her spreading my cum over her pussy and clit.

"Jesus Christ," Cas says, shaking his head. "You're a fucking dream."

"How do you want me?" she asks.

"Naked all day, every day," Cas tells her with a grin.

But I have a specific idea about this too. I scoot up the bed. "Come here, Caroline."

She rolls to her stomach and crawls toward me. I cup her face and kiss her deeply, then move her so she's reclining against me. I pull her legs apart, draping them over mine, spreading her wide for her other men.

"Fuck her hard," I tell James. "I guess I didn't wear her out yet."

A ghost of a smile—a very pleased, almost smug smile—crosses her lips.

I lean in and say against her ear. "You're going to feel us all day tomorrow," I promise.

"Big talker," she teases.

But then James thrusts into her and she gasps.

I smirk at her and brush her hair back from her face. "You okay?"

Her eyes slide shut in pleasure. "So okay."

James thrusts again and again. "God, I love fucking you."

Then he pauses and grunts as Cas thrusts into him from behind.

"Oh yes, God," Caroline moans. "Fuck us both, Cas."

And he does.

His thrusts drive James into Caroline and I feel every pounding stroke, too.

We're all connected.

I play with her nipples. We take turns telling her how gorgeous she is, how good she is, how much we love her, how this is just the start of things between us all, and then James says, "Rub her clit, Grayson. Make her come again."

"I'm so close," she says, her voice ragged as the back of her head presses into my chest.

I reach between her and James and find her clit. The sensation of James fucking into her and my hand adds to the heat of it and I circle her clit then pinch it, and just like that, she's crying out and coming apart.

James stiffens and empties into her a moment later, then Cas shouts James's name and comes as well.

Everyone collapses onto the bed, a tangle of limbs and heavy breathing.

Caroline is draped over my chest. Cas is curled around James. James's hand is splayed over Caroline's hip.

"God, I love you all so damned much," James says. "This is perfect."

Caroline stirs on my chest, giving a happy sigh. "This couldn't be better."

Cas gives a grunt of agreement. "I can't believe you really thought you could leave us."

I try to stifle a chuckle, but she feels the vibration in my chest. She lifts her head and gives me a look.

"Too soon?" I ask.

But then she smiles. She looks at James and Cas. "I can't believe it either, honestly. There's nowhere else I'd rather be."

James rolls his head to look at her. "Well, just know, as of right now, if you ever leave, we're coming after you." His gaze slides to me. "I'm very close to a millionaire who would happily come with me to chase you around the world."

I slide my arms around her and squeeze. "Damn right."

She gives me a sweet, sexy smile. "Hmmm…that sounds kind of fun."

"It does," Cas says. "Wait 'til the kids are a little older and we'll all follow you all over. Evie and Noah would be great world travelers."

I'm startled to see her eyes fill with tears suddenly, but she's smiling at the same time. "That sounds amazing. But maybe I won't run. If we all go together I can sit in first class, right?"

I laugh and run my hands up and down her back. "Absolutely."

Then she wiggles and slides off of me, then off the bed.

I prop up on my elbows. "Hey what are you doing?"

She gives us all a big grin as she backs toward the bedroom door. "Just thinking that having you all chase me sounds fun… and we can do that right here without anyone actually leaving." Then she runs out of the bedroom.

I look over at James and Cas.

James is grinning and shaking his head. Cas is already off the bed and pulling on his boxers.

"I think it's good there are three of us," James says. "She's going to be a handful. And on top of those two babies, she's gonna wear *us* out."

"Yep," Cas says, starting for the door. "And whoever catches her gets his hands full of her first…next."

Laughing, James and I jump off the bed and dive for our clothes.

And as I hear Caroline's happy shriek from the next room, I realize the best part of this is I don't even care who catches her first, because this is going to be amazing for all four of us all the time.

CHAPTER 36

Cas

"ALL UNPACKED?" I ask as Grayson and Caroline come out of his bedroom, looking disheveled.

Caroline is giggling and flushed.

Grayson looks satisfied and smug. He's carrying Caroline's empty suitcase. "Yep."

"If you can call dumping all my clothes on a chair unpacking."

"Then what took you so long?" James asks with a grin, pulling the takeout boxes we've just arrived with out of the bag with one hand, Evelyn on his opposite hip. "We were gone for thirty minutes picking the food up."

I reach into Grayson's kitchen cupboards and pull out plates and bowls, Noah asleep in the baby carrier I have strapped to me. We're going to have to sort out dinner better than this in the future and nap times and schedules, but for today, it will do. It's only been two days since Caroline came flying into the gym, a little spitfire of emotion, telling us she's in love with all of us.

We've got details to deal with, but we're all so fucking happy with this outcome it's ridiculous.

"I might have fucked our girlfriend," Grayson admits.

Caroline pretends to look sheepish. "It's true. There might have been some fucking involved in the unpacking process."

"Shocker." This is something we've already discussed. Grayson and Caroline can have sex with each other whenever they want, like me and James. I set the plates on the counter next to James and give him a kiss on the side of the head.

"Where are you taking that suitcase?" James asks.

"We're throwing this suitcase in the dumpster because she's not going anywhere."

"Grayson." Caroline throws him a look of disapproval. "What if I want to, you know, take a trip to see my mother? Or go to New York with you?"

"I'll buy you a new one. This one makes me angry. It almost went with you to Colombia."

She laughs. "You're ridiculous." Then she leans over the kitchen counter to eye the Thai food. "Mmm, thanks for picking this up." She gives James a kiss, then runs her hand across his back as she shifts around him to kiss me.

Affection is free for the offering and taking at any time, between anyone, with anyone else around. That's another thing we agreed on. There isn't any jealousy between us and we don't want there to be. Open communication and open affection. That's a solid foundation for our new relationship.

Grayson opens the door to his apartment and sets the offensive suitcase in the hallway. "I need to text Kyle."

Caroline stiffens. "About what? You told her not to come over tonight, right? Fucking Kyle."

"Why does Kyle annoy you so much?" James asks, lifting a piece of chicken to Caroline's mouth and easing it between her lips. "Eat this. You sound hangry."

"I am hungry," she says, chewing the chicken. "But I'm not *hangry*. I just don't like how pretty Kyle is. She's been in this apartment every night for weeks while my boyfriend is asleep in bed in the other room. It pisses me off the way that suitcase pisses off Grayson."

"Well, we can't throw Kyle in the dumpster so put that

thought out of your head," I tell her, pulling out silverware from Grayson's kitchen drawer.

James laughs.

"Are you sure?" Caroline teases.

"Kyle saved my ass and allowed me to sleep," Grayson says. "Nothing more, nothing less. Don't hate so hard on Kyle."

"She's so...put together. And gorgeous! Don't tell me you didn't notice," Caroline insists.

Grayson looks genuinely confused. "Is she gorgeous?"

James and I exchange a look.

"She's gorgeous," James tells him.

"Absolutely the full package," I agree.

Caroline wrinkles her nose.

"Huh. I honestly never noticed," Grayson says.

Caroline rolls her eyes.

"It's not Kyle's fault you're jealous." Now Grayson is smirking a little as he picks up his phone. "I'll text her now."

"You're firing her," Caroline reiterates. "Just so we're clear."

"We're clear." He types quickly and then shows her the text. "Good?"

"Thank you for all your help, but I no longer require your services, effective immediately. I will pay you for the next four weeks and give your agency a very positive review."

I just raise my eyebrows and start dishing pad Thai onto plates.

"Good?"

"Good."

"Send." Grayson taps his phone with a flourish. "But we're keeping Jane, right?"

"I feel like we need a full recap of all our decisions and plans to make sure we're on the same page," I say. "Let's do that while we eat."

"We're having a family meeting?" Caroline asks. "I love that. It's a great idea, Cas."

"Kyle texted me back," Grayson says.

Caroline yanks his phone right out of his hand. "What did she say?"

Grayson's hand is just hanging in the air. "Sure, you can have my phone. No problem."

"She wants to know why you're firing her."

Grayson reaches for his phone. "May I?"

"Of course. I'm not going to text her."

Grayson types and shows her the screen.

She reads it aloud. "It has nothing to do with your performance. My girlfriend is jealous of how gorgeous you are... Grayson! What the hell?"

I start laughing. "You walked right into that, Caroline."

"Hit send?" Grayson asks her.

"No. God. Fine. Just tell her whatever. Just not the truth, which is that I'm jealous." The corner of her mouth lifts up in a smile.

"I knew it!" Grayson reaches behind her and tugs her against his chest. "But you have nothing to be jealous about, ever. I haven't had eyes for any woman but you since the second you strolled off that elevator, all tits and long legs and a perky smile."

She laughs and leans back against him.

I'm enjoying their banter. I like having a full apartment with our family, Evelyn trying to eat the noodle James has handed her, James talking to her as he pours wine with one hand. He's head over ass for Grayson's little girl.

Hell, our little girl. She belongs to all of us now. Just like Grayson and Caroline will be parents to Noah.

I would have thought my reaction to that would be on par with Caroline's feelings toward Kyle, but they're not. My son will only benefit from having people to love him.

"Answer Kyle. She's probably fretting." Caroline pulls away from Grayson and gives Evelyn a kiss on the cheek. "I just love you so much, you little cutie."

"Oh, now you're worried about Kyle's feelings? I can't keep up." Grayson obediently texts though and puts his phone in his pocket. "That's done. What can I do to help?"

"Put all of these plates on the table." James pops Evelyn into her high chair.

Grayson does what James tells him without question. It's interesting to me that a man who is used to being in charge is so easygoing with the three of us. Oh, sure, he's still demanding as hell and thinks money can solve everything, but I like his energy.

"You know, there are very practical advantages to being in a poly relationship as a formerly single dad," Grayson says. "There are a lot of hands to help."

Caroline carries the wine glasses to the table beside him. "There really are. You can fly to New York whenever you need to on business and leave Evelyn here."

"Or take you with me," he protests.

"It depends on what is going on. I am planning to get a teaching job, but I'll probably only be able to sub this school year since it's already started."

"What did your employer with the international school say when you quit?" I ask. "I know you felt bad about putting in your notice."

She nods. "I did. But the assignment doesn't start for four weeks. I wanted time to acclimate. But it's still not ideal. I have to reimburse them for the travel stipend they gave me."

"That's easy enough," Grayson says. "I'll pay that. What is it, like ten grand or something?"

Caroline laughs. James snorts.

"You really have no idea the value of the dollar, do you?" I ask him, wryly.

"That's almost my whole salary," Caroline tells him. "No, it is five hundred dollars."

"Oh." Grayson has the decency to look sheepish. "Just tell me where to send it."

"I can pay for it. I do have savings."

"I want to," Grayson insists. "Think of it as payment for my grumpiness and general lack of understanding of how to do basic daily tasks."

Now I'm the one who laughs. "I still can't believe you didn't know how to use a can opener. My mind is blown by that." I had found him staring at it last night when I asked him to open a can of tomatoes.

"When am I opening cans?" Grayson protests. "What even comes in a can?"

"Tomatoes." I shouldn't be as surprised as I am. I've met Grayson's mother. She doesn't lift a finger in the kitchen.

"We should grow our own tomatoes," James says, taking Noah out of the carrier on my chest and putting him in his swing.

"I agree," Grayson nods. "Sounds very healthy."

Caroline isn't saying anything. She's just beaming at all of us.

"What?" I ask her.

She shrugs. "I love you. All of you. Sure, this is practical for any number of reasons, but you know what isn't practical? How we feel. It's big and bold and beautiful and warm and incredible."

That makes me pause in pulling the carrier off over my head. "Perfectly said, gorgeous," I murmur, my throat tight.

Grayson takes a seat next to her. "We need to toast to that." He raises his wine glass.

"To cutting a cased opening in this wall to make these two apartments into one," I say, raising my own glass.

"Ooh, I love that idea," Caroline says, lifting her glass. "James?"

"To living and loving with my best friends, who happen to be the loves of my life. And to finding an office space for Grayson because I can't be a stay-at-home dad with a nanny and him underfoot too. I'm a patient man, but not that patient."

Caroline laughs.

"To finding out I got full permanent custody of Evelyn," Grayson says.

Everyone gasps and gives out congratulations. James claps him on the shoulder.

"Bravo to that," I say. "There is a Dutch saying. A hundred

hearts would be too few to carry all my love for you. That's how I feel right now."

Evelyn gives a happy shriek and throws a noodle.

We all laugh.

"Cheers," Caroline says. "To the future."

We can all drink to that.

Thanks for reading Three Dirty Dads! For more of Caroline, Grayson, James, and Cas (plus the babies!) here's a free bonus scene:

http://subscribepage.io/2otF6R

Read More Emma Foxx

Read more Emma Foxx for more *steamy, fun why-choose rom coms! No cheating, a guaranteed HEA, and the guys are all about her.*

Puck One Night Stands

Four Pucking Christmases

Seriously Pucked

Permanently Pucked

Icing It

Some Like It Hot

Light My Fire

Three Grumpy Groomsmen

Spicy Short Reads

www.ingramcontent.com/pod-product-compliance
Lightning Source LLC
Chambersburg PA
CBHW032357310726
48973CB00007B/2050